Half Moons
and
Maiden Names

A NOVEL BY H. CHARLES DILMORE

NEW YORK

HALFMOONSANDMAIDENNAMES.COM

First Edition I July, 2010

ISBN 0982522436

Cover design and photograph © H. Charles Dilmore.

Printed in the United States of America.

HALF MOONS
AND
MAIDEN NAMES

PROLOGUE

At first, she didn't recognize the horse hooves coming up the dusty drive. *Two steeds. Trotters. Medium wagon.* She kept her eyes focused on her needlepoint while one ear absorbed the sounds below. As with music, she knew that a revealing lyric would show itself.

And when she heard his whistle, she knew.

She set down her embroidery and with two fingers waved aside the sheers.

Carter appeared in the barn doorway just as the dust cloud caught up with the wagon, overtaking it in a shower of dirty gold. He pulled off his gloves and wiped his forehead with his sleeve.

Abram hadn't moved. His legs dangled off the back of the wagon, shoeless, shirt ripped. Shane leapt down from the buckboard, wielding his Winchester.

She could barely hear him from up here. "You missin' a black boy, boy?" He stamped it with his sinister, trademark laugh.

He is the most self-centered man in Mississippi!

But something about Shane—the way he moved through life—made her react, and she touched the base of her throat. Her mind tried to ignore what her instincts sought to recall.

Shane spoke again, tilting his head to indicate the woods where he found Abram.

Carter called to the man, and Abram hopped down, bare feet knowing the dust of this place once more. Carter took note of his feet, then led him into the barn. Shane followed, rifle pointed at the ground, but Carter backed him out and he lipped off, gesturing with his free hand.

She released the drape and stepped back from the window. Shane wiped his nose, looked up to where she likely stood, then looked down the driveway and spat. He climbed back up on the wagon and yanked the reins. The horses fought at the bit, protested then surrendered, backing up. *He'll never get them turned around in that space.*

With flash and brutality, he did. And when he had them aimed, he whistled at the team, stood halfway to absorb the speed, and shook the reins like he was racing the devil for first dibs on hell. And, somehow, he had the wherewithal to look up at her again—saw her this time—and pointed, fingers in the shape of a pistol.

She looked around the bedroom as if she couldn't remember why she was there. Her eyes happened upon her needlework and she gave a reflexive nod and went back to it.

Carter lead Abram to his big desk and sat behind it. A bale of straw supported the end that was missing legs, and the thing sloped like the deck of a listing ship. He leaned back and found his favorite afternoon angle, the chair creaking a two-legged warning.

"Do you like working here, Abram?"

The question hung like the shaft of light that filtered through the hayloft window—if it weren't for the dust, it would be invisible.

When no answer came, he sat forward. "Abram!" Now the man looked at his master.

"Have I fed you well?"

"Yes, sir."

Carter started a new question, but was perplexed and blew only air from his cheeks. He blinked and sighed at the puzzle before him.

"Abram, why? Why do you run?"

The man responded only with his eyes, and they widened as if he were entering a trance. He stared at a spot on the floor as if watching a play, as if witnessing events in miniature.

"What is it?"

Abram spoke as if channeling. His eyes remained fixed on that spot of floor, the stage that haunted him.

"Last night, I heard thunder. And remembered that I left my longshirt on the woodpile out back the house."

He stopped and looked at Carter, secretly hoping that this much story would somehow, magically suffice.

"And?"

"I went back to fetch it."

"And?"

"And... I heard sounds."

Carter bit the inside of his cheek, turned his head to the side. His patience was slipping, but he refused to prompt the man, again.

And Abram sensed this. "I came around the corner, and saw the Missus. Up there. On the porch. I could tell it was her because the light lit up her..." he waved a finger in front of his eye to depict "glasses."

Carter locked his fingers on top of his head, thinking, *What? Was she bringing in the dog? Was she fetching her book? What!*

But he let silence own the room, exhaling slowly. He sensed that the next words would be like a lead ball—small, but so destructive.

"Sit, Abram." He motioned with open hand. "Sit down."

Abram pulled the chair back, although there was already plenty of room to be seated. He sat hunched forward, elbows on his thighs and studied his hands.

"What happened, Abram?"

"I saw Mr. Becker. Behind her. Kissing on her, sir."

"Mr. Becker."

"Yes."

"Mr. Becker, who brought you back."

"Yes, sir."

It was Carter's turn for quiet. His eyes were empty, seeing but not seeing. "You're sure it was Mr. Becker."

Abram reached into his pocket, then extended his fist. Carter hesitated, not sure he wanted to know what was concealed, but he positioned his hand under Abram's.

The thing fell into Carter's hand and he studied it, then he leaned back in his chair again. "Abram?" he asked, sounding weary.

"Yes, sir?" For the first time, the slave made eye contact. The men were now communicating on a knowing level, bonded by shadows of last night.

"Can you please stay? I would like you to stay."

Abram swallowed, nodding as he answered, grateful. "Yes, sir. I would like that."

Carter looked off, the dusty shaft of light holding his attention, changing, never changing. After a time, he looked at the old clock. It had stopped, but it was nearly lunch time. He stood and placed the *thing* in his pocket.

"Have you eaten today?"

"No, sir."

Carter moved forward, spoke low. "Wait here."

He walked, grabbing Abram's shoulder as he passed, and his hand touched bare skin. His shirt was torn from the collar down the back, as if he'd caught it on a nail and run.

When Carter returned, he had a plate of leftover turkey, two buttermilk biscuits, and a tiny glass bowl of honey. He nodded, and the two men started eating off the same plate, without utensils, silently filling up their emptiness.

They dipped into the same honey, overlooking the sticky crumbs left by the other, the burden of words behind them, now.

"That last piece is yours, Abram."

"Sir?" he asked, out of respect.

Carter slapped his midsection. "I'm full up."

They finished and Carter gathered his thoughts, considered the swarm of bees inside him. If he spoke slowly, carefully enough, they might fly off, safely, and not swarm.

"Can we keep this to ourselves, the story of the Missus?"

"Oh, yes, sir."

"Abram, things are gonna work out all right. Let's put in a good day's work today."

Abram headed out to the field. Carter walked into the stall area. Tara nickered, eyes wide, excited at the prospect of being sprung today. Sheba was less vocal, but interested nonetheless.

"Hey, girls."

He walked past them into the empty stall and unbuttoned his pants. The mares watched without enthusiasm. He looked around while his stream hit the straw, the straw from the last cut of spring, the straw from up on the ridge meadow. And now, time for the autumn harvest.

He suddenly felt nauseous. There was a rage inside of him, but it was lifeless. It had no energy behind it. He buttoned up, saddled Tara, and hitched her at the side door.

The Intricacies of Simplicity

the only path
to love or freedom or greatness
is the path taken

Sarah Jane heard the screen door and looked up from her baking.

"I need to ride into town." He avoided her eyes. Because he knew their power. Because he needed to despise her right now. "Anything you need at the mercantile?"

She wiped her hands on her apron, then turned and reached for her list. It was where it always was—clipped, under the lip of the cupboard. She could have found it in the dark, blindfolded. Everything she needed, she documented. Everything she documented, she needed preserved, precise, protected.

"List," she said, looking at it one more time, as if memorizing it before she released it into his custody. She added, "If they don't have enough blue fabric, I can work with a dark green, okay?"

Carter looked at the list—tallying the written order and the verbal addition—and nodded. "Green, okay."

"Dark green *if* they don't have blue!"

"Yes."

And he was off. Without good-bye. Without I love you. Down the dusty drive, down the path that split the tobacco fields and led to the road into Hattiesburg. The sun was sultry, but the angle was changing, every day a little lower, a little more golden, fading.

He could have galloped all the way into town, but this felt good, the trotting. Tara's head bobbing as the road climbed. Her rhythm moved through the man—butt, back, body—and beyond, to his psyche, as if the horse were demonstrating how to move ahead, how to endure, carry on.

Carter considered what lay ahead, just three miles down the trail. And when they crested the highest hill, and when he saw the church steeple and water tower, he fingered the pistol at his waist. In his mind, he read the shocking headline of the weekly newsprint, detailing with horror how Carter Monroe simply walked in and emptied the pistol into Mr. Becker.

He pondered the notion that the calmest of men could lose control, could act on impulse, and he marveled at how easily one could find himself in such a deliciously dark situation—boxed in, coiled, then lunging.

His relationship was dead. War was marching closer to him, to his land, to everything he had ever known.

So he rode, fetching supplies that would string them along another day, another week, maybe a season. Or maybe fate would see him caged.

He hitched Tara in front of Key's Mercantile and pulled the saddlebags over his shoulder. While he glanced once more at Sarah Jane's handwriting, he clicked off the pistol's safety.

When he pushed open the door, a little bell rang, and Robin Key looked up from her work. She stopped what she was doing and locked eyes on him, as if she expected him, as if he were right on time. She looked up at the clock.

"Good afternoon, Mr. Monroe."

"Afternoon, Robin." He was halfway to the counter. "How are you, today?" And his eyes went right, should his target occupy one of the tea stools.

"I'm pretty good. What can I help you with?"

"Well, got my list." He read from the top, and she fetched the items.

- 10 pounds flour
- 2 pounds lard
- 1 pound soap

- 1/2 pound sugar, if she had it
- 1/4 pound coffee, if she had it
- 6 yards canvas, any color
- 6 yards cotton fabric, dark blue
- 1 piece chalk

"And can I have a look at your cotton work shirts?" He noticed the back door was ajar.

"Buttoned or pullover?"

"Pullover, please."

She opened a small, hinged door and pulled one from within. "This is a size Large. Twenty cents."

Carter held it up to himself, then smelled it. "Nice. Okay. Do you have seven of these?"

"Uh, yes. Yes, I do."

She tallied the order and he paid. While she made change, he loaded the items into the saddlebags, food in one, textiles in the other, and let the flour sack stand alone.

"So, how are things, Robin?"

She looked up at him, then lost count of the change and started over. Then she dropped a coin on the floor and it rolled under the countertop and toward his boot. He picked up the nickel and handed it to her.

"Robin?"

She closed the register drawer, "Oh!" then realized she had not given him his change. "I'm sorry. One dollar and five."

He placed the dollar in his wallet, the change in his pocket. Again, the damn nickel fell, landing at the base of the same boot. He remembered that it was his left pocket that had the hole, and transferred the change there.

Then his fingers detected the cuff link.

He pulled it out, studied the "B," and offered it to her. She looked, then met his eyes, then looked down, into nothingness. She put her hand out to receive the thing, like it was cursed, like she simply had to accept it.

"Where was this found?" she asked in a near-whisper.

"My back porch."

When she took it, he closed his hand around hers—her delicate knuckles, her piano fingers. She felt the caress of his thumb, the warm hunger of his calluses. Each hand—his and hers—held the promise of unlimited potential. Yet each clung to possibilities that would forever lie sleeping.

He let her go after just a couple of seconds, long enough to leave her imprint on him for weeks, strong enough to build a proper fire inside herself—smokeless, but smoldering nonetheless.

When he left, he considered stopping into the saloon. Not because he needed whiskey but wanted the company of men, of noise, of the possibility of a badly tuned piano and the ruckus of drunken song.

But he had goods that were sensitive to heat, and decided to head for home.

Tara was as eager to return home as she was to leave it. In both directions, something called to her—adventure one way, companionship the other. The horse was led not by ego, but by the simplest desire to please.

Carter patted the side of her neck, hard enough to make a manly, spanking sound. "G'girl, Tara."

He tried to become the horse, to live by the same calm, to move through this life one ride or one plow session at a time. He considered how letting go of his higher intelligence might actually make him a better man.

Enlightenment through simplicity. A higher state via sacrifice. Peace through numbness.

But he had to deal with this life, had to reconcile things that were out of place, had to clarify things that were confusing. The weight of this made him sigh, slouch in the saddle. And, again, he envied the horse.

As they walked up the drive, Tara quickened her pace, knowing that her stable mate was near.

Carter thought he caught a glimpse of a bird entering a birdhouse —one of the three that he built for the coming winter. He watched as he passed, but failed to detect movement. He craned his head as long as he could, then decided that he had seen but a shadow.

The help was bent, stooping low to pull the first ripened leaves of tobacco. Next week, the higher leaves would be ready, and the workers could stand upright.

Hattie stood when she heard the hooves. Carter touched the brim of his hat and she returned a wave. One by one, the others stood to see the man returning on horseback, each waving.

And behind him, while his eyes were on the help, the house wren peeked from its new home—the yellow house—then flew to catch another moth.

In the Mind

the pen and the ink
can ne'er say enough
can ne'er properly trace the heart on parchment

but it's beneath the ink
in the simple, childlike trying
that we reveal our truest, sweetest intent

After lunch each day, Carter went behind the barn, to the shady spot where the help relaxed from one to two. There was half a chalkboard, and those who wanted to learn the alphabet could. Those who wanted to hear Carter read aloud were read to.

"The world outside will one day be yours," he would say. "I feel this in my bones. And when that day comes, you will want to be *equipped*. Focus today, and you will become more."

Logan and Abram slept off their lunch, and that was fine—the day was long, and Carter didn't impose. Most participated. And from time to time, the laughter would wake those who rested, and it grew louder when sheepish, sleepy eyes blinked to see the source of the racket.

They started by singing the alphabet. And always, there was a little, nervous laughter at the end. Then Carter wrote on the chalkboard. All eyes were on him as he produced letters, two sentences ending in dots.

"Who can read this aloud?"

James tilted his head as he decoded the words, but he wasn't ready to volunteer. Mary Ethel brought her hand up, but only to her shoulder.

"Mary Ethel?"

She smiled. "I don't know *all* of it."

"That's okay. Read what you can."

She stood and came forward, near enough to touch the words. "I am... a good worker." She punctuated each sentence with a head nod. "I am... a good..." She pointed in the air, her tentativeness out-muscled by determination.

"Peer... peer-so..."

"Per..." Carter offered low.

"Per... per-so... n." She had it solved, but needed only the confidence to say it completely.

"Per-sone."

"Yes!"

She whispered the word to herself, still not realizing her achievement.

"From the beginning. You have it, Mary Ethel."

"I am... a good worker. I am... a good per-sone."

"You *are!*" He put a hand on her shoulder. "A good person."

Awkward rumblings came from the group. Logan and Abram would not sleep today. They were curious about what was taking place. And even though the sentence was resolved, Carter asked if others would like to read it.

Hands went up in the air. "James! Come up." Carter reached his hand toward him. "Come on up." James touched each word on the board.

"I. Am. A. Good. Worker. I. Am. A. Good. Person."

Carter looked at him with wide eyes. "Yes!"

Now everyone wanted a turn. *Perfect.*

Carter wanted them to carry away a message of inspiration. "Today, each of you *had the chance* to show something. And today, each of you *took that chance!* And I am very proud of you!"

They meandered back to work, and when they got there they found Carter already between the rows of tobacco. He worked with them for the first hour, then went inside the barn to attend to his afternoon paperwork.

I will so miss this.

Waves of Oneness

not every wave
can bring a treasure to the shore
but every wave is essential

Crickets rehearsed before the scheduled darkness. And the breaths of the western sky grew shallow until finally, silently ceasing. And even after departing, its spirit lived on in a seamless, ethereally blue robe.

Then it simply was time.

Carter fetched his short leather coat—the one that his sister made him—and went to the bench by the rock wall. When he sat, he drew a deep sigh that signaled the end of the workday.

He reached inside and unbuttoned the little, secret pocket there. His fingers found his pipe and the pouch of herbs that his friend had supplied. He loaded but a thimble full. Before closing the pouch, he stuck his nose inside, sucking his cheeks like he was relishing sweet, hard taffy.

He swallowed as if the aroma were drink, such was the perfection. He always admired how wine connoisseurs did their tasting, though he'd never had his lips to a glass.

He regarded the sky one more time, felt the pulse of the earth, and struck the stick match against the side of the box. He squinted against the fire so that his eyes would not be robbed of their night sight, pulled a breath or two, and shook out the match.

The night was so still that when his lips drew on the pipe, the little round furnace made the leaves and stems and seeds crackle like tinder at a village bonfire—warming every spirit, reflecting in every eye, completing his communal circle, albeit a circle of one.

He held a half-breath and felt the smoke expand, teasing his throat. To keep from coughing, he released a little through pursed lips. The rest, he slowly exhaled through his nose, tasting the same sweetness as before, but now in ghost or spirit form. Before the herb was lit, it held the intriguing scent of a woman. That same woman was now a lover, inside of him, promising with her eyes. And always, his gratitude joined hands with his disbelief, the notion that anyone could enjoy him so.

In the time it took to let in three tokes, he felt it—the oneness with something greater. Maybe it was a Spirit Guide. Maybe it was the ether, the universe. But he was now connected. He sensed that something heavenly had its arm around him, assuring and protecting. And he reciprocated, his man-child reflecting back the honor, the gratitude.

He tapped the pipe on the arm of the bench, and the last remaining sparks flew for their final, glorious moment and burned out, returning as ashes to the earth. He left the pipe there to cool, though if the night were chilly, his pocket would absorb and appreciate the warmth.

He didn't notice when the crickets had started this particular movement—seemingly in sync with one another—but he noticed them now. So perfect was the symphony that he tilted his head to comprehend their beauty, and they became one.

He heard no wind, but felt the cool night air tiptoeing in. And when he turned his cheek to discern its direction, the air stopped, insisting on anonymity. He smiled and they became one.

She would wonder where the hell he was. And she would pace, then stop and cross her arms. And the help would say "Excuse me, ma'am," and walk around her. And for his seven minutes of glory he would pay.

And when he arrived and sat, she would decide whether to command her eyes to bore through him or to gaze only downward, silence be his punishment.

And he would chew very slowly, never faster than the tick of the mantle clock, always as calm as its pendulum. And his eyes would go there to appreciate the perfection of the timepiece, and they became one—the gears and his inner workings, the keyhole and his secret dream.

And he would mix his peas with his mashed potatoes and smile, and they became one.

The Bird and the Whistle

emulate someone
stimulate someone else

Abram sat on the stoop, back against the beam that held the crooked porch roof. He worked a little block of wood with a pocket knife while the others smoked. The *flick, flick* of shavings was steady and didn't go unnoticed.

"Where'd you get that knife, boy?"

Abram kept his focus, answering in a sing-song. "From Carter. From Master Carter."

"What? He just *gave* you that?"

He stopped what he was doing, perturbed. "He *asked* me if I might like to *carve* somethin'."

"And then he just *handed* you a knife? You sure you didn't steal it?"

He wanted to walk. Walk away from them! Down the driveway and up the road. Keep walking up, like the map showed, up to the north. *And when I get there, I'm gonna wear a fine, new suit, with silk and buttons. And shoes! The shiniest shoes you could ever want. And then, I just might work on a farm. And have my own desk, my own chair, and lean way back in it.*

But for now, he had to deal with these people. And they laughed when he finally came out with it. "Don't *any* of you have a dream in your head? Is *this* all you got for the rest of your days?"

Oh, yes—they laughed. They had a good time over that one.

And it was several minutes before his hand stopped shaking and he could continue his carving. But then his heart wasn't into it, so he went inside and flopped down on his bed. It was hotter than hell in here, but he'd had enough of the noise. He preferred this heat to the idiocy outside.

He reached under his bed for his sack and fished around. When he came up with it, he placed the thing next to his own, side by side. *Master Carter's is much better.* It was smooth as glass, simply detailed, and shaped perfectly like a fat, little bird. Place your mouth over the tail feathers and blow. Three holes on the bird's back let you change the tone of the whistle.

I could never do it this good.

"Sure you can," Carter had said. "It's like anything—comes with practice. Copy mine. Copy it ten times, and you'll see improvement each time."

Carter had handed him the whistle and Abram's first block of wood. Then the pocketknife. *Out of his own pocket!* Carter had slapped Abram on the shoulder and left his hand there.

Night Thoughts

we know we are awake
when dreams dream us

Sleep was impossible tonight. Her breathing was like the seashore, steady and calm. But his mind raced like a water bug, with no destination but frantic to get there. Ironically, he'd felt calm all day. But now, now he could not silence the questions and fears that taunted him.

There was a time when he was able to feel passion, able to feel jealousy, able to muster the courage to make demands and fight back. But somewhere along the line, he realized he and Sarah Jane had but a business relationship.

Oh, yes—she *needed* him. She needed him in order to get ahead, to bring in the harvest, to be the muscle of the operation.

But for everything else, he was just a placeholder, a stand-in. She hadn't run a seductive finger over him in a long, long time. She shared the fire inside only when she sensed that this arrangement might be slipping from her grasp. She cried the sweet, pathetic tears of helplessness only long enough to bring him in, to ink the contract, to make it binding.

Maybe Shane Becker was right—maybe Carter wasn't man enough. Not man enough to satiate her, to get his woman pregnant. "You need to put more *men* on the job!"

Maybe Carter Monroe wasn't meant to have a child. And if she *did* get pregnant, how would he know if it was his child or Shane Becker's?

And then what? Live out his days in fear? Wait until the child became a man and see whom he resembled?

Craziness. Stop it! Sleep.

But he lay there, sheets damp and cast off, wondering how she and Shane had married, divorced, and were lovers again. He couldn't fathom how one could return after such an explosive break-up. He found it totally illogical that she could make love to a man whom she cursed, who sent her into raging fits, who caused her to scream in a voice more like a man than a woman—such was her passion, her hatred, her fire.

At some point in the night, he dreamed. As if rescuing him, his psyche sent him what he required.

Sea spray, once again. His first night on deck, once again. The black ocean beneath a moonless sky. Shadows and silhouettes. Men and masts, sails still taut and snapping on the midnight watch. The rising and falling as the ship heads... heads... somewhere. Somewhere vital, important.

He seeks the faces of his crew. Each appears confident, dauntless. Only he is unclear. He holds the ship's wheel, and they entrust him. So he sails on. He touches his face and finds a beard, traces of salt.

Up ahead in the distance, a lantern, the shore, and the ship fights him for control. It goes there despite his steering orders. Everyone else is joyous, and they leap onto the pier and head for the first tavern. Someone whistles for him to join. He looks down at his feet. He wears the shoes of a child. He is eleven, twelve, too frightened to go inside. He wants to get back out to sea, but the men need to drink of this port and do things that men do.

That Certain Thursday

how many divine secrets of the world lie sleeping
dressed for love, adorned in treasure
ne'er to rise from their bed

For months, they had planned, quietly scheming, talking between rows of tobacco, hushed conversations about this new land, energizing their dream.

They had waited for spring, when the rivers were high and the snow had melted up north. Carter had seen snow before, and it made travel difficult, impossible when you're on the run.

Now they would wait for that certain Thursday.

Thursday was Sarah Jane's day to go into town to do her banking and to have lunch with her lady friends. When she was a safe distance away, they would take a road to Leaf River, then cross it to the east.

After that, they would simply head north, or "up," as Abram was fond of saying. They would cover twenty-five to thirty miles per day. And they would avoid all main roads or travel only in darkness, if that's what it took to get to New York.

And they told no one. Not the closest of friends. And both—master and slave—lay awake many a night worrying about the details, the feasibility.

Carter assembled a pack and kept it hidden in the barn, at the ready. Bedrolls, tent, maps, compass. Canteens and the spyglass. Tobacco, though he didn't smoke it. Two bottles of southern mash whiskey, though he didn't drink the stuff—more for bartering purposes. The bow and arrows. The Winchester rifle, the Colt pistol, and the Derringer as a backup. And bullets, lots of bullets. If nothing else, they could make a lot of noise in a pinch.

And the violin, and bow, and resin—that's if everything fit.

And there would be danger. Traveling thousands of miles without detection was impossible. And who be the enemy? There was no clear delineation between North and South, between intolerance and acceptance. One could stand in a spot and be celebrated by a host family or be judged and shot by the lady next door.

They would make the journey one county at a time.

And now it was March. And now the world up north would be waking from its frozen slumber. And now it was time.

Carter and Abram chose this Thursday as their secret departure date, and their skin crawled at the thought of heading out. And yet they thirsted to begin.

So it was shocking when Wednesday came and Sarah Jane announced that she would run her errands *this* morning, not tomorrow.

The cold sweat of irony kissed Carter's forehead. He had no choice but to hitch Sheba to the wagon. He fumbled with the harness, dropping the girth strap twice. He was exasperated when the mare would not take the bit in her mouth. Then he broke the cotter pin off the hand brake and couldn't locate a replacement. He finally fashioned one out of a horseshoe nail.

When Sarah Jane opened the pistol cabinet, he felt the color leave his face. "Darling, where's my Derringer?"

"Oh! I was oiling it. Climb up and I'll fetch it."

With his back to her, he unbuttoned his pack. The horse turned her head to him, quizzical. He found the little, single-shot pistol that he had hidden there.

"Here we go."

He held it by the barrel so that when he surrendered it, it was aiming at his forehead. *She wouldn't.* She took it by the butt and placed it in her jacket pocket as if the thing were a coin or clip or hairbrush— just a little something she might require later on.

She gave the reins a sharp, little snap, and the horse headed out of the barn. "I'll return around four o'clock."

"Good luck," he waved.

As soon as she was on the driveway, Carter ran to the row of crops. Abram was carrying a full basket of tobacco.

"Abram!" He motioned for the man to come to him. When Abram continued carrying the load, Carter yelled again, motioning. "Set it down. Right there! Yes!"

When Abram was ten feet away, Carter spoke low. "Get your gear. Meet me in the barn. We're going."

Carter hustled to the barn and saddled up Tara. Then he hoisted his pack and tied it to the saddle. Though he had planned this for months, he fidgeted at the prospect of forgetting something.

Sarah Jane had left him one pistol short. He put the little box of Derringer bullets back in the pistol cabinet. The Derringer would have been useful only in extremely close contact. On a whim, he took another pistol and ammunition and stowed it in his pack.

Abram walked in. He was only loping, but out of breath from the excitement. "She gone?"

"Yeah. You ready?"

"Yeah."

The plan was for Carter to ride, Abram to walk. *The converse would cause alarm.* Once they were in darkness, isolation, or friendly territory, they could exchange places.

"Here we go. Calm, now. We're just heading into town."

They made it down the driveway without any of the help seeing them. *Okay, first leg is done. Smooth sailing.*

When they hit the main road, Carter could see the tracks from Sarah Jane's horse and wagon. He gazed far ahead to see if he could see her, to ensure that she could not see *them*.

They weren't a mile up the road when they saw a horse and wagon coming toward them at a fast trot. "Wait!" Carter squinted. The wagon was too far away to determine the owner. "Into the trees!"

He steered the horse into the ditch, up the little slope, and into the brush. Trees were twenty yards ahead, and he cantered to get there. Of course, Abram would have to catch up, but the horse blazed a nice, little path for him.

Carter reached the tree line, wheeled around, and waited.

Carter couldn't see the wagon until it was dead-even with them. "Oh, shit!" Abram hunched low and squinted. It was Sarah Jane. Had she forgotten something?

They had planned on four to six hours of travel before Sarah Jane got home to discover them missing. As it was, they'd had twenty minutes. *So much for smooth sailing!*

They had no choice but to continue through the woods.

After a full hour, it was still slow going—underbrush and low branches. Carter and Tara blazed the trail, staying as true to north as possible, but avoiding marshes and hills that would wear Abram out. Still, they were muddy and branch-whipped. Abram bled above his left eye.

The strategy was to stay in Mississippi as long as possible. Something about Alabama made Carter feel skittish, something instinctive told him that the rule of law there was primal—even more so than in Mississippi.

They would cross Tennessee, then straight "up" into the quickest route through Kentucky. They weren't six miles from home, yet they felt like the world was flying.

First Migration

there is something about fleeing
about instinct and wits and sense of danger
that makes the calm that much more wondrous

The early going was especially rough. They slogged through thick, wooded areas and battled gnats in the swamps. Man and horse fought just to make forward progress.

Until they finally skirted Hattiesburg to the east, Carter kept looking left, half expecting to see Sarah Jane on the road, arm and index finger extended like a lightning rod. *How sadly ironic if this plan were thwarted before we've fled the area.*

Once they were out of this county, they would be strangers. They could move onto the roads and be but simple travelers.

Their story—that Carter was taking this slave to a new master— had been rehearsed back home. Always their *destination* was "the next state to the north."

Eventually, they hoped, they would be able to travel freely, day or night, without the need for fabrication. But freedom was a concept that neither could firmly grasp. The notion was incredible enough to Carter; he could not fathom what it meant to Abram.

At five-thirty pm, the rain began. Abram had been on the horse an hour. He looked back at Carter—both had the same idea. They found a small hill, went there, and Abram halted the horse and dismounted. Carter untied one of the packs, pulled out the first of two tarps, and spread it on the ground.

"Wanna take her bridle off? See if she'll eat."

Then he set up the little tent. The wind gusted, blowing the door of the thing like a canvas ghost. It spooked Tara. Her rear end pivoted, knocking Abram on his ass. All three were so dead-tired, so wet and weak and worn out that everything was just stupid-funny.

Carter gave Abram a hand up. They stashed the saddle, the guns —anything that couldn't take the rain—inside the tent, then climbed in after.

There was just enough room to lie down, barely enough to roll over. They peeled off their wet clothes and huddled in a blanket each. When they were settled in, they shared a canteen, ate a biscuit or two. They were cold but ravenous and the crumbs caught in their throats. They coughed and caught their breath and watched the rain.

"You realize, don't you," Carter offered, licking a crumb off his thumb, "that we're actually on our way out of here? On our way north?"

"Yes, sir. That feel pretty good."

"Hey. Call me Carter."

Abram chewed, nodded, quietly reflecting on this new direction. Carter continued, "In my book, you're already a free man. So... let's get used to it."

When night fell, they were still hungry, but too tired to leave the tent and rustle up more food. They considered lighting a fire, but didn't want to attract attention this close to home.

"Let's leave here as quietly as possible. Once we get north, we'll find our new rhythm," Carter explained.

He went out to check on Tara one more time. He poured water into a cupped hand, and the horse sucked from it, her lips sweet and soft on his palm. Then she chewed the grass that was still in her teeth. Carter patted her neck, scratched her mane and forelock.

"You're a g'girl." Then a whispered, "I'll see you in the morn, okay?"

They slept like the dead, spirits leaving the land they knew for a world they did not. But the learning and the knowing would come with time—they just had to let it wash through them.

The rain was finished with them, and the softest echoes played along the forest floor and its canopy. And when the night was at its most still, Abram had a night terror, and it scared the daylights out of Carter. The high tone of voice made his blood run cold. "Shhhh. Shhhh," Carter soothed.

Then it was quiet, again. And the forest paused for a good long while, until it was safe to resume its tip-toeing and whispers.

Carter didn't sleep much after that. His pulse was racing. His psyche put him on high alert, and every leaf that stirred was amplified by fright. He listened for Tara, but the horse made no sound. *Okay, a good sign.*

At some point, sleep reentered the tent and touched him on the shoulder. He slept, but lightly. The quiet was broken by the occasional cough or other man sound inside the tent. But soon he was *back aboard the creaky, wooden ship that carried him and his shipmates closer to a strange and lovely shore. Again, the faces in the moonlight, the low and even voices of men on deck, the wave that would hit the ship just right and cause that wonderful sea spray.*

When he woke, the veil of the world was being lifted, blackness replaced by gunmetal grey. He blinked to comprehend his whereabouts. Abram was facing him, staring at the cold fist Carter held at his chest. He stared so long, unblinking, that Carter cleared his throat, curious as to what held his attention. But Abram was not affected.

"Mornin'," Carter whispered. Still, Abram's eyes remained fixed. Carter felt his pulse quicken, worried that Abram was dead, or catatonic, or...

Abram coughed, bowed his head, and tried to wake his mouth, raise saliva. Then he exhaled and saw Carter observing him. He was groggy, somewhat uncomfortable. He yawned and rubbed his face.

Carter asked, "Do you always sleep with your eyes open?" Abram turned to him, one eye open, so he clarified. "You were sleeping with your eyes open."

"I was?"

"Yeah. You were staring at me, but not seeing me."

"Oh," was all Abram could muster.

Carter pulled the tent flap and peeked outside. Both men grunted as they got up from the damp ground. Carter looked around the perimeter, gave Tara a nod, then moved off to the edge of the little campsite to relieve himself. Then he dug into the food pack and pulled out a couple biscuits.

"No gravy, but we can pretend." Abram took his, and raised it in thanks. "Think we can do twenty-five miles today?"

"I do."

It took effort to get their wet clothes back on. And it was the first time Carter ever heard Abram swear. They took down the tent, loaded the packs. They gave Tara some water and they were off.

And that day, Thursday, they saw not a soul from sunup to sundown. They heard horse hooves once, and quickly moved from the edge of the woods to a deeper spot, then waited. But no one came. And Tara snorted as if amused at their ridiculousness. But more absurd was that Carter took the snort to heart. *Maybe we are being ridiculous. Maybe it's time to get on that road and travel the way we deserve.*

But something nagged at him, warned him that he might be recognized. They were still in Mississippi—someone could be passing through and know him by sight or remember their description, if questioned.

We've planned this for so long. Caution is warranted.

So once again, they moved closer to the road where the going was a little easier. They were not free, but they were ever hungrier for freedom.

28

They made good time. The sun was hot in early afternoon, but rain gave them a welcome break. Conditions were fair enough that they made about twenty-three miles.

They walked deeper into the woods, until satisfied that men had made trails through this section. They stopped, but Carter held up his hand, and slowly turned three hundred sixty degrees, getting a sense of the place. They were vulnerable after sundown, and another minute of evaluation was energy well spent.

"Good."

They had twenty minutes before nightfall. They unloaded their packs. Carter had Abram pitch the tent, then pulled out the map. He spread it on the ground, pulled out his compass and squatted.

"Ever use a compass, Abram?"

He looked up from tying down the tent. "Compass? I seen one, once."

"It's pretty easy to use. Look." He demonstrated how to align north with the black end of the needle. He placed the compass on the map and showed where north would take them—from their origin to their destination.

"Abram, if something happens to me, the compass is the most valuable thing you have. Take the compass—it's always in my left front pocket."

Abram hesitated.

"Take the compass and you will find your freedom."

"That's what you tell us about readin'!"

"Well, yeah. That's true, too!"

"I was always too dog-tired to stay awake for readin' time!" Even though it was Abram who admitted it, Carter felt like it was he who failed. *I should have forced the issue, insisted.*

"We can work on it on while we travel." Realistically, Carter knew that it would be damn near impossible to travel, keep a look out, and learn to read. *But "damn near" never stopped me from tryin'.*

He pocketed the compass and folded the map, stowed it.

"Abram, pretend I've been shot dead. Where is the compass, and how do you use it?"

"Pocket."

Carter fetched it, handed it to him. Abram studied it, as if he had found a ruby or sapphire, so Carter prompted him. "Where's north?"

Abram held the compass, rotated it until the N aligned with the black end of the needle.

"Excellent." Then he expanded. "N. North. North begins with 'N.' Let's make our first letter."

They crouched again, and Carter "erased" a spot in the dirt. He drew an "N." "See? Up, down, up. Now you do it. Up, down, up. Looks kinda like the trim on a barn door, huh?"

"Yeah."

"Good. Now make an 'N' wherever you see dirt." He stood. "And say 'N' each time you make one. I'm gonna fix us some dinner."

He opened the food pack and pulled out the little skillet. He added some dry beans, opened a tin of spice and sprinkled it in. Then he added some water. He stirred it with a fork, then let it set. He casually looked over at Abram, still drawing N's. Then he mashed the beans with his fork—just enough so they'd soak up the broth and thicken, a cold stew.

He smelled the mixture. If he were eating alone, he would have added more spice. But he'd been accused of being too liberal that way, so he let it be.

They sat on the ground outside the tent. Two men, two forks, one skillet. And they went at it. Sure, it would have been twice the meal had it been warm, but this was fine. It filled the emptiness. It tasted pretty damn good and Abram said so. Somehow, the simple meal felt like a reward at the end of a tough couple days, a turning point.

"In a couple days, we can have a fire, eat a hot meal." He added, "Once we're out of Mississippi."

"When will that be?" Abram asked.

Carter went though his mental maps and notes, and sighed. "I think we will cross the state line in ten days. It's a tall state!"

They sat back. The evening was still, and not a breath of wind disturbed the peace. The insects and amphibians were well into their evening choir, organized, coordinated. Somewhere, a stick broke and Carter's eyes went to it. He watched for a full minute—a patient hunter. He knew that a creature of the animal kingdom could easily outlast a man, so he always made a point of watching a little longer.

He stood. "Want to give Tara some water?" Then he walked deeper into the woods to take care of things. As he squatted, he could hear Tara grinding her teeth after she drank.

"It'll be better when we can have a fire. Then we can carve a little, before bed."

But tonight, their bodies and spirits were still growing accustomed to the rigors of the journey, to the demands of constant watchfulness. And in the darkness, they were comforted. Night was their shield, and they lay down, heads falling, falling back, trusting the arms of darkness to catch them.

Abram slept without a night terror. But when he awoke in the morning, Carter lay on his belly, left arm outstretched, locked. His left hand pulled and held taught the catgut bowstring, the arrow in firing position. His eyes locked on a target that Abram could not see, but he knew to freeze, quiet his breathing.

But he pictured the worst. A posse of slave hunters? A night doctor? He wondered how many, and what action he should take when the arrow flew. His eyes went to the ammo pack. He had never fired a pistol, but knew what the trigger was for.

And then, without warning, the bow string slapped in the air like a whip and the arrow was away and buried. Carter remained completely frozen until an unexpected smile crept across his lips. Abram watched him get to his feet and disappear through the tent flap.

When he returned, he had removed the arrow from the badger—it was inedible—and cleaned the tip in the dirt.

"How did you know he was out there?"

"I heard Tara. Somethin' spooked her. Figured the bow would be quieter."

Abram was amazed that he had not even heard Carter fetch the weapon. *If I slept through that, what else would I miss?*

The Vanishing Point of Days

planning, ingenuity, and fortitude
are inoculations against desperation

Each morn after they broke camp, they ate an apple that Carter fetched from the food pack. And each morn, the apple would be progressively softer, having traveled and aged, being jostled and bruised.

When Carter handed one to Abram this morning, the man turned it over and over before taking a bite. "Soft."

Carter said nothing. Abram bit. "Oh." He didn't chew the piece in his mouth, but showed the brown that his bite revealed.

Carter still said nothing. He bit his own fruit, discovered the same, and went right on eating, smiling. He found it ironic that a slave balked at food that the master considered edible. But rather than feeling incredulous, he had fun with the situation.

"Sweet, huh? Yeah."

For now, this was the best they had. Rotten apples were keeping them alive; and adding some humor made them more palatable.

The man on horseback had responsibility for two hundred seventy degrees of lookout duty; if he spotted man or beast or residence, he reined in the horse. If he saw food or water, he would say so. They filled the canteens at every opportunity, even if they still had plenty. And when they came upon a fruit tree, they would eat as much as they could on the spot, then replenish the food sack.

The man on foot was charged with keeping up with the horse and with lookout duty for the ninety degrees to their rear. They discovered that it was smarter for the walking man to hang back about ten paces from the horse so that he was more apt to hear anyone approaching from the rear.

But despite their watchfulness, they had time to daydream, to reflect. And the farther they got from home, the more deeply Carter thought about Sarah Jane.

She caused him much anguish. She inflicted the most hateful pain. She questioned him so thoroughly that he questioned himself. She admonished him for his inability to help her bear a child. He was "a tree without leaves, without fruit," she said. "Unable to render shade or nourishment," he thought pensively.

But unlike a tree, he had precious mobility. And the power of thought, and choice. And he believed that even without leaves or fruit, he had seed within him—if not to propagate, then to inspire.

Every man—even the down and out, even the lost—has a purpose, be it to build or to serve, to learn or to teach, to drink of love or to live off the memory of love. Carter could turn a field or build a fence. He could manage a farm or he could cut the hay. He could share a bed with a woman or he could sleep with the horses.

He sighed. *I am a simpleton.*

And this morn, as he trudged ten paces behind the horse and finished one of the last of the rotting apples, his mind went to her.

He breathed and smelled her in the air, her scent so vivid that he found himself listening for her voice. When he looked to his right, his heart leapt—half expecting to see her there.

Virgin sunlight used its kiss to open the spaces between the trees, now, landing dappled on the sweet, sanguine berry bush, as if this place were designed to attract such kisses, dreaming of its own first lover.

Sarah Jane would wake and go without breakfast, he thought. Through another morning, she would worry about him. She would think the worst had happened or, he mused, she would piece together all the hints and curse his name.

She would find something that he loved—a treasure—and smash it. And when the help appeared with broom and pan, she would dismiss them so that she could walk on the pieces, crush them further throughout the day.

Eventually, she would find the map—the one that he drew by hand, the one that led south, to the sea, to the fishing boat that he once saw in a painting, the *Sweet Little Lass* out of Mobile.

It's likely that she would hire a man to find and fetch him. But the man would come up empty and return to her a failure, for the *Sweet Little Lass*—according to Carter's barber, went down in a storm and all were lost.

The ruse would buy Abram and Carter a lead of another week or two.

Yet even with all of these things in place, and knowing all he knew of Sarah Jane, he did miss her morning kiss.

Before her eyes were open, she was an angel, an earthy, hungry angel. Before she realized where she was, she wanted him. Before she pushed him away, she loved him because he was a man.

He pictured her afternoon surprises in the barn.

Sarah Jane would return from a ride, thirsty and invigorated. He'd come in from the rows of tobacco—gloved and shirtless—and pull the saddle from her panting horse. He'd coax the bit from the mare's mouth and hang the bridle on its wooden peg. Then he'd turn to find her reclined on the bale of straw—head sideways, as if posing for a portrait, beautifully nonchalant—skirt up to her chest, daring him to have her.

And he would have her.

And he would show her his strength, for that is what she required. And to her he would surrender his power, reveal his weakness. His passion and his tears were not merely for this pleasure—they were for the love that she withheld, could not feel.

And after, she'd leave without a kiss and march straight to the house, leaving half of his love standing in awe and half running down her leg, the warmest part of him already cold.

And he would use a lead rope to walk the horse, to cool her down, and to come back to the earth, himself. And the mare would nudge his shoulder a time or two while they walked, as if she understood, sympathized.

He thought of her, his Sarah Jane.

His chest felt warm. But he sighed, and realized once again that the warmth was probably because of him, not her. He was loved for his utility. And now, walking behind the horse, he declared once more that he required more than that.

And when it came time for Abram to walk, Carter waved him off. "I'm good." Felt good walking today. Felt good to be under his own power.

They were on a good trail, worn and clear, and heading pretty much straight north. They passed a lone rider coming the other direction, and the man smiled broadly. He led a second horse behind him, and Carter noted the whiteness of his teeth, the fineness of his attire.

Late in the day, he decided he might ride the last hour before sunset. "Abram, when we get to that ridge, maybe I'll mount up."

Abram raised his hand to tip his hat. And at that moment, the shot rang out, and Tara bolted left, and Abram fell. Carter dove, eyes trying to match the shooter with the sound.

"Abram!" he yelled in a whisper. "Abram!"

"I'm okay!"

"Are you hit?"

"No. Just my..."

Another shot rang out, this time from their port quarter. Tara had slowed by now, shaking her head, some fifty yards away, then came to a stop and sniffed some tall grasses.

Carter slid a pistol to Abram. "Stay low." He pointed, "Aim there. Fire only if I yell fire. Stay here."

Carter came to a crouch, then sprinted so that Abram, Tara, and he made a triangle. He searched frantically for the source of the second shot, but saw nothing. He waited. He knew that he was on defense but refused the notion. He sprinted again, this time spraying three shots as he ran toward the approximate location of the second shooter. He came to rest, crouched again, behind a tree. He looked back to Abram and could barely make him out. *That's good!*

He kept scanning the horizon, surprised that he had yet to locate a skittish horse, a telltale bandana, a flash of steel. He debated running to Tara and grabbing the rifle, but decided he would scare her and become a target.

So, on his own count of three, he ran again toward the second shooter and fired twice more, leaving himself one more bullet. His adrenaline made him crazy, and if he saw the shooter, it's likely he would have pummeled him to death without spending his last shot.

But he found nothing, not in the brush, not high in the trees. So he ran back to the original scene, reloaded, then repeated the charge-and-fire procedure in an attempt to flush out the first shooter.

And again, he found nothing.

He started back to the scene, but thought of Abram aiming at him.

"Abram!"

"Yeah?"

"I'm coming out. Do not fire."

"Okay."

He ran to fetch Tara. He walked the last twenty feet, hand out, clicking his tongue. Tara nickered. It was enough to convince the horse that everything was safe, and he took the fallen reins.

He took the gun from Abram, and clicked on the safety. "Put it in your belt. Let's ride the hell out of here. Ready?"

Carter stood in the stirrup and climbed into the saddle. He gave Abram an arm up, and Abram sat just aft of the saddle. Carter wheeled the horse and trotted her to the road. As soon as they hit the dirt, Carter spurred her and they galloped. His adrenaline was still surging, reins in his left hand and pistol in his right. *Three shots left.*

It felt good to be moving, but both men were scared witless. They were sweating, but cold. Carter leaned into the horse's neck, and Abram pressed up against Carter's back. They were flying!

After two minutes, Carter reined Tara in a little, and they slowed to a trot. He sensed that Abram was taking the brunt of the animal's roughness, so slowed to a walk, now. And as soon as they did, Carter steered them off the road and into the woods. It was darker here, and Carter took them as deep as they dared venture.

Then they halted. Abram climbed down, holding his shoulder. Carter came down now, then immediately fetched the rifle.

"Abram, let's get the tarp down." Abram did. "We sleep in the open tonight."

They slept in shifts; but at some point, they both crumbled, unconscious.

Carter woke before dawn and smelled smoke and couldn't get back to sleep. He thought about the shooters, where the hell they came from and where they went. He was hungry, groggy, stiff. *The trail is hell. I miss my bed.*

He decided that both would ride from now on, as long as Tara held out. And he wondered if they should travel under cover of darkness. They would, as soon as they were out of this area. The bullets still had him bristling, jumpy.

As the sun peeled back the night, Carter woke Abram. Before the man was on his feet, Carter explained the new plan.

"We ride until noon, then sleep. That way, we travel only at night." He sensed that it might be too early for Abram to comprehend this much, so he summed it up, "No more of this gettin' shot at shit!"

They geared up, ate an apple, and made their way north. After two hours, they came to a swamp, impassible. "Oh, to hell with this!" Carter reined the horse to the road.

The swamp that prevented their travel granted them a gift—the road was so much easier, almost luxurious! And their spirits were lifted. It was ironic to think that just hours ago they were fired upon. Now they were traveling in high style, though hungry, beat, and dusty.

They decided to press on past noon, stopping around two. They went straight back, into the woods, and built a fire. Carter made his bean and spice dish, heated this time. And they shared the skillet, audible moans celebrating the deliciousness.

"So, we'll sleep until dark, then travel through the night."

Of course, sleep at this hour was elusive, more like napping. And around five, Carter took his bow and arrow and headed deeper into the forest. When he returned, he carried a rabbit, which they dressed and baked and devoured.

"What a day, huh? It's like a feast!"

Abram didn't stop chewing to talk. "This is delicious."

Just to have the fire was marvelous. It was hot out, but the crackling was soothing, the flames mesmerizing. In a sense now, they had taken a step away from *fleeing* and taken one toward *arriving*.

And in the night, they had free rein on the road. They met a wagon or two—one actually sported lanterns—but they recognized no faces and were themselves anonymous. An hour into the nighttime travel, Carter had Abram come up and sit behind him. Tara could handle this, carrying two men at a walk. She had hauled wagons full of everything from fieldstone to barrels.

Now, over a week into their journey, they had found the rhythm. They had weeks of travel ahead, but things were getting easier. They were fed, rested, and were now carried. They were granted a glimpse, a hint of the life that was to come.

Fo' Sister

...ngels get confused...
...cripts and roles they're forced to play
...play they must and with compassion

...Ie ran to the barn to fetch a bucket, bare feet slapping dust and ...w. The doors were partially open, just enough for his skinny, twelve-year old body to slide through sideways.

But he misjudged the step up and while his body made it through, his feet stayed outside. He landed sideways, face in the straw. And when he lifted his head, everybody froze.

Mama was bent at the waist, her eyes wide as saucers, bottom showing. Master LaFontaine stood behind her, chewing tobacco and bumping into her. He spoke in a language foreign to Abram, in an animal's voice. "Akua!"

And something told the boy to leave without the bucket, without brushing off, just get the devil out of there.

And he ran. He ran without a plan, first toward the field, then toward the smokehouse, then behind it. He sat by the woodpile, out of breath, mind reeling out of control. What he saw caused a powerful confusion of energy to explode inside of him.

He felt the tears come, wracking tears that caused his gut ...tighten.

And something else, something new—an incredible sen... anxiety, and then... and then... a release. An extremely ... angelic sensation.

And then his spine hurt, down low. Way down low. ...went away and he was aware of the wetness.

41

He was late with the bucket, and caught the switch _from
Leonard. But when Master LaFontaine walked in, he _from_
Leonard to "Stop! Leave!" And he talked low to Abram. An _at_
him a square of chocolate.

And Abram never got the switch again.

That night, Mama didn't say nothin' about what Abram saw. N
that night, not ever. But she was extra sweet to him at supper, strokin
his head as she passed. And when she kissed him good-night, she
said, "I love you, Abram," and kept her lips pressed against his
forehead for the longest time.

The next day, Master LaFontaine asked Abram if he wanted to
work inside the house from now on. "I think you would like it,
Abram. Cooler inside. You won't be sweaty or dirty near as much. I
think you might like it."

So Abram started that morning, sweepin', scrubbin' floors and the
bathtub. He brought in firewood, herbs, chickens—whatever the
ladies wanted.

He also stood around a lot. Didn't know where to put himself. At
night, he had a lot of unspent energy and had trouble falling asleep.
So he did a lot of thinking, pretending, dreaming of what was next for
him.

That Friday morning was the first time that Mama got sick. But
opened every morning. And the ladies seemed to huddle
d wring their hands, and notice Abram watching. And
ng bad was happening.

s morning, candles burned in every front
ning. Mama was upstairs. The lady of the
ft to have dinner with relatives.

tudying the paper snowflakes,
sheet below. _How long does it_

42

he heard Mama cry. She was crying really hard. He
But, see Grace talking to Lettia. She looked down at him,
looked a some linens, then walked downstairs and across the
han came within ten feet, holding out her hand.
rod him out the back door and across the yard, past the
, past the smokehouse, to the swing. She signaled for him to
nen just pushed him. Just pushed him.
as minutes before she said, "Baby's comin' today."
didn't know what to make of it. There hadn't been a baby in
use for a long time. He didn't see what all the fuss was about.
the baby comes! Wrap it in a blanket and bring it out to play!

For seconds at a time, the swing lifted him from this earth, December kissing the nape of his neck. And in his ears the rush of Christmas wind lied, *This shall never end!*

And in mid-swing, and in his childhood rapture, he heard Lettia scream, screaming from the back step. And Grace ran from him, apron and bonnet flying. And he watched his bare feet drag in the dust, dragging until the thing came to a stop. And the wind died with it.

He slumped, and in his gut knew to stay away.

The next day, Master LaFontaine called for him. He went to the barn and saw the long pieces of wood set across the saw horses. The place smelled like pine, and LaFontaine realized that Abram had never seen saw dust before—he saw a couple piles on the floor, then looked to the ceiling to see where it came from.

LaFontaine demonstrated. "See? If I saw through the wood"—the saw huffed as he made a few passes—"this is what is left behind." He handed some to Abram. "Soft, huh? Smell it. Good, huh?"

He dusted off his hands. Abram mimicked him. Then they got down to business at hand. "Do you remember when Master Chet died, and we had a coffin for him?"

Abram shook his head.

"Well, I thought we'd make one for your mama." / silent, so he continued. "Yeah, we'll make a nice one, so she was She'd like knowing that you helped build it, Abram." *ll*.

LaFontaine showed him how the pieces would fit. Then 1 eight nails from a brown sack. Seven went between his lips eighth, he nailed into a board, then stopped when it just pe through the other side. Abram was distracted, mildly fascinated his master didn't swallow the nails. The man pulled a nail from l. lips, and hammered it in, repeating this until eight nails were ready to be hammered home, into the corresponding piece.

When the boards were matched, LaFontaine had Abram take a few whacks with the hammer. Abram held it with two hands, taking great pains to hit the nail precisely. But the nail bent before it was halfway through, so he was instructed to drive the next one.

When the same thing happened, LaFontaine said, "Ah-ha! I know what you need." He reached into the brown sack and retrieved a nail. "Put this in your lips." The boy looked incredulous, but took it. "Not too far, now. There."

Incredibly, the boy was able to drive the third nail home. "One more tap!" Abram hit it a little deeper. "One more!"

He drove the rest home. LaFontaine straightened the two bent ones and took care of those. The sides of the coffin were now joined to the head.

"See? It's taking shape. Good job."

They repeated the procedure, adding the foot. Then the bottom, requiring twenty nails, was joined with the rest of the box.

They stood back and looked at what they had made from nothing. Boards and dust and nails became a resting place. Abram sniffed, and wiped under his nose. LaFontaine lifted the cover, just to show how it would fit.

"Maybe we should paint something on the top. What d'ya think? A cross? A flower?" Abram didn't reply. "A bird?"

Abram liked that idea, so LaFontaine went to the cupboard and found some black paint and a brush. He reached to his ear, hoping to find his pencil there, then found it on his workbench.

He leaned over the coffin lid. "What d'ya think—a flying bird?"

"Yeah."

"Yeah, good idea," he said as he set the pencil in motion. With just a couple curves, they witnessed the birth of a bird in flight. LaFontaine showed Abram how to dip the brush, spread the paint, use the horsehair to make a sweeping stroke or a thin line.

Abram wanted to do more—he liked the feel of the brush. So LaFontaine sketched a cross below the bird. It flared out at the four ends. They both liked the look of it.

And when they were done, they both felt a mix of emotions—a sense of accomplishment for crafting a worthy bed for Mama, for LaFontaine's lover; and a profound gloom that her skin and bones and spirit would be laid to rest, sealed, buried, and over decades remembered, forgotten. Generations would wonder who she was, would wonder her name, her legacy, her laugh.

But no one would see her eyes again. None would know her glance—its flame had gone out. And that simple fact was hardest to understand, the most profoundly difficult to fathom.

"Do you know," LaFontaine said, leaning back in his chair, "Do you know that most boys are taken from their mothers when they are babies?"

Abram looked up at him.

"Oh, yes. They *do* this so that the master has *control* over the boy. So that *everything* that came before is erased."

The man leaned forward now, his face close to Abram's. "But I don't work that way! I think a family—even a Negro family— deserves, *deserves* to live together, to make a life, to..." he gestured with his hands, as if they would find in the air the right way to finish his thought. "...to have the love of family."

He leaned back again, his face in darkness, his mind on Abram's mom. "Your mama was a beautiful woman. And we will all miss her, son. You had some good years with her."

When Abram was stoic, LaFontaine asked, "Didn't ya, son?"

"Yes, sir."

The men set Mama in the coffin. She wore the best clothes she owned—her houseworker outfit—and held dried flowers that the Missus had cut and hung at the end of autumn. They asked Abram if he wanted to kiss her before they put the lid on.

He looked down at her, licked his lips, and shifted his feet in indecision. He was frightened. Scared that she might wake up, grab him. Scared that she might open her eyes and take him with her.

He said nothing, only shook his head and continued looking down. Besides, he was holding his new baby sister.

So the men put the lid on, and when Abram saw the two symbols he painted, he felt a stab in his throat. Later in life, someone would ask if he'd ever painted. In his mind, he would see the lid as if the paint were always fresh. But he would lie, "Never."

They placed her head to the east, in anticipation of the call of Gabriel's trumpet.

He held his baby sister graveside, and afterward, people commented at what a good brother he was—he kept her from crying. She kept him from crying as well. He focused more on her, sleeping, than on the surreal scene before him.

And sure—he thought about tossing baby in the hole with their mama. After all, it was baby who dragged Mama by the foot. Death came when baby arrived. But numbness was his savior. And when the service was over, Master LaFontaine told him to go swing for the afternoon. "No work today, son."

And LaFontaine brought Abram a hard candy on a stick. It was green—Mama's favorite color. Abram had never tasted anything so sweet before. And when the master walked away, Abram felt the sniffles come on. He blamed the sucker—it made the roof of his mouth a little raw, and so the tears naturally came.

And he sat on the swing, facing away from the house, but did not swing. He hung his head. And he thought about digging up Mama and giving her that last kiss.

And he felt the guilt of failure. He sensed her disappointment, pictured her shedding a tear, longing for his last kiss but bound and gagged by death.

He knew he could never get that moment back again.

And that night, without pack or plan or provisions, he would leave his bed and walk through the door, not caring if it squeaked. Then he would run, past the outhouse, down the driveway, toward town.

And the moon followed like a dog that won't listen, won't go home. And the trees that shaded him during daylight now failed to recognize him, decrepit strangers against the sky.

He slept in a damp meadow that at dawn turned to mush. He woke shivering, uncontrollably so. He got up in the near-dark, realizing that his trousers were soaked through, his butt cheeks unable to dry, despite the friction of walking.

And he had no idea where he wanted to go.

The others would be up and eating by now. The thought of food made him hungry. He hadn't eaten dinner last night. The last thing he ate was the green candy on a stick.

He turned the next corner, following the dusty little road to the cemetery. There was no fence, no gate, just a sign he could not read. He crossed the site to the mound of earth and could not believe that his mama was there. He stared at the wooden cross that Master LaFontaine made, the symbols like hieroglyphics, a code he could not decipher.

But he walked to it, and knelt, and traced the carving, and pretended to read. "Mama. Died two days before. Coming back another day. After she visits heaven."

He looked at the fresh earth before him, put his fingers straight down into it, and pushed. He pushed his fingers as far as he could, wiggling them when he was near elbow-deep to gain another inch or two. The cold at that depth shocked him, but he pushed and wiggled deeper.

Then he stopped. He wished to reach her and he feared reaching her.

The wind blew, and—as if shaking him both to his senses and to irrationality—he suddenly feared that Mama would reach up and grab him, so he pulled his arm out, panting. He sat back, dirty, thirsty, and watched the hole slowly fill back in, mud patching the wound of the earth.

Traces of daylight crept up behind him, then past him until the cemetery was lit by a damp grey. It could barely be called light, but it was enough to sting his eyes.

He stood and stumbled, his mind blank, his tummy empty. He shook the dirt and mud off his arm, and walked.

He walked down the dusty road and turned left, back up the driveway. It looked strange, foreign to him in the daylight.

He saw no one until he got to the fields.

"Abram!" Everyone looked up. Abram didn't answer, he just walked down the row and took his place among the others in the sea of tobacco plants.

He breathed deeply, taking in the sweet scent. He felt like he'd been gone forever. Working inside the house was disconcerting, unnatural; and he'd missed the plants, the neat rows, the feel of this place. And, after just one night, he'd missed the things that even a slave considers a comfort—his roof, his bed, his breakfast.

And yet he would run again—always to nowhere, always in confusion. And always he would return before the day was through.

$he

who can say
where the inner child is born
and how it views its place in this world

Sarah Jane married—against her father's wishes—when she was fifteen. He was afraid. Afraid of the pain—for her, for him. He was frightened of childbirth, at the notion of her pregnancy and delivery, for it had robbed her of her mother, him of his wife.

"You don't understand!" he pleaded. "You don't realize what a man requires, Sarah Jane! It's... it's animal! You have no idea! *Enjoy your childhood while you can!*"

"But, Daddy...!"

"Listen, there's *time* for that!" He gripped her shoulders. "*Later, Honey!*"

She stormed out. He thought it was in anger, but it was in frustration. *How can Daddy be so blind?* She'd had Shane since she was twelve.

And less than a month after the wedding, she was with child. Shelby was born on her own sixteenth birthday. Tad was born eleven months later, and Henry a year after that.

She was a good mother. She not only raised her children, she also built a farm—first eggs, then poultry, then tobacco. She parlayed the business like it was a math game, plowing profits back into the business and growing it exponentially.

Shane made wagon wheels. He didn't make the best wheel around—not the smoothest or cheapest or longest-lasting—but he knew how to delight his customers. He chased orders. He created a need and the means to fulfill it. And he would happily work day and night to finish an order, sleeping only when the spokes and rims and cogs were assembled, delivered.

When he focused, he was tough to match. But sometimes, he was entitled to undisciplined free time, and took it even when it wasn't convenient to Sarah Jane.

Where *he* was intermittently lackadaisical, she was driven, focused, relentless. She was not content with the same customers as last month—she required more and greater challenges. She thrived on growth, skirting the frantic edge, deadlines and near-impossibilities.

So arguments spilled over, from his wheel shop to her barn, then across the grass to the house. From the kitchen up the stairs, to the bedroom. From the wash basin, pitcher droplets on the floor, leading to the bed. Voices and passions highly charged—his her equal, hers his match.

Bed was where they made their final stand, where they came to communicate in their language primal. Bed seceded from the state of normalcy, immune to the day-to-day, and blurred the business at hand.

But midway through their sons' childhoods, Shane packed up his tools and headed to a new place in town. As much as he loved her rain and thunder, Sarah Jane's emotional storms were too much for him.

By the time their three sons marched off to join the state militia, their mother was but thirty-six years old. She walked them into town, but refused to watch them parade off with the troops—said she had a time-sensitive delivery to make. She kissed them, held them, then rode off without looking back. When she got home, she spent the next three days in her bedroom, darkened.

Soon, she was running a farm operation that grossed a thousand dollars a month. And although she lost her best workers that day and the economy was in a shambles, her business sense kept the place afloat.

She worked late every day of the week, pushing herself until she dragged herself upstairs and fell into bed. Often, she fell to sleep in mid-prayer, seeking protection for her boys, but was pulled down into unconsciousness.

She rose before the sun. And each morning, her first thought was of her boys and the daily realization of the danger they were in, of her helplessness.

Whistles Heard

as we march into every new state
—albeit uninvited and through the back door—
at least one of us will enter a smarter man

On the trail, there was no time to carve, no time to even think about whittling. But one afternoon while Carter was hunting with bow and arrow, Abram pulled from his coat pocket the bird whistle that Carter had given him, the template which Abram was instructed to copy.

He held it lovingly, like it was a real bird, a house wren. He ran his thumb along that sweet spot where the back meets the tail feathers, the place that quietly demands to be stroked and loved.

He noted the delicate perfection, though his own hands were incapable of such detail. He marveled at the symmetry, though uniformity may forever elude him. He admired its smoothness, though his own knife may never achieve the same.

In that moment, he wanted to cry for its exquisiteness and to crush it, frustrated that he would never match its glory.

He heard a twig snap, and looked to see Carter coming through the trees. He raised up two rabbits and smiled triumphantly. Where he'd previously used the bow and arrow only for recreation, Carter now refined his skill and felt a quiet pride for his accomplishment.

Things were good now—they made slow but deliberate progress north. The daylight hours were increasing, which meant fewer available traveling hours at night. But Carter used the light hours to hunt and cook, and the two celebrated and feasted daily.

Abram was now writing the alphabet in a ledger book, first copying the letters, then creating each from memory. After they ate, Carter quizzed Abram until he could recite or write each letter on demand.

The trail was enough to challenge any traveler. But Carter wanted their downtime to be productive. So, his secondary goal was for both men to be better equipped for the world once they reached New York. If Abram could read and write—even just a little bit—his standing in the world would increase. And if Carter could provide for himself, be self-sufficient—then he, too, would have a better chance at survival.

Their last hour of daylight was usually spent packing up, breaking camp, killing the fire. But just before that final act, they would get as close to the coals as possible and soak up the last of heat. In the flames, they would conjure images from home—the farm, the people, the hum of life they left behind.

And less certain, less clear, were images of what lay ahead.

They were night travelers, deliberately against the grain, creeping up the middle of the sleeping world. And the road quietly obliged, unfolding one county at a time. During transit, they barely spoke, a good ear turned to potential danger.

So, with such a narrow field of focus, their minds went to a place neither had been. The North. New York. Northerners. Yankees.

And it scared the devil out of them.

Fellow night travelers were cause for heart palpitations, suspicion. Horses were openly curious, but men... men were guarded, intentionally dark in shape and low of voice, each party cloaked in the nefarious. Hushed pleasantries were exchanged, but with pistols drawn, concealed under coats.

And once they passed, Carter would rein the horse to a halt and cock his good ear, ensuring that the hooves faded, becoming one with the music of the night world.

And in daylight they slept, hidden from the world as if in darkness, dreaming less and less of the comfort left behind and more of this place they called "The North."

Tonight, on the horse—just a couple hours into the evening's ride —Abram nodded off to sleep. It was for just a second, and his forehead banged into the back of Carter's.

"What the...?"

"Sorry. Sorry." Abram readjusted his seating.

Carter was surprised that Abram's mind went to sleep—there were so many ways to occupy it. Carter's thoughts went there, went to where he imagined Abram was, what he might be going through.

He knew only fragments of Abram's formative years—thirteen of them spent on the LaFontaine farm. He was orphaned. He had a younger sister. *Probably still at LaFontaine's.* He'd spent four years with Sarah Jane and Shane before Carter arrived, then two more.

He was a good worker. Quiet. Chose to sleep during study time rather than learn to read. But it's easy for a young man to focus only on the need at hand and not plan for the future.

Or maybe his instincts told him that he had no future.

At any rate, he and Carter had one thing in common—they both felt the need to fly. They both decided to risk everything to find freedom, to at least *try* to find it.

And it was strange how the conversation came to life.

"How big is Mississippi?" Abram asked one day, during a ride into town on the wagon.

Carter considered the question, trying to conjure a way to describe such scale. "Think of it as a big rectangle. It's tall, kinda narrow side-to-side. If we rode down, south, we would come to the Gulf of Mexico in..." he pondered, "three days.

"If we rode right, or east, we'd be in Alabama in two days. If we rode left, west, we could be in Louisiana in two days.

"But if we rode north, up, it would probably take twelve, thirteen days to make Tennessee."

Carter let the information sink in. "Big. Big place."

He wondered where Abram's mind was. His *own* mind was a little overwhelmed by the size, by the dimensions of the states. And the only reason he had any grasp whatsoever of the layout of the country was from reading and from his early days in Georgia. He reckoned that anyone who had any less experience would find the scope utterly perplexing.

"What are ya thinkin' there, Abram?"

His insight gave Carter instant pause. "I was jes' thinkin' about what happens next."

"Next?"

"Yeah. What happens if you and the Missus break up the farm. Like Master Shane and her did."

It surprised him that Abram—and probably the others—had worried about their welfare when Shane left the farm. *Of course they would worry about their fates. Everything they depended on was in limbo.*

That day, Carter thought about reining the horse to a halt and discussing this further, but really had no idea what to convey. So he let the sound of the hooves continue.

And it worked. The sound was always soothing—the constant beat, the dependability, the easy pace. The horse was like a clock—no need to count the beats. Just let the sound fill you, and time will do its own thing.

When they got to town, Carter paid for the supplies and the two men loaded the burlap sacks and various boxes onto the wagon. Carter handed the canteen to Abram. "It's gonna rain."

Abram drank, and handed the thing back. Carter added another meteorological observation. "Damn, it's hot." Then he drank.

"You nigger-lovin' sonofabitch!"

Both men froze, and their eyes went to the boardwalk, the bench, the boots and brown teeth. Carter finally swallowed the gulp he had taken, and wiped his mouth with the back of his glove. He screwed the cap back on the canteen, eyes narrowing on the man.

"Why doncha jes' marry the boy!"

Carter put a foot on the step and pulled himself up on the buckboard. "Let's ride." Abram followed him up. Carter reined the horse back, back out of the space, then gave a "click" to head for home. They saw the man lean forward, mouth moving and one hand gesturing, but couldn't hear.

They rode three miles in silence, but Abram sensed that Carter still fumed. What he didn't know was that his master fantasized about *knocking a hole in that good-fer-nothin' bastard.*

As they unloaded the wagon, Sarah Jane came down from the house. She didn't address Abram; he was invisible to her. "You remembered my yarn?"

Carter froze. "Oh, hell."

She thought he was teasing. "Oh, come, now."

"No, I... there was this... I knew there was one more thing, and... I forgot it." The *good-fer-nothin' bastard* had made him forget that last, essential item.

"Dammit, Monroe! I ask ya fer one lousy thing, and you come back without it! What the hell am I supposed to do for my shawl order?"

Carter said nothing, but he beat himself up for forgetting.

"You sure as hell remembered yer tools! And yer seed, huh! Didn't ya?"

He manhandled the last burlap sack, shouldering it to the barn. He hoped her voice would trail off, but it followed, chasing him like flame chases a stream of turpentine. He swallowed every retort, the venom intended for her and *that good-fer-nothin' bastard* back in town.

"All right, all right! Lemme unhitch the wagon! I'll fetch yer goddamn yarn."

"Now why is it *my* goddamn yarn? Am I the one who forgot it? Huh? Is this *my* fault, now?"

He was in such a huff that he threw a bridle and a blanket on the horse—no saddle. *Just get me the hell outta here.*

And he rode hard down the drive. And the intentional dust made a barrier between them. And he felt impressive. And he felt stupid. And he hoped that when he got to town that someone dared to cross him. And he spurred on the horse, and added a *"Yeeaw!"* so that the mare knew he was serious.

And before he even hit the road, he regretted his decision to leave the saddle in the barn.

When he got to town, his tailbone hurt. He slid down from Tara, and the blanket slid down with him. It hit the dirt and he felt equally dusty, clumsy. He hitched the horse and spied the bench—empty. Then he walked inside the mercantile.

"Well, Mr. Monroe. We haven't seen you in a while!"

He smiled at Robin and looked around like he was merely shopping, knowing full well he had something very specific on his list, something do-or-die.

"Robin, can I get three batts of red yarn, please?"

She softly vanished, then reappeared, talking. "Now, I only have two red. I expect more in a couple days." She was at the counter, close enough to touch. "Can I interest you in a pink?"

Carter could not believe his ears. Sure, it wasn't Robin's fault, but the thought of enduring another tongue-lashing back home just made him tired. Very tired. Dead-dog tired.

"Really? No more? Like, not even a partial red one that we could —I dunno—fluff up and make it look like a whole one?"

He was talking like a sleepwalker, monotone. Robin studied one eye, then the other. She had an inkling of what was going on in Carter's world today.

She patted his hand. "You wait right here."

He did. He waited. He leaned on the counter and looked around at the bins and baskets and buttons, the needles and fabrics. He heard a back door slam shut. And in a minute, he heard it slam again, and there was Robin.

"Ta-daaa!" She held up a batt of red yarn. It had no label, so she removed one from a pink batt and wrapped it around the red. "There. Good as new!"

Cater gave a grateful smile, but with mouth closed. It was a smile of humble satisfaction and no more, like when you dodge a bullet— *yer alive, but someone's shootin' at ya!*

As Carter approached his horse, he noticed the blanket was off. He scanned the ground beneath the mare—nothing. He looked on the boardwalk, as someone may have seen it fall and hung it on the rail. Nothing.

He stopped walking and did a slow scan of his horizon. People milled about as if scripted—a man limps across the street, carrying a chair, his free arm swinging with each step. A boy swings on the hitching post in front of the barbershop. A man exits the saloon and scratches his belly. The butcher leans against his doorway, smoking, squinting. He sees Carter and nods.

Carter nodded back, then gave a little run and kicked his leg up over the mare. He reined her, then cantered out of town. When the way was clear, he tucked against the horse's neck and looked back to his left, hoping to catch a careless clue—someone laughing, someone victoriously waving his rogue blanket. Nothing. No one.

When he got home, he realized how much he'd perspired. He sweated against the red-dyed yarn that rode inside his shirt. He was relieved to discover that the color didn't bleed, but the batts were a little damp.

So he took his sweet time unbridling the horse, brushing out her coat, then watering and feeding both mares. All the while, the sun crept from the barn—its departure inaudible, profound.

He leaned on the stall door and just watched, just listened—the nosing of the hay and the grinding of the grain. And he let the beautiful horse smells enter him, venture like smoke, like good medicine, up his nostrils and into his psyche.

How is it that a beast can emit scents as evocative as a woman on a Sunday walk? Then he smiled as all things quietly made sense. *These two are mares, after all.*

And when he finally made the walk from the barn to the house, he saw Shane's horse munching on the dry grass in front of the porch, reins loose on the ground, the stallion right where the other man left him, huffing and wet.

Carter felt like his home was not his own, like his woman belonged to someone else, like his life's purpose was to serve another. *It's no wonder I sympathize with the help—I'm prit-near a slave, myself!*

When he got inside, she had already served Shane. His mouth was full of biscuit or soup, and he raised his glass when he saw Carter. "Hey!"

Sarah Jane stopped what she was doing and just looked at him. She expected to be scolded, or dared him to do so. She was sweetly vulnerable, but prepared to lash out, latch on. Carter laid down the yarn and went to the basin. As he washed the road from his hands, he put himself in a safe place, in his emotional cocoon.

"Everything go okay in town, Dear?"

"Uh-huh," he said without emotion or eye contact.

Shane took a big bite, then talked through his food. "Did ya find yer blanket?"

Everything in the room halted. He felt dizzy, like his heart just *stopped*. Carter shot Shane a look, feeling his pulse in his neck, now. Shane stopped chewing, sensing that Carter just might draw and fire on him, right there in the kitchen.

But no weapon was produced, and Shane burst into a hideous laugh, proud that his little trick was about the funniest thing he'd ever seen.

Carter dried his hands on his shirt, thinking *I'm gonna ride away from you low-down bastards—gonna dust y'all!—and never have to see your faces again.*

"Any regrets?"

Abram leaned to the side to better understand his traveling companion. "Huh?"

"Are you happy we left the farm?"

"Yeah. I think so."

"Okay, Abram, tell me the alphabet. Tell me a word that starts with each letter."

And the horse kept moving. And the night moved with them. And the letters of the alphabet came as well, like the slow, steady pace of the hooves. And every night brought them closer to the north edge of Mississippi.

Blankets and Wood Nymphs

and every morn shall birth surprise

Just before sunrise, just one day from the Tennessee border, they stopped. Carter dismounted and held up his hand for silence. Tara shook her head, exhaling through her nostrils but not forcefully enough to snort—she seemed to sense the command for quiet.

They had stayed to the east of Walnut. Carter had no idea how large Walnut was, but they were so close to the northern Mississippi border now that he didn't want to jinx it—the more invisible they were, the better.

So here they were—midway between Walnut and Corinth, not sure if the dirt they traveled was public or a farmer's personal road. Carter stepped off into the field, faced Abram, and gave him the "wait" sign. Then he ran up a small rise to get a look at things from a higher perspective.

Abram watched his figure grow smaller, then creep, then stand with hands on knees. Abram looked around, nervous about the approaching daylight, nervous about standing still. Until now, they had hidden themselves before sunrise. Today, they were flirting with the event.

A dog barked about a quarter mile off. Not a worried bark—just a notification. Carter stayed low, walked backward, then turned and ran down the hill. "Let's keep going," he said, licking his lips. "I think we're good."

He climbed back up, and they cantered for a mile. To their right, a farmhouse became clear. Strangely, the dog was silent. *Maybe he was let inside.* As they passed the property, Carter slowed the horse to a walk and pointed.

Over the split-rail fence at the property line, a quilt hung—pretty, but out of place. The morning breeze was barely discernible, but enough to flap the bottom left corner back and forth, like the tail of a fawn learning to graze.

It was hard to make out the design of the thing, and impossible to decipher the colors; but Carter *was* familiar with the lore associated with it.

He just wasn't sure if he should trust it. He loved the notion, but was dubious about the way men could twist it, create a trap. *If I consider everything a trap, I will never be ensnared.*

Again, the dog barked—this time, from the hill Carter had explored, and again, a single bark. He sniffed and traced the man's tracks.

Carter debated for several moments whether to approach the house, determine if he and Abram were welcome, learn if the residence were in fact an Underground Railroad station.

He hemmed and hawed. They were not starving. They were relatively healthy. On the other hand, it would be luxurious to have a bath, to eat off a plate, to sit in a chair.

The dog approached at a trot, but when his eyes met Carter's, he slowed, bowing his head, lowering his tail, wagging sheepishly.

"Hey, come here, boy." Carter squatted.

"Careful," Abram cautioned.

"He's okay." By now, he was in Carter's arms, pirouetting with excitement. "Yeah, he's okay. Aren't ya? Yeah."

Tara turned, sniffing. She shifted her weight. Abram was equally restless. "We should probably go," he said in an adamant hush. His eyes were on the house. His instincts were warning him.

Carter stood, taking another look at the house, the quilt, the dog. If it were a trap, it was a beautifully inviting one. *Traps always are!* He nodded slightly, then moved to the left side of the horse, and climbed up. He hated passing up an opportunity, but he respected his instincts and could live with or without indulging.

They cantered a mile or two up the road, leaving the dog and blanket in the morning dust.

When they came to a meadow of tall grass, Carter steered them through it and into the woods beyond. They were too tired to set up the tent, so they slept on the tarp, under the thin canvas of leaves that sheltered them from the morning sky.

Halfway to sleep, Carter's subconscious reminded him that this might be their last day in Mississippi. Finally, a milestone! *Oh, that does me good.*

He woke around noon, opening just one eye, and had a look around. Tara was lying down, her nose just above the ground. The woods looked different than just this morning—thinner, and Carter questioned his choice of sleeping location. *Must not get sloppy, now.*

Abram still slept. Carter came to his knees, then reached for water. Finally, he rose and headed east, away from their site, taking the canteens and bow and arrows with him.

He climbed a short hill which had beckoned with the clump of white birch at the top. Their leaves made a *Shhhh* sound in the breeze, and their bark was the brightest thing in the wood.

Just before he made it to the top, he froze, heart instantly pounding. He pursed his lips to calm it. There, not fifty feet ahead of him, stood a man, facing the same way Carter faced, peering from behind a tree.

Carter's eyes went to his left then his right in search of cover; but there was none, and he stood there, vulnerable, exposed. He reached behind him—careful not to let the canteens clank together—found an arrow, and readied it.

He waited a full minute for the situation to resolve itself, but the man did not move. He didn't scratch, didn't look around, didn't move. Carter carefully shifted his feet, so long was his waiting.

Finally, Carter cleared his throat—not fully, just a little, and pulled the bow halfway back, just in case. Nothing. He cleared his throat again, louder this time. Still nothing! *I might just launch this thing, just to wake his ass up!*

But at that moment, the man turned and trotted down the hill. His hair was long and black, his skin the color of earth. He was in such a hurry that his eyes failed to detect Carter until he was practically on top of him. But his reaction to Carter was the same as his reaction to a tree—he simply went around him.

He stopped when he came to a wide oak, the tree between himself and the top of the hill. When Carter saw this, he trotted to a tree of similar diameter.

When nothing occurred, he carefully looked back over his shoulder at the stranger. The man's eyes were fixed on the birches. And right then, Carter heard the voices, their laughter.

He peered with one eye, bow half drawn, arrow eager.

First, the redhead.

Hair graced her shoulders and half of her back, skin so white it glowed in the dappled light of the forest. She stopped before reaching the top of the hill, then turned back and laughed. She dropped something, and her trio found it uproarious. When she bent at the waist, Carter felt blessed for being a man.

When they all made it to the peak, Carter saw the reason for the other man's presence—the three women were too wet to dress. They carried their clothes and innocently played the part of wood nymphs. Their hair was coiffed by nature, already forming crimps and curls and perfect ringlets.

And they were totally unaware of the two men who watched. They were but fawns, having preened and bathed in sweet water, now returning to their safe place.

Carter pulled himself so he was completely hidden by the tree, then he glanced back at the man. The stranger was so completely entranced that he, too, was innocent. His eyes were focused on the three beauties; Carter was invisible to him.

Carter looked back and watched the three making their way through the forest, meandering, blind to danger, teasing without realizing they did so. *Why do they clothe themselves at all—such incredible, breathtaking beauty. Dear God, such simple, exquisite perfection.*

And when they were out of sight, the man walked toward Carter. He stopped ten feet away, close enough that Carter focused on his black, sharp eyes, his nose like a beak. At his throat was a necklace, the likes of which the white man had never seen—five strands of the thinnest bamboo, strung horizontally, parallel, perfectly spaced with a black bead at the ends.

The man regarded Carter with the same fascination. Finally, Carter broke the spell, extending his hand to the man.

The man looked, but did not accept the handshake. Instead, he let a smile come. And he spoke.

"Ne-zhoni." He gestured to where the three had graced the hill. "Ne-zhoni."

Carter turned his head a couple degrees, but refused to take his eyes from the man. "Tò. Aoo'?" The man was shaking his head, now. So, Carter turned and walked toward the hill, and the man simply joined at his side. They walked together up the hill, through the stand of birch and down the other side. It was then that the glassy, little pond revealed itself.

The Indian pulled off his shoes and stripped. He waded in, and Carter tried not to noticed how feminine he looked from behind, how attractive he would be if he were a woman—the hair, the skin, his thinness.

Ten feet out, the pond dropped off and the man was in up to his chin. He swam, dove so his hind quarters broke the surface, and disappeared below.

It had been days since Carter had a bath—a shallow stream bath at that. So, he followed suit. When he got down to his underclothes, he took one last look around, then shed them—clothes would not dry in time for his next ride.

The Indian smiled and pointed at him, happy to find him enjoying the water, then dove under again. Carter did the same, passing the man six feet below the surface. The water was crystal-clear, and surprisingly warm.

After, Carter dried himself with his shirt and struggled to pull on his clothes, now tight against his skin. The Indian treaded water in the middle of the pond, visible only from the mouth up, his black hair behind him like a family of soft, tame snakes. He watched Carter, his eyes indecipherable. *Even his demeanor is of a different language.*

Carter pulled on his boots and grabbed his bow, his arrows. He nearly gave a wave with bow in hand, then thought it might be misread as a sign of war or victory. *To hell with it.* He waved it anyway. It *was* a victory for the two of them, a simple, shared conquest.

The Indian gave the slightest bow of his head, then dove beneath the water once more.

Carter was happy to smell a fire—Abram was awake, expecting Carter to return with food. Unfortunately, he was able to bring back only a squirrel and a bird that he could not identify. Still, it was better than brown apples.

Carter couldn't help but detect the mild disappointment in Abram's eyes. "There's *nothin'* out there!" But they cleaned the animals and cooked their meat until it crackled.

The meal wasn't entirely unpleasant. It was no stew, but it felt good to chew on something, swallow something warm. And they had been fortunate—the trail had provided enough. They were far from starving.

"At some point, we're gonna get a home-cooked meal."

"You think so?" Abram asked, genuinely excited.

"I do." Carter leaned back and looked into the fire. "I do. Something tells me Tennessee will have something for us, a nice surprise."

They were quiet. Carter handed Abram his canteen, and the two drank from the water where Carter swam.

"Nice pond right over the hill, there." He wiped his mouth. "You wanna grab a bath?"

"I don't know."

"You should. Do ya good." Then he added, "Get the road off ya."

Abram scratched himself, debating, knowing he should take advantage and get washed. "Any snakes?"

"No snakes. But, umm… watch for the Indian."

"The who, now?"

"Ya might run into an Indian out there. Good man, though. His words… they sound like a song."

"A real live Indian?"

Letters of Tears

Dear Carter,

I know why you left. I know I failed you, failed us.
And I know that wishing won't bring you back.

It's been a month and I don't know where to send this. Or if you even made it
out of town.

I thought you went to Mobile, but couldn't find you, there. Yes, I looked. Yes,
I chased the night air, came up empty. I thought I sensed you 'round every
blessed corner, or down a lane that you would love. And I was so ready to
love you.

But it's as if you sailed away. Into the sunset.
And I know I deserve this. I was mean to you.
I didn't know I was hurting you.

I lie. I knew. I just didn't know how much.
I feel out of breath, out of energy.
I didn't realize how deeply my spirit was tied…
such is your allure.

You might think you left without me.
But your spirit offered its arm and mine accepted.
And I shall rock this porch should you return her, should you return.

Sarah Jane

Can Help You with that Heart

compassion
is the awesome force
of the gentle

Her hair was the color of sand, and the wind treated it as such, blowing fine wisps at her edges, oasis and mirage, a promise and a lie. Men would try and men would fail to mimic that wind. She had but to turn her head and new wind would find her, enticing her with promises of its own.

Carter entered her stage just days before Christmas, 1858. He was helping to load a wagon with feed, chicken wire, and lumber. He had no idea it was her wagon—he was simply following orders. But she watched him as he worked, singled him out among the others. She saw in him a light brighter than the Christmas lamps that in an hour would be lit here in town.

She was acutely aware of the time and needed to be home before dark. But the man intrigued her—he was working hard, but he wore a smile, joked with the others, and seemed to relish the chance to hustle, to carry more than his share.

And he was... well, pretty. Pretty in a rugged, cultured sort of way.

It's not that his eyes were beautiful—they weren't gem-colored, they were dark. But they gave off sparks when he smiled.

It's not that his body was all that incredible—he was tall, a bit thin, and not powerful-looking. But he had a grace about him. His step was eager. He was driven, focused.

And she immediately envisioned him working for her, smiling at her, kissing her. She sensed that they would get along well, and in her mind she already had a place for him. If she needed to move people around to accommodate that vision, then she would.

They wore no rings of marriage. They were united by no priest or God or medicine man, but felt blessed nonetheless. Both yearned for something fresh—for the opportunity to believe in something magical, for strings that tethered but did not bind, for a song that played purely out of love.

And—for a while, at least—every sun that rose was celebrated. Their love of thirst and thirst for love was rediscovered, quenched, and as if from a cistern of rainwater it gushed, consecrated by their own personal angels, sweetened by love, by lovemaking.

In the darkness, they declared every moon phase their new favorite, wondrous.

They stood barefoot on creaky floors, and when they shed their garments, the fatigue of the day was shed with them. Their hands finally found something soft and they gripped hard, desperate not to lose it. Their lips brushed the curves of their daydreams, skin sweetened by perspiration now dried to a whisper, articulating their most excruciatingly personal fragrances.

Each was reunited with their lost spirit.

But, over time, there were cycles that they badly wanted to arrest.

Each half moon that hung in the sky was a reminder of their incompleteness, a symbol of what was divided, an icon depicting seed or egg and neither could find the other, could bring it into light, could align and fuse.

The lunar ovum. The celestial seed.

The half moon had the face of a woman, turned to the side, seeking *something else* in the darkness, never facing forward until it was too late, until she closed her eyes and faced the earth, a failure in full spotlight, lit but only by another, never by light she herself could offer or reproduce.

And on those nights, she would face away from him, face anywhere but toward that window. And when her breathing finally signaled sleep, he would let himself inhale fully, happy that sleep had coaxed her but sad that he could not bring her such a simple gift. And he wondered how a man like Shane Becker could bring her gifts of three… three sons, and Carter could not bring just one.

When she slept, he loved the notion of bringing her a daughter. *A daughter would change her entire world. And how they would laugh.* But when they argued in the light of day, when he saw what she could be when she held her ground, a realization socked him in the gut—she would quite likely be a terrible mother to a daughter.

And so he lived with half moons of his own—resolve and indecision, belief and ambivalence, deep longing and mere half-heartedness.

By some miracle, he could grow tobacco where no one could—plants that towered, buds and leaves and fragrance that made one's mouth water. And for seasons, now, he saw to it that the bounty was harvested, prepared, and sold. Under his hand, acres would flourish.

And beneath his kiss, a woman would take his very best and with it touch the stars! But the emptiness, the absence of fullness, these were a mystery that fed upon itself and grew as a wedge, invisible but splaying the two and leaving only question marks and accusations.

She sat in the creaky bedroom chair that overlooked the back yard, the chair that once held an article of clothing of his. With two fingers, she moved the bedroom curtain lace to the side. The mare swished black flies with her tail.

She misses her stable mate, her Tara. She is half without her. She yawned, surprising herself, then thought, *Maybe it is I who is barren. Perhaps my time has already come and already passed.*

She let go of the lace, touched her belly. Three had come from her, but it was likely that none would follow. If somewhere the spirit of her little girl—who looked and laughed like him—waited by a stream, would she wait an eternity or would another claim her, love her as her daughter?

The stream would run forever, infinitely patient; but such could not be expected from a child. *The spirit of a child deserved to be born.*

She climbed into bed and curled into a fetal position.

Maybe I am the girl. Maybe it is I who must forever wait. Maybe this river will flow for eternity but I will be here, never claimed nor understood.

Fireside

freedom and slavery
often share coats of the same color

This night, they feasted. Two pheasants between them—much too much to eat—but they gorged themselves, fullness an unfamiliar feeling, their taste buds relishing fresh bird on open fire.

Abram was tearing into a wing when he surprised Carter. "Do you miss the Missus?"

Carter stopped chewing and looked at him. He swallowed, then took a pull from the canteen.

"Abram, I need to share something with ya." He cleared his throat, looked into the fire, then looked back at Abram. "The Missus and I... we were never married."

"What?" His eyes were wide, his expression would not have been more exaggerated if someone had told him the world was ending next Tuesday.

"We were in love, but both had been married before." He carelessly poked at the fire with a stick. Embers flew and hit the pheasant that remained on the spit. "We didn't want to go down that rabbit hole, again."

He tossed the stick on the fire and sighed. "Damn good thing."

"You were married before?"

"Huh? Yeah." It felt funny to speak her name aloud. "Elizabeth, Liba. Sweet little Liba, over in Americus, Georgia."

Abram was direct. "Did she die off?"

"No, nope." A smile came to half his mouth. The other half masked pain. "No, she, uh... she thought I could bring her the world, could cast away all her demons." He looked right at Abram. "Couldn't! Couldn't quite do it for her."

Carter pulled the second bird off the fire. It was a shame that they couldn't preserve this one, save it for tomorrow, but it had to be eaten. While it cooled, Carter showed Abram a little trick.

"If you really wanna get some good iron into your body, break the bones when you've cleaned 'em off." He snapped one, revealing a thin, brown line. "Suck the marrow out of 'em."

He demonstrated. "It's good for ya."

Abram did the same. "Can't really taste it."

"Right—ya can't. But it's good for your blood."

While the next bird was still quite warm, they dug into it. The meat easily fell away from the bone, its sweetness so incredible that the men were content to leave it on their tongues. They swallowed only when they had to, when they realized that they still had much more to eat.

They had been on the trail for a month, and had yet to spend a nickel. Some days, they felt as though they were barely surviving. Others, they were blessed. They were living off the land, compliments of a giving Mother Nature.

It was funny, really. Sure, they were sacrificing, to some extent. But no one nagged at them to perform, to fetch, to turn out the light. Their only responsibility was to keep moving.

And the next day, when they crossed an invisible line into Tennessee, Carter made sure he marked the occasion so that it was memorable to Abram. He came down off the horse and hugged the man. He slapped his back and said, "Congratulations. You are one step closer to winning your freedom! You are one state closer to New York."

And he had Abram recite their intended path, the little, semi-nonsensical word jumble that Carter had taught him to memorize. "Mississippi, Tennessee. Kentucky, West Virginia. Pennsylvania, New York."

In some ways, to Abram, the woods they stood in this afternoon felt a lot like the woods they stood in when they were back in Mississippi. He would think the same when they reached each state, and it would befuddle him, as if it could be a big joke—a journey of circles. And at night he would dream that they woke up back on the farm, having failed, and he would be back in the rows of tobacco, bent and picking the first of the ready leaves, feeling their stickiness on his fingertips, their sweetness, leaves the color of leather, gold.

Often, Carter looked at Abram and wondered how he perceived the world, wondered how he regarded his place in the world. Most times, he felt like Abram was content to be given an instruction, a duty—and he would perform it, all day long.

But if Carter failed to give an instruction, Abram would sit and look around at the world, scratch himself, lean back, wait for something to come to him.

Such was his perception of Abram's perception, his understanding of Abram's understanding. One could find fault in both sides of that —in Abram's ambivalence, in Carter's presumption. Or one could simply let it be. Carter, for one, thought it was fine.

Hell, look at me—I'm the complete opposite! I am free to go where the hell I want, but I'm forever restless! I've always gotta be goin' some-damn-where!

Endurance and Incentives

nothing makes us feel
more far away
than something from home

nothing makes us feel
more distant
than closeness

Leaving Mississippi was cause for celebration. But the change was dramatic—the road immediately became challenging, and Carter discovered that state borders were fixed, hard, for geological reasons.

Tennessee was like another world.

Neither man had encountered hills of such magnitude and number. Nor had they experienced such a feeling of smallness. For every mountain that became their focus, their northern star, they would have to cross ten. The psychological strain—to aim for a distant mountain and not arrive there for two, three days—wore on them.

And Abram was the first to break.

One Saturday, he tripped over a root, stumbled, and caught himself. Then he just wandered off the road and sat down. Carter slowed the horse, wheeled back around, then halted.

He let things set a spell before speaking.

"You all right?"

"Can't do it." Abram's head was between his knees. "Can't do it."

Carter looked up the road—the way ahead. He sighed and looked back at Abram.

"You wanna ride a while?"

"No."

"You wanna…"

"*No!* I'm *done!*"

"Yer... what?"

"I'm *done!* Not goin' no farther."

Carter rubbed his face, smoothed the beard that surprised his hand each time. He had not seen a mirror in a month—didn't need one, really. The hair was some kind of progress meter, a calendar.

He came down off the horse, then led her by the reins into the woods. "Come on." Abram sat still for another minute, then got up and followed.

Carter set up the tarp. "Why don't you get Tara undone." And Abram went to it while Carter built a fire. It felt strange coming off the road so early, peculiar to surrender at this early hour, weird to break with the regimen that Carter had so enforced day after day.

By the time Tara was free of saddle and bridle, Carter had a little fire going. Daylight wasn't for another several hours, so there would be no hunting. He went to his pack.

Down at the bottom, beneath his spare shirt—the one reserved for Arrival in New York Day—was a brown bag, home to two pounds of dried, jerked beef. He separated two strips, then closed the sack back up.

Abram came over and sat. The fire felt good. Carter handed him the beef and he bit it, started to chew. Carter looked at his piece. He smelled it, turned it over in his hand and thought about where it came from, where it had been.

"Know who made this?"

Abram said nothing.

"Kelly Wood made this. You remember Kelly Wood." He would forever speak the first and last name as one, as if neither was recognizable without the other.

"I rode up one day, smelled the most amazing smell—meat, smoke. Almost smelled like somethin' you'd put in your pipe. Well, he was makin' that dried beef, pressing the water out of it. I never knew you could do that to meat."

Carter bit off a piece—it was like shoe leather, but the taste was phenomenal. He closed his eyes and went back to that day. Ridin' up, smoke in the air, and Kelly Wood comin' out of the house. The door slammin' and that blonde hair just hittin' the sun.

"Well, hey, Carter! What do ya know?"

They wandered, talkin' about work, about women, about nothin'. They shared a pipe, the herb that Kelly Wood grew on the south side of the barn. Wind chimes flanked his little garden—bells and glass and flattened forks that made music when the wind-spirits sauntered through, blessing all that grew, sacred.

And whenever they met in this place, Carter felt like he was living inside of his mind, separate from his body—new dreams and dimensions, potential that was hidden from view just a few tokes ago.

And they would stare, ever-deeper in thought. And one would give a little laugh and share the notion of one day hunting together, though they never would. Or traveling for traveling's sake, though that, too, would remain but a dream. Or building a dance hall and having music every night, though Kelly Wood somehow sensed that his days were numbered and this dream, too, would live only in the mind.

And at the wood's edge they would relieve themselves, and Carter would start laughing about something halfway through, and Kelly would say, "Damn! I can't even go! What the hell!"

Carter chewed that first piece of jerky as long as possible, extracting every last sensation, and picturing his friend, sending a silent hello. Even Kelly Wood had no idea of Carter's plan or whereabouts. No one knew. The only person Carter had told was the slave now sitting beside him.

"This is good."

And now, sitting by this fire, Kelly Wood seemed so very far away, a lifetime, as if he existed in a book that came before Carter's time in this world.

But then he thought about the things they discussed, dreamt about. And he felt content, rather funny, rather full.

Gertie Comes Inside

the darkest of dreams
cannot compete with reality,
the disasters of life

Carter never told a soul about the horror he witnessed when he was a boy of twelve, about the morning that Gertie screamed bloody murder, the voice like a jungle cat being ripped in half.

And how they flew from the breakfast table, spoons and placemats flying with them.

Smoke poured from the shuttered window of the slaves' quarters, like black water through fish gills, hinting at the hell within. The same from under the eaves, noxious steam about to blow the lid off a kettle.

Dad tore open the door of the guesthouse, and smoke took him to the ground. So he stayed down low and stumbled inside. If there were a fire, the smoke was too thick to see it. Carter stood helpless as Dad pulled Mimi out, dragged her down the two steps and laid her on the ground.

Frantic, he said, "Get her some...! Get her some water!"

He ran back inside and by the time Carter fetched a pitcher, three more lifeless souls lay in the dirt, there. "Tom. Tom! Here. Drink. It'll be good for ya."

But Tom would not drink, would not wake. Not for water, not for nothin'. Nor would Mimi. Nor Hannah, nor Lewis, Webster, Harriet, George. All of them, seven souls, sleeping peaceful-like, making not a sound, arms at odd angles like puppets dropped.

And Mom came out, kerchief to her mouth, the deepest grief in her eyes. When Carter saw her, his blood ran cold, as if he had *required* her reaction before the reality struck him, sank in.

And when the smoke cleared, he helped Dad lay them straight, lay them on their backs, place hands on chests. Then he staggered sideways to the woodpile, retching, his body trying to throw up the breakfast still on the kitchen table.

And when he returned, Dad stood in the doorway, peering through the smoke, letting daylight in. Dad heard Carter cough and he spun, thinking one of the victims had awakened. And his eyes were so very wide—desperate for a glimmer of hope, but there stood Carter.

And Gertie just knelt in the dirt and wiped the seven cold foreheads, soothing them, offering peace when no deeper peace could be had.

And from that day forward, Gertie slept in the house.

Not well. Seven restless souls frequented her bed, unaware of the hour, caring not that she required peace of her own. And she would walk the earth in a stupor, empty and unseeing, a slave unable to pick, or fetch, or serve even herself.

And the little cast iron stove that Dad installed—to take the chill out of their night—was in its compassion merciless. Its flue was found shut, and he would forever ponder whether it had failed or if the help had simply forgotten to open it before their night fire.

The events of that day robbed Gertie of those she loved most in the world—kin and kindred. Her life was spared because she had crept over the little hill and down the valley to comfort a cousin who was experiencing her first menses. But in exchange for her survival, she would learn the weight and depth of guilt. She would puzzle the mechanics of fate. She would know intimately the intricacies of chance, the fragility of life.

The pain that Dad carried was different from Gertie's—while hers was in the heart, his occupied his shoulders, and the weight was visible. Anguish and guilt were cruel outlaws, and Dad was only too aware that they lay out there in the hills, watching, whispering, reminding him that this was on him.

Carter would observe this of his father, maybe without understanding what it was that he was seeing. Still, what he witnessed shaped him, worked his ideals, chiseled deeply certain notions, like *skin color means nothing,* like *all should come sit at this table, and* that *all should sleep in this house.*

Carter shed tears for the women, but his connection to the men was deeper. He felt accepted by the men, a part of them. It was profound to him how vital the men were in life, and to see them silent was surreal.

And he cried for George, the big man who clapped his hands and called "Carter, man!" just 'bout every day. Hard to believe that booming, bass voice would never resonate in the yard—not ever again.

And he cried for Lewis, the skinniest man he ever saw, who still had peach cobbler in him—cobbler that the boy brought him after supper. And he ate it off Carter's dessert plate, foregoing the fork, using those skinny fingers to experience what Mama had made in the white kitchen.

And for Webster, buried with worn harmonica that matched what was left of his silver hair. And never again would that music serenade them in the noon shade or by the evening fire.

Carter would learn in time what the three departed women meant to him; but it would take the eyes of another to help him understand.

Dad bartered his favorite horse for seven simple coffins. The woodworker was gracious—he helped Dad and Carter get the seven to the site, stayed for the service, even helped lower the souls. Afterwards, Tonga was tied to the man's wagon and off they rode. Dad watched that stallion as long as he could, the thing looking back over his shoulder as he trotted, fighting the rope, eyes white, not comprehending.

It took an hour to shovel, lay some stones, place the crosses.

When they got home, Dad sketched where the seven rested, printed their names and spoke each aloud. He dated the record and put it in the drawer with old invoices, letters. *Who is ever gonna see this?* When he closed the thing it squeaked, the bones of an old man. He leaned back, pictured his steed fighting the rope, and wept without making a sound.

And Carter would read to Gertie that night, words penned by another. His words were too young, provided inadequate comfort. But pages from a book... they were sufficiently mesmerizing. And she rested.

And at a chapter's end, he would look to see if she wished for more. And her eyes would be on his face. Not meeting his glance, not on the lips. But deeper, looking through him, at the spirit level.

And at age nineteen, she would become literate. And at sixteen, he would taste his first kiss, first love. And—as it should be in the world —the new generation would rewrite the pages of love, would redefine color and tone, would throw on the fire the cruel rulebooks of their elders.

And—as it has been for eons—young lovers would be cast out of Eden, shunned, made to question what was already perfect, holy.

Through Smoke, a Child

if you are brave
seek the path that lets you see inside
but prepare for what you will likely find

"Why do you do that?"

Carter furrowed his brow and looked back at Abram. He rolled smoke around in his mouth, extracting the flavor, tracing the very biology of plant and leaf and bud.

"Why do you smoke before bed?"

Carter exhaled, almost regrettably, but still let his tongue and cheeks make love to the taste, lips guarding the exit of his private boudoir until they were finished, satiated, had what they wanted.

"Helps me, ummm… helps me sleep."

He'd hidden it from Sarah Jane—at least hid it from her sight. She knew he smoked. She knew when. She just didn't understand why he couldn't smoke what *she* had planted, what *they* grew for their livelihood. She suspected that it was because tobacco wasn't his idea —it was Shane's.

"It has *nothing* to do with Shane! I just don't care for tobacco. Can't explain why. I'm just… I prefer this."

Tobacco didn't make him hear crickets that minutes ago sang unnoticed. And not just their call, but their purpose and plight. Tobacco didn't let him *become* a cricket, inhaling evergreen at the base of a juniper and assigning self to a single star.

Tobacco didn't make him *sense* that an oak tree some forty feet away was communicating with him, leaves and roots vibrating on *his* frequency.

Tobacco didn't make him think of carving something beautiful, of praying to the spirit world, of thoughts so elegant and right they made his hair stand on end.

When he smoked, he and all things—*all* things—spoke the same language. Stones. Birds. A dripping water pump. Everything lived. Everything reached to connect. Everything demonstrated that magic still breathed in this world.

When he smoked, he thought things that during the day were impossible. He let in the possibility that his enemies were his brothers. He shed his ego. He became less a man and more a loving, spiritual entity.

And it was frustrating when she would smell it on his kiss and accuse his passion of being herb-induced—which was ironic, because he loved her and wanted her body every, *every* night.

"Maybe... maybe this is my little escape, Abram."

The man was more than a little incredulous. "What do *you* need to escape from?"

Carter considered Abram's angle, wondered if Abram pictured Carter's world idyllic. "I dunno. Sometimes, I just need some quiet time. Don't you need some alone time?"

"I reckon."

So Carter was surprised when Abram reached, asking for the pipe without asking for the pipe. Carter handed it over and watched the end disappear. The little fire leapt to life and made Abram's face surreal, wooden. Carter smiled at the man, but also at the connection, the sharing, the notion that someone else might experience this.

"Now hold it a little," Carter coaxed. "Take in some fresh air. Now, hold. Hold." When Abram was unable and let the smoke escape, Carter reassured him, "Okay."

Abram coughed. He handed the pipe back and walked away a few steps, coughing some more.

"You okay?" Carter drew slowly, as if barely sipping, now. His eyes were on the man. "Watch. A little smoke, and a little fresh air. Gotta mix it."

Abram watched the demonstration, then tried it again. This time, he didn't cough. But when he was done, and when he exhaled, he flapped his arms and dropped his head low. "Oh, God!" He staggered, and Carter helped him sit back down on the log.

Carter let him catch his breath. He looked in the little bowl of the pipe, then tapped it against the wood where they sat. A tiny cherry of fire came out, and Carter put his boot heel on it. Abram still hung his head, almost to knee level, and Carter put his hand on his shoulder.

"You good?" Abram shook his head, and Carter looked around, remembering vigilance, remembering to monitor the area, ever a trespasser.

In minutes, Abram talked about his sister, and Carter described his. Neither had seen a sibling in years, but Carter had the privilege of communicating via mail, though he felt guilty about that and kept it quiet. Instead, he offered some hope.

"Someday, I think you will see her again."

"You do?"

"I do. I think there's a change comin'. I think shit's gonna be different. Maybe not next year, but in another chapter of this life."

Abram was still. His face hinted that he was puzzling great things, but his demeanor was soft, quiet. And Carter wondered about the shape of his thoughts, his view of the world, his dreams.

"We got any more of that... that... hard meat?"

"Jerked beef? The shoe leather?"

"Yeah! The shoe leather."

Carter fetched some, and, with effort, tore it in two. Both ate and smiled, enjoying the deep taste, the breezes and ghosts and events from earlier days.

They slept without pitching the tent—it felt warm enough. Besides, the night bugs were tuning up for a symphony, and it felt nice to be among them.

He looked over at Abram—under his blanket, on his side, hands under his head. Even with eyes closed, he wore a soft smile tonight. This was unusual, but welcome.

The night bugs steered Carter's mind, commandeered him back to Georgia. Way back, even before... her.

It's summer again and the streets are lamp-lit, hot, spilling over in celebration. A band plays and a storm taunts, schemes on the black horizon. It's the last night of the carnival—and the conductor drives the tempo faster to outsmart the rain.

He pondered the way the music's focus was handed off from trumpets to flutes, from timpani and snare to clarinets.

Somehow, that's what the night bugs were doing tonight—they played their part, sans sheet music, and then they listened. If no response came, they repeated their passage, but were often interrupted midway through until everything became perfectly chaotic or perfectly in sync—he couldn't discern which.

The weather over the next several days was pleasant, but the terrain was unyielding—steep rises and steeper descents, and they averaged about half the mileage they expected each day.

"Mississippi, Tennessee," Carter began in a sing-song.

"Kentucky, West Virginia," the man answered from atop the horse.

"Pennsylvania, New York," Carter finished. "Know what I think, Abram?"

Abram looked down, reins loose, easy in his hand.

"I think Tennessee is showing us the hardest climbs of this journey. I think the road gets easier when we hit Kentucky."

"It do?"

"We'll just take it slow," he huffed. "Yeah, we'll just... let's just enjoy the view."

He wanted to make promises, to paint a picture of prosperity, to play up life to come in New York. But in reality, he had no idea what life would be like, there. It could be the new world. It could be the same old world but with an annoying accent.

The *survivor* in him knew that a place—any place—is what you make of it. But the *realist* knew that every city and town and village had a personality, an attitude. And the *believer* in him knew that one did not have to accept what was dealt, demanded... one could create beliefs of one's own, decide what to accept, choose what to be.

And he would.

And he would do what he could to instill this in Abram, because the man deserved it. Because Abram had been through a lifetime of hardship already. Carter sighed as they headed down the latest slope and worried that the man had already succumbed to what he was dealt, had already decided that this was the way his world was to go.

But Carter believed that there was a child inside of that man. And if he had to rip a door off its hinges to locate him, he would. He would pull Abram—no, he would *entice* him—through this new portal and *announce* his freedom and *demonstrate* how to stand his ground.

Soon. Has to be soon.

The Horse of Danny Roots

when we are reflections
in the eyes of a creature of God
our life is affirmed

but when those eyes forever close
we face in the same moment
mortality and eternity

When they first spotted him, up ahead on the side of the dusty road, he was coaxing the horse to stand. Even from this distance, you could tell that he was barely pulling on the reins—more persuading than pulling.

And, at that point, the horse was alert, head bobbing, showing that she heard and understood, but *could* not obey.

By the time they reached him, the man had sat down. And the horse relaxed with him, lying completely on her side now. Even when she noticed Tara—and she did make eye contact—she did not raise her head.

Carter sensed that the man was less concerned about his transportation and more about the beast. And when Danny Roots looked up at him, Carter just nodded, quietly understanding.

Finally, Danny Roots said, "Never shoulda brung her." He smiled without feeling a smile, bit his cheek.

Finally, Carter offered, "What can we do, stranger?"

Danny looked off, "Oh… I dunno."

But he knew. He knew.

Carter came down off his horse and laid a hand on the neck of Danny's mare. "How far you going?"

"Forty Forks. About two days walkin'."

"We can carry your gear for ya."

90

Danny absently said, "Yeah," but his eyes were on her. He snapped back to reality. "Oh, yeah. Thanks." He rubbed his chin, and kept his hand to his mouth, a monotone, "Maybe... reckon that's what needs to happen."

It wasn't until they removed her bridle and transferred Danny's gear onto Tara's back that introductions were made. Danny extended his hand to Carter, then to Abram, which pleased Carter. Danny and Abram would lead Tara up the road, and Carter would follow only when Danny was out of earshot of the pistol.

Danny wrung his hands, looking around as if he might forget to bring something. As the two were leaving, Carter called out, "What's her name?"

Danny uttered it one last time, but it caught in his throat, escaping in inarticulate pieces, and he was forced to repeat it. "Maggie."

She was beautiful, a Palomino—tan, blonde. Time had kissed her with a perfect dusting of grey at her eyes, forelock, fetlocks. And Carter contemplated what kind of magnificence it took for one to be down, down for good now, and yet to retain such grace.

Only her ribcage moved now, lids were heavy, peaceful, like she knew that it was here that she would come to rest.

He had been here before. His first week in Mississippi, his steed went down at a gallop, and Carter was forced to assuage the beast's agony left-handed—his own right arm and clavicle were broken. Carter had bitten clean through his tongue, and the sound in his right ear never fully recovered.

He figured it would take Abram and Danny Roots ten minutes to be away, but he gave them fifteen.

He rested a hand on her neck, played with her hair. He felt compelled to kiss her—in that deep place between her girl-lashes—and she exhaled with a voice nearly human. He pulled away and she nodded just once, her eyes locked on the sky over Carter's shoulder, across the road, above the field. Blue would be the last color registered.

He covered her head and neck with his sleeping blanket, and weighted the corners with wood and stone. He trudged up the road, then trotted to catch up. And Danny Roots was relieved when Carter explained that he hadn't had to use a bullet, that angels took her.

Danny looked away and wept, but no tears came—just the wracking, and just for a moment. "You boys..." he choked, "hungry?"

When Carter had the opportunity, he stashed her lock of hair in his saddlebag. He had no idea how he would one day honor her, but he felt obliged to act on the sacred impulse.

They walked until two pm, then sat in the shade and ate a bit, drank. Danny Roots shared hard bread and goat cheese, and a tea drink sweetened with sugar. Carter wanted to ask about Danny's home, story, destination; but they needed to move. At supper, they could share more, and Carter looked forward to this, to exploring the journey's new—albeit temporary—element.

And somehow, the road seemed less rugged with three. Danny's heart was heavy when he thought of Maggie, but he stayed close to Tara, and rode when Carter and Abram brought him into the riding rotation.

"Oh, she's a fine girl," Danny Roots said after just a mile in the saddle. "Smooth and sweet." He slapped her neck. "Ain't ya, girl!"

H omes and Hosts

wondrous
the invitations
to play on another's stage

An hour before sunset, they stopped on a hilltop and Danny Roots pointed south-southeast. "Selmer. Nice town." Then he turned to Carter. "What's your sleeping plan for tonight?"

"We pitch a tent. Make a fire. See if we can rustle up a rabbit or..."

"How 'bout we stay with a friend of mine?" Danny interrupted.

Carter thought about it, but before he could speak, Danny added, "Could sleep under a roof. Maybe see if he's got somethin' in the kettle."

"Well," Carter started, looking at Abram. "We're good. We're good with the tent."

"Aw, nonsense. You fellas helped me out of a pinch. It's the least I can do for ya. Besides, Dusty owes me one!"

They came down off the hill and turned east. Danny Roots pointed at the house, a dark two-story in the distance. As they got closer, they heard kids playing and a dog barking, and evening fog rose to meet the purple twilight.

Danny yelled and Dusty and the dog came out to meet them. Carter tapped Abram's leg, and Abram dismounted, but not before Dusty noticed the Negro atop the horse.

"What the hell are you doin' out here, Rooty?"

"Jes' checkin' in on ya, ya ol' geezer!"

"Wasn't expecting you until tomorrow."

"Yeah, I left a day early. Thought I smelled rain. Thought I better get a move on." Then he spoke low. "Maggie went down. These boys picked me up, carried my gear for me."

Danny introduced Carter and Abram to his friend.

"Beautiful place ya got here," Carter complimented.

Dusty brought them into the yard, and as soon as the first oil lamp was lit inside the house, the smell of food hit the men. Coulda been a stew... something with beef or lamb... whatever it was, it about knocked 'em over.

Dusty led them closer, calling over his shoulder, "You boys hungry? I believe we got enough to feed an army."

They tied off the horse and stepped up on the porch. Carter hung back, so Abram did, too. *If Abram's not invited in, I'll eat out here with him.* Danny saw this, and pulled Dusty aside. To mask the awkwardness, Carter spoke to Abram. "Be nice to eat out here," he lied. "So nice out." But nothing sounded better than sitting down to a table. Sitting in a chair! Seeing people, a female, kids.

Danny came back out onto the porch. "Dusty ain't sure there's enough room at the table, so how's about we eat out here in the porch chairs?"

"Good." Carter was disappointed. A part of him wanted to be back out in the woods—at least the woods treated all men equally.

But seconds later, he was surprised by the flurry, the plates of food and... kids! Everyone came outside to join them on the porch. Dusty was last, somehow carrying four chairs at once.

Carter and Abram met Dusty's wife, Doris, their kids—Beck, Angus, Sallie, Sadie—and Doris's sister, Rosetta. And, somehow, not surprisingly, the easy smiles of the women struck him deeply. *Can't explain how... it's just the reaction in my cheeks, my eyes, and arteries.*

And then he thought of the irony at hand—leaving his woman behind, having endured more than he could stand, so running away. Far away! And then... the first woman he meets on the trail is regarded as a goddess! *Uncanny! I'm such a fool!*

But he would be more foolish to turn down the offer to sit directly across from Rosetta. And he waited before sitting, waited until she was in place, and then he came down to eye level and she modestly met his glance, silently defining the magic of moments.

"Sorry we only have day-old bread, Gentlemen."

"Oh, please…. This is perfect, Doris."

"Yeah," Danny Roots added. "These fellas ain't had a home-cooked meal in about a month!"

At that, Rosetta looked directly at Carter, surprised.

And the moment for the first bite of the warm, thick stew arrived. Beef and carrots and potatoes—three playing as one. And they tried not to rush, tried not to appear gluttonous. Heavens, it was so delicious it was sad to swallow. Each bite was medicine for body and psyche.

And it just felt wonderful to be seated in a device invented for hind flanks—just the right height, just the right amount of tilt and support. And light spilled from the lantern at the front door, and eyes on the far side of the table picked up the source, reflected it—each time a glint and a sparkle.

No one asked the reason for their journey—only where they came from and where they were bound.

"Mississippi, Tennessee…" Carter looked to Abram, who had a mouthful of bread.

"Kintucky, Wess Virginia…" at which the kids laughed.

"Pennsylvania…"

By now, Abram had tucked his food into one cheek, so he sang out, "Newww Yorrrk!" and everyone roared at his enthusiasm.

"My my, that *is* a long journey," Doris exclaimed. "Surely, something good must be waiting for you."

Carter just nodded, pretending to be chewing, wanting to leave it at that. Thankfully, no one pressed him further. And Doris mentioned, "I have kin in Pennsylvania."

Carter and Abram were only too happy to finish the bread. They scooped what was left of the stew with the remaining crusts.

And when they were finished, Carter offered to wash the dishes. But Doris waved him off. He gave an exaggerated shrug to Rosetta, but she also shooed him off, but with a shy smile.

So the men walked out into the yard and talked. After a minute, Carter considered asking if the men would like to share some whiskey —he had stashed some for bartering—but he neither wanted to stay up late nor deal with inefficient travelers in the morn.

He walked Tara to the barn, made sure she had water, then treated himself to some time in the outhouse.

He sat, fed and full, enjoying yet another semi-comfortable seat for his backside. Without warning, the miles behind him crept up and pushed down on his shoulders and he suddenly felt fatigued beyond comprehension. He nodded and leaned forward so far that he thought he would fall.

Did I just fall asleep out here? He had all he could do to stand and push the door open. When he got back to the men, he was seeing double, felt outside of his physical body.

"You men care," he started, "if I find my place to sleep in the barn?"

"Carter, did you want to catch a bath?" Dusty offered. "We've got some water on the fire for ya right now."

"Oh…" He shook his head like he'd just come out of a round of fisticuffs. He scratched his good ear. "I suppose that does sound…" he searched for the words, landing on, "awfully fine!"

When it was time, Carter told Abram to go ahead, "Go first."

So Carter sat by the fire and tried to hold up his end of the conversation. The ladies made some sort of hot tea—spicy, almost pepper-like on the tongue. Felt wonderful to have something hot going down him. Just having his hands around the tin mug was pleasing.

96

"Who plays the fiddle?"

"Oh, that would be Rosetta."

"Really!" Carter sat up, came to life. "What do you like to play?"

"Oh, mostly hymns. When no one is around, I like to create my own songs. Just simple stuff, and…"

"No kidding!" Carter interrupted. "Well, I would love to hear you play." He thought he detected shyness, and didn't want to pressure her, so he added, "Sometime."

"I reckon I could play a little somethin'."

She tightened the bow and tuned up. She held the fiddle using just her chin—bow in one hand, tuning peg in the other, and the notes bent fore and aft until all four pleased her.

There was almost no silence between the tuning and the start of the song—she began immediately.

Warmth. Depth. A simple verse and melody.

Carter wasn't sure if what he was hearing was melancholy or extemporaneous or holy, but the notes knew how to find him—through his good ear to his soul, through his other ear to his chest. On the latter path, the notes could have moseyed, unbuttoning his shirt with finesse. Instead they ripped it open with a purpose, sending a low and steady voltage through him.

And sitting there was surreal. More than a month on the road, sleeping outdoors, total focus on moving, on advancing. How divine to sit, to come in out of the wind, and to hear music from an angel.

He studied her eyes. At first, he thought she was watching her fingerings. But he realized that when her eyes weren't closed, they were focused on nothing, nothing of this world—she simply had to place them somewhere.

He heard a waltz, then a lullaby. Baroque, then something modern, free of form. He noticed the muscle in her forearm, the curves that revealed and hid themselves as she powered the bow.

Carter took the opportunity to look around the room, to see if his reaction was aligned with that of the others. But he allowed himself only a second or two, then his eyes returned to her.

And when she finished, her fiddle went to rest position, automatically, as if she were accustomed to performing, finishing, receiving thanks.

Carter set his mug on the floor and clapped. The others smiled at his enthusiasm and joined in. When the applause died, Carter looked toward the stairway. "That Abram is missing one heckuva show!"

"I have one more, if you'd like to hear."

"Oh, Rosetta! You could play into the night!"

Her sister laughed at that—out loud, but then covered her mouth —happy that the stranger's attention was on Rosetta.

She started on the lower, thicker strings, and made the notes tip-toe—sneaky, light steps at a 1-2 count. But after a moment, higher notes were woven in and some sort of tension escalated. Still the 1-2 count, but more complex, more emotional, now.

Carter felt her aura, felt how the room became hers. He noticed her feet, her stance, like that of an archer—one foot on the target, the other angled for balance. He admired her strong foundation, but also her femininity. And at that moment, the music slowed, slowed, and her bow traveled along one, long note.

And then it returned to the tip-toeing. It felt nice to be back in the familiar. And it was different, now. It had a lilting to it, a lightness and an occasional slurring, as if the notes had been around the world and came home with the hint of a swagger, more confidence.

Carter happened to look at Doris. She wore a smile but closed her lips when she saw Carter. And he felt privileged to be among these two sisters.

And when she was finished, Rosetta curtseyed to the applause. And Carter asked where she was trained, and thought about the fiddle he had left back home, back in the barn. He felt simple, dwarfed by her talent, but was happy for it as well. He had his kind of music, his reasons, and she had hers.

Carter excused himself and went to the barn. He returned with two shirts, and undergarments tucked inside those, out of sight, a change of clothes for him and Abram. Funny, to wait on Abram as if he were a son.

He headed toward the stairs.

"Say, Carter," Dusty called. Carter turned, holding the clean clothes to his chest. "Not sure what kind of timeline you're on, but might I entice you and Abram to stay on for a few days? I've got some carpentry work to do, and sure could use the help."

He saw Carter puff his cheeks and make some mental calculations, then added, "I'll make it worth your while."

"What kind of work?" Carter felt very tired. The thought of sleeping under a roof had been a sedative in his veins, blurring his thought process since before dinner.

"We're gonna add a room onto the side of the barn. Some roughing-in, some roofing. Why don't ya think it over during your bath."

Carter took the clothes to the top of the stairs and dropped them outside the door. He returned for two buckets of hot water off the fire, then went back up the steps.

"You good in there, Abram?"

"Yeah," came a weak response. Carter heard him rise from the tub, feet on the floor. A second later, Abram said, "Come on in."

Abram stood there, wrapped in a towel, staring, staring at nothing. *The warmth's got him. He's knocked out.* Carter smiled, noticing the thinness of Abram's legs. They looked like a girl's legs. Out of his clothes, Abram looked slight, even smaller than in his man clothes.

Abram still stood, so Carter yanked off his suspenders and pulled the shirt over his head. Then off came the boots, socks.

Carter wasn't gonna stand on ceremony, so he unbuttoned his pants, dropped them, and slid into the water. "Ooo, dass nice." He cupped his sensitive parts with two hands, until the heat was tolerated. Then he just leaned back and let the warm have him, to his chin, then to his nostrils. And if he had gills, he would have gone beneath the surface, letting his head and hair and scalp have what the rest of his body was loving. *Why must I come up for air?*

Abram sat on the floor now, still wrapped up. Then he rocked. "Are we leaving tomorrow?"

"Huh?" Carter hadn't *forgotten* about Abram, but in his reverie the voice caught him off-guard.

"Are we leaving tomorrow?"

"Well, that *was* the plan. But Dusty asked if we wanted to stay for a couple of days, do some work around here, eat well, bathe!" When Abram was quiet, Carter asked, "What do you think?"

"It's nice here."

It sure was an unexpected pleasure! *Warmth in all its forms—food, bed, females.* "Dusty said we could help him put an addition on the barn. It might be good to do some work, get off the road for a while. Aren't you cold, man? I brought you some clean things."

Abram dressed in front of him. He donned the shirt that Carter bought one of the last times he was in town.

And his mind went there, to that day, to Key's Mercantile, to Robin. So ironic that Shane went to her. It was as if he trolled the world with a wide net and Carter paddled behind in a shabby canoe, taking what was cast off.

Sarah Jane would be happy back with Shane. She belonged with him. They had a history, a foundation. He could satisfy a part of her that Carter never quite claimed as his own. *Though God knows I tried.*

It was a bit like breeding horses... sometimes, the most orchestrated pairings go awry, fail, because there is something that the horse knows that the breeder does not.

"You can go downstairs if you like."

But Carter sensed that Abram was uncomfortable. "Or you can wait for me."

Abram sat back down on the floor, so Carter grabbed the washcloth and went to it. This was heavenly. He pictured a day, an invention, a fire beneath a tub that would keep the water warm all day long. *I would never come out. If I had visitors, they would find me here. If they wanted to talk to me, they would need to come in.*

It was hard to stand. He felt weak from the day, the month, the warm water. He used Abram's towel to dry off, and then pulled on the clothes. They felt good. Tight, small, but fresh.

He carried the buckets and led Abram downstairs. Everyone was still by the fire, and all eyes went to the two.

"There they are! Feel better, gettin' the road off ya?"

"I'm tellin' ya—that was heaven-sent. Thank you, Doris!"

The men said good-night to their hosts and walked across the yard, the house light losing its grip, surrendering them to the musty darkness.

In the barn, they spread their sleeping tarp, grabbed the blankets, and sprawled out together. After deep sighs, the blood sang, steady in their ears. They felt their breaths returning home, theirs again, warm in their chests.

It felt strange to see to a ceiling—the boards and beams and bales of straw—and not a sea of stars.

They rolled over. It was cold tonight, and they pushed up against one another for warmth—backside fitting against lower back, calves and feet pairing off, finding matches. By now, they thought nothing of proximity, nor of the novelty of men touching. Warmth was merely an essential component of survival.

And there were times during the night when one would roll over and face the other in the dark, and there might be some confusion over who occupied the next space. A hand would graze and come to rest upon a hip. A pelvis would innocently thrust, the mere act of nocturnal stretching, repositioning. The little brushes, the inadvertent cheek against a shoulder were never more than that.

An hour after sleep began, Carter heard a mild commotion up at the house—a wagon and horse snort. He opened the barn door just an inch. A buggy and white horse. A dark figure was welcomed inside and stayed for about ten minutes.

I don't believe he's deliverin' eggs—not at this hour of the night!

A voice of caution made the hair stand on the back of Carter's neck. A big part of Carter wanted to wake Abram, to pack up and be gone before sunup.

This ain't the way we go down! This ain't how we fail!

But he was cold, so he lay back down on his blanket, pistol trained on the door.

Sometime in the night, Abram had a wicked dream. Carter woke immediately, realized what was happening, but not before his skin iced over.

"Shhhh… it's okay. Shhhh. Abram. Abram!" He had a hand on the man's shoulder. "Shhhh… it's okay." It seemed like the terror was over, but now he wept, carrying something agonizing, profoundly sad.

Carter decided the terror was the better emotion to endure—at least terror could be battled. Agony could not be slain or defended against. It had to be endured, internalized, worn.

Abram rolled onto his belly and put his face in his hands. He sniffed through his nostrils and dealt with a pain.

Carter propped himself up on one elbow and rubbed him, shoulder to shoulder. In a way, Abram felt like a son—which was ridiculous, because they were roughly the same age. Right now, though, he was a boy in a man's body, running from something Carter could not see.

He couldn't tell if tears were flowing, the face still buried, the reasons private. But the sniffles sounded moist, so Carter kept rubbing, now and then grabbing a muscle and working it, giving strength, until Abram rolled onto his side.

"It was the night doctor."

Carter leaned in, straining to hear.

Abram continued, "He came here. He found me!"

"Shhh… you're safe."

"I run all day and then I run all night. And I don't know why. Where? Where am I goin'?"

"Shhh... It's okay."

Abram wiped his face. "Tired."

Carter didn't know if he meant tired, so ready to sleep, or tired of running, or tired of being a slave. So he just said, "Yeah."

"Am I even gonna *like* being a free man?"

Carter started to answer, then realized he had no words, so he just blew lightly. He closed his eyes and they burned, having slept just two hours before waking. "Yes. Yeah. You will. You will have your freedom and you will love it."

"Is it gonna feel different for me?"

"Yeah. It is." He wanted to erase the question marks and focus on strength. He wanted to give hope. "You are gonna do great."

"Yeah?"

"Yeah… you're gonna get a job. And you're gonna come home, and have a little wife, and… and read. And fix your dinner. And walk on the street. And be someone who is respected!"

At this, Abram rubbed his eyes and kept his hand there, covering them, overwhelmed.

"It's okay. It'll be okay. Stick with me. Yer gonna do great."

Making a Room

only in the bricks and stones we lay
only in the paint, and shapes, and words
do we outlive our names

Carter got up before the sun and carved by lamplight. He felt compelled to do this one thing, even if it meant missing that last hour of sweet slumber. When he was finished, he turned down the wick, thanking the flame before it was swallowed.

Doris fixed them an oat meal for breakfast, sweetened with some kind of crumbly, brown sugar. Rosetta collected the dishes when they were finished, and she laid a hand on his shoulder as she leaned in to take his bowl and spoon, and every simple thing was amplified.

How… how do women do that? How is it that the most innocent touch is more medicinal than any snuff or tonic or spring water?

Before Danny Roots rode off to Forty Forks, he embraced Carter and Abram. "I sure appreciate what you fellas did for me."

"Pleasure, sir." Carter gripped his hand, wrapped around him, and slapped him soundly on the back.

When Danny opened his hand, he found the horse hair that Carter had braided and strung through the wooden flower born just this morn. *Maggie.* The mane reminded Danny that his horse walked in the spirit world, the flower that she would forever live.

Danny could say nothing, but let his eyes speak.

Carter slapped him on the back again. "You ride safe, now."

He mounted a horse of Dusty's and headed for the road. And as he turned away, Carter made a mental note to reload chamber one of the revolver.

The men proceeded to the barn and Dusty showed them his plan, a pencil sketch. He wanted to create an annex at the south end of the barn. "So Doris can do some indoor gardening, grow some herbs, and set a spell in the sun."

He described his vision for a set of windows built right into the sloped roof, a wall of sky. "We need to dig some good-sized holes for the corner foundations. We'll take the wagon over to Roscoe Mills and fetch a load of lumber." He smiled, "*Then* we can have some fun!"

They decided that the digging would be the hardest task, so they started there. They measured the intended dimensions of the new space. Dusty stepped "inside" to get a sense of the new room, then had them push the marker for the new wall out another four feet.

"I'd hate to make it too small, right?"

Six posts, three walls—a room that joins to the existing side of the barn. It was more ambitious than anything Carter had tackled, that was for sure, and it excited him.

It took all morning to dig the holes. After the first, Carter peeled off his shirt. Around ten, Rosetta brought out a wooden tray with mugs of sun tea. By now, Abram and Carter were soaked right through their pants. They were tempted to guzzle the drink right down, but they did all they could to make it last.

Rosetta didn't dilly-dally—she pretty much collected the empty mugs and headed back inside. Carter grabbed his shirt and wiped the sweat from his eyes, which then focused on the woman walking away. Her hair spilled out the back of her bonnet, and she walked with a sort of formality that was out of place on a farm.

Not that I mind.

It was seventy-five degrees and humid, yet he shivered, then looked to see if anyone had noticed.

At lunch, the adults and children ate in the shade, happy to be done with the first aspect of the project.

"Did you grow these beans, Dusty?" Carter shoveled another forkful in his mouth, chewing slowly, letting the flavor escape with nowhere to run.

"Yeah, over beyond the corral. Got a little patch fer growin'."

"They're incredible."

When they finished, the men hitched the wagon. Carter rode Tara, and Abram rode up on the seat with Dusty. The ride to Roscoe's was just plain enjoyable. It felt nice to be riding *within* a town, and not just riding *through* it.

They were a quarter mile from the place when they smelled the pine dust and the afternoon air was as mouth-waterin' as pickle juice, but sweeter. The smell registered in Abram's senses, but his consciousness pushed away the connection to the coffin he and his previous master had crafted and painted that dark December.

They rode through mountains of rough timber, strategically marshaled and stacked. And as they made their way closer to the mill, the noise increased and the timber became boards and beams, blinding white and drying in the sun, all perfectly dimensioned, standardized.

Dusty brought the wagon to a halt and hopped down. "Be right back."

A couple bearded workers loaded 8 x 8 beams for a fellow customer, and each time they passed, they eyed Abram and Carter with suspicion. Carter had never seen a lumberjack before, and his eyes met theirs.

They wrestled with another beam, then looked again. This time, one of them spat. The other followed suit and it was clear which of the mutts was the alpha male. *I tend to do that—peg the pack leader.* The subservient one slapped alpha's back and said something that Carter wasn't meant to hear.

That's when Carter got off his horse.

He covered the distance to the two men without running. When he was within eight feet, he stopped, hands on hips.

The men were were rugged, splintered, inland sailors and they moved within striking distance.

"Lookin' fer somethin', fella?"

Carter spat in response—not well, but the sound was authentic. He raised his arms and let loose a barrage.

"Vous travaillez? *Vous travaillez?* Mais nous manquons toujours la fin! Les Duponts arrivent dans une heure!" Carter looked at the sky and gave a short laugh, here. "Allez! Ne discutez pas tout les temps!"

When he finished the monologue—excerpts memorized from French class back in Georgia—he folded his arms and cocked his head at an angle, challenging the men to compete, deal with him.

The alpha male threw his hands up and walked past, bumping his shoulder, but only slightly. "Yer just an ass, mister—you can *stick* your Chinese!"

The other man followed, also lost for words of merit. But neither repeated the word that had so *incensed* Carter.

He walked back to the wagon, shaking off the adrenaline. He looked up at at Abram, still perched on the bench seat. And Abram asked, "What did you say to them?"

"Pffft! It was French. Learned it back in school. Can't remember what it means, actually."

"What... why did you talk French?"

Carter looked at the ground. "I knew that if I spoke English, I would say something bad."

Abram grew quiet, and Carter wondered if he appreciated the fact that Carter would tangle with any man who threatened physical or psychological warfare on Abram.

Carter was surprised that—of all the times when he stepped up to do the deed—the perpetrator often backed down. Ironic, because Carter had only been in one fight in his entire life. It was quite possible that he was *all talk*.

Sometimes, that's all that's required.

Abram surprised him. "That's like that time in town, when that man called you a nigger lover."

Carter was surprised that he remembered that—neither had spoken of it since.

"Abram, they are just ignorant people. But here's the thing." Carter shielded his eyes from the sun. "Just because someone *says* something doesn't mean they're right."

Abram looked down, but Carter wanted to make sure he got it. "You can believe what *I* tell you, what people who *love* you tell you. The rest... they can go to hell."

He put his hand on Abram's shoe, and squeezed it. He squeezed it real hard, so Abram would remember. "This is your world, too, Abram. As much as it's mine, it's yours."

Change came so slowly. If a dog is beaten down, it's hard for that dog to regain his confidence, but the next litter had a chance. Generations of the Negro had been battered, scarred. And change was painfully slow. *But this is the 1860s! It's time to be modern!*

Dusty came. And they drove the wagon around to the back of the mill. And the two goons who got the French lesson helped load the thing. Carter wondered if the solo horse could pull such a load. But they took it slow, and everything was fine. He rode ahead a few paces to keep the workhorse focused on his mare, keep him inspired.

And when they got back to the worksite, they unloaded and stacked. Boards and beams and nails and pegs. Carter tried to envision how things would be hewn, chiseled, joined.

Dusty turned to Abram. "Ever done any woodworking, Abram?"

"Yes."

"Awww, great!"

Carter was puzzled—*He has?*—but only for a moment. The days of carving seemed a world away. And he rubbed his fingertips together and found the sweet, fresh knife scrapes.

They used nails to tack a horizontal, header beam to the outside of the barn, eleven feet up. "Don't drive them in all the way, if you can help it."

They used a tool that Dusty borrowed from the mill. "It's a twist drill." Carter inspected it. He was at a loss to describe how it operated. "How the heck?" The thing looked like it would only wobble.

"He said to put your shoulder into it, then crank it." And sure enough, the bit ate into the wood, spitting out neat shavings. Abram caught a couple. "Warm!"

They took turns working the drill, until six holes dotted the header beam. Each hole tunneled through the beam and into an existing stud inside the barn. Then they drove pegs through the beam, making the connection as solid as rock. They pulled the nails back out, to be reused elsewhere.

Next came the 8 x 8 uprights. Each was guided into a hole, which swallowed four feet of them. Rock and rock dust were backfilled, then dirt. Everything was tamped and checked for plumb. The beams had become mighty columns.

And from each column, a smaller beam—chiseled to fit—ran up to the header beam. These beams became joists, and each was drilled and got a peg run through it. Every piece became a secure component and each strengthened the other.

By suppertime, they had birthed the skeleton of a room, the bones and structure of a space, and in the sunset Dusty's pencil sketch was realized.

And when they stepped inside the ribs and chest and shoulder blades, the space had already altered their voices—it enhanced their presence but made no echo. The voices were there and then gone. History would preserve these men, but in deep and utter silence. They might be recalled but not remembered. *Is that not the same as forgotten?*

Dusty carved "1861" on a beam in a corner that only the most observant would find. And in carving, he too became but a ghost to future generations. And only the most reverent would wonder about this day, about these people, about the care they took in making something worthy and lasting.

Each would go on to explore the physical world with great gusto and desire, then in their tiny locales go silent and return to dust—touched by the blessings of this life, yet gripped by its profound sorrow.

But someone from the waking world would place a hand upon these beams, would trace the numbers, and—like joining ends of two morse cables—bridge the real and ethereal worlds.

An artist of the twenty-first century would defy all logic and purchase *Home with Barn on 20 Acres—Seller Motivated* sight unseen, and on a whim follow a calling and migrate a thousand miles to be there. *Just because.*

And the artist's sensitive spine and vivid imagination would understand that this sunroom was annexed for life-giving purposes, that its builders had life-stories that could fill volumes, that the faces and hands and hearts of brethren were now hers as well.

A Month of Dust

the sun still makes me squint, react
but since you've sailed I can no longer feel it
on my cheek

She had lost track of the days, of the names that went with them. An outsider would reconnoiter that she was making ends meet, that she was still turning a profit, doing well for herself despite the slope on which the world was sliding.

And they would be correct—she *was* managing.

But she was also merely surviving. Sleepwalking, unfocused, threadbare. Stand her up next to Sarah Jane of autumn and she is but a faint shadow, a winter shell, unresponsive to light or touch.

She walked across the drive, skirt slipping off her hips, the hem picking up dust. She pushed open one of the big barn doors and went to his desk. Still, it dominated the space, displacing huge volumes of life, of energy. But now that he was gone, the water level of her life had dropped several feet. Days once cradled by seas of contentment were now exposed, weathered.

Did I not see what he meant to this place? What he imparted?

Her eye went to to the dirty window and she followed. Seven wooden wrens looked out from their dusty perch, staring, waiting for the return of their creator. Sarah Jane lifted one and stroked its back, wiping a month of dust from its little head, from its tail feathers.

She brought it to her lips and blew, letting her first three fingers become those of a girl, improvising a nonsensical song. She stopped, then played again, this time letting each note play longer, endure, mature. She played for him a love song, a lullaby.

And it felt inadequate, lost inside this big ol' barn like a bird trapped, helpless but by choice, unable to see the door still ajar, blind to her own chance for freedom.

She dropped the wood into the pocket of her apron—leaving six—and walked outside, across the drive, up to the house.

The help met her in the upstairs hallway with an armload of linens, her nightie. "Ma'am."

Sarah Jane continued in silence, latched her door, and lay on her bare bed. She pulled the spread over her and stared at the wall. She thought about writing, but it would be just another note to herself, not worth the ink or paper, not worthy of her own energy.

Carter,

To say I miss you is but an echo inside a hollow tree. My bark has fallen, branches heavy. The wind blows through me and I curse its every origin, west to east, north to south.

Sometimes, I think that the rules of this world—edicts intended to guide and preserve us—in fact cause our demise. I was happily married, then unhappily so. Gloriously in love, then discontent with the love that once lifted me.

And now that love has released me, I realize that it took with it my breath, my oxygen. There is no more sparkle, no more flame. Everything in my heart has ceased.

For weeks, I was angry at you. But left alone with my anger, I went nowhere. Anger has dried over. I cannot blame you for running... perhaps I would have run as well.

I have said this all before. And I repeat it because my words go nowhere, only to the wind. And every week that passes I know we are farther apart, less likely to ever be together again.

I only wish I...

There was a knock at the door, faint, like a child's. "Yes?"

Mary Ethel peeked in. "Will you be wantin' a drink, ma'am?"

"Come in."

She carried a glass of lemonade and a napkin and slowly walked across the creaky floor. Sarah Jane rose up, but remained on the bed. She drank from the glass, then placed it against her cheek. "Hot today."

"Yes, ma'am."

"Thank you for this, Mary Ethel."

"Yes, ma'am." She turned to leave, almost animated in her attempts to miss the squeaky floorboards, and Sarah Jane wanted to rip up every one until the squeaking came no more. *It's too much a part of us, of Us, of him and me.*

But she just let her head drop and tilt, and she stared at the place where he would undress at night, the place where his clothes would drop.

And she could see his bare feet, his legs walkin' him to her, those thighs, the love in his hands.

And she felt in her tummy the same muscles tightening, the mini-jolts and surges, the warmth that found every delicious part of her.

She set the glass down and pulled the bedspread over her again. Her hands went where she was warmest, just to pretend, and only for seconds. And she slept. And when she woke, it was only darker, nearer the setting sun. *The end of days,* she said aloud.

She rolled over and felt a muted stab, her abdomen. She reached for the pain and dug the little bird from her apron. Still, she marveled. *How is it possible to smooth something so rough, to shape the shapeless? He took a tree branch and made a sculpture, music.*

She blew through its tail feathers again, this time producing only wind and dust in the setting sun rays.

Life Surges

sometimes
places, the magic ones
should remain unnamed

too the people
the beautiful spirits across our path

for neither the hum of the hillside
nor the curve of her face requires naming
and neither risks being forgotten

Their hands had been well occupied all day—a new kind of work for Carter and Abram—sawing, chiseling, drilling, fitting components together. And if the sun had remained another ten hours, the men would have worked right through. Such is the satisfaction of building.

But the day was just a thin, violet line, now, low in the sky, and the smell of supper at the house was winning their attention.

"Let's eat, men!" Dusty's words finally rang, and they put away their tools.

And the eldest daughter, Beck, met them at the front porch. Her instructions were to hand each a warmed washcloth. And the men brought the damp cotton to their faces, taking away the dirt of the day, and came inside.

And the place glowed, golden lamplight and the faces of women. And the men were suddenly weak, at the mercy of hunger.

Plates were filled and the adults sat at the table. The children each occupied a tread on the stairs and were only happy to do so. And they sat staggered right and left on alternating steps, quickly finding the best arrangement.

And it appeared that fate placed Rosetta directly across from Carter, but she and Doris knew better. And that they made it look natural was a testament to their skill.

And Dusty raised his mug and proposed a toast, "To the new project—the one that will let sunshine in—and to the unexpected help that will make it possible!"

And the mismatched glass and tin and stoneware cups met and clanked above the table. The kids on the stairs toasted as well, all giggles, and the adults mimicked them.

Carter felt his face flush and he looked into the eyes across from him. And he realized that he was seeing not just a pair of eyes, a graceful chin, a lovely smile—he was seeing an entire spirit, and every part of her *felt* beautiful.

And he tried to eat as slowly as he could, almost worshipping the flavor that these women created. And he repeatedly thanked them. And when he noticed that Abram did not, he brought his friend in. "This is just delicious, isn't it, Abram?"

"Oh, yes. It's very good."

And after dinner, the men talked about the next steps of the project. Carter nodded, but could not help noticing the women cleaning up, the trips they made from table to basin, the sheer number of plates and utensils, the pots and the pans.

And before things settled down, he walked past the women on his way outside. "Thank you again for that divine meal, ladies."

"Oh, you're welcome, Carter," Doris replied. "So glad you liked it!"

"The gravy," he paused, unsure how to describe his gratitude, "the flavors just brought everything together."

"Oh! Well, it was my sister who was responsible for the gravy and spices."

Rosetta smiled, "I had a *little* hand in it. Mostly, I was her little helper!"

And he stepped out onto the porch. As soon as he was out of the women's sight, he made a dash for the little house.

When he got there, the door was latched, so he knocked. A little voice came from within, "Occupied!"

"Oh! Okay!"

He danced a little. *Wow, I really...* But the door opened and out she came.

"Sadie!"

"I'm Sallie!"

"Oh, of course! I'm sorry, honey. Dark out here."

He watched her for a few steps, until she was out of earshot. Then he leapt inside and pulled the door shut. *If I were king, I would have one of these of my own.* He abhorred this vulnerability. *Everyone would have their own little house.*

When he exited, no one was there to follow. Still, he held the door and swung it open-shut, open-shut several times, sucking the air out as best as he could. He was embarrassed to leave it shut, but no one deserved to walk in on a stray raccoon.

He was halfway to the house when he saw a figure. He knew by the white apron that it was Doris or Rosetta.

"Hello," he called out, still advancing.

"Hello," she replied, though not clearly enough to reveal her identity.

"Nice night!"

"Mmm... it is." She rubbed her arms. *Rosetta.*

They sat in the chairs in the grass, just before the porch, just barely touched by the house light. And they commented on the stand of pines, silhouetted against the night sky, and stared. It was quiet enough to hear their breaths; he swore she could hear his heartbeat.

"Feels nice to work on something new."

"How long will the project take?"

He cleared his throat. "Well, I've never built a sunroom before, but it looks like it will take a week or so, as long as Dusty approves of our work."

"And then…"

"And then…" he echoed. "Then we'll be thinkin' about heading north, gettin' Abram up north."

"What do you do back home?" she asked. "For a living?"

"I ran a farm. Tobacco, agriculture. Lots of hens, too. Eggs."

"Funny… you never smell like smoke."

"Ahh… I don't smoke tobacco. Funny, huh?"

"Do you have slaves?"

"Well, the woman," he paused, "that I lived with did."

"You weren't married to her?"

"No, just living together. Two years." He looked off. *Two years. Where did they go?* He came back to her. "What about you? Ever been married?"

"I was married at seventeen." She sighed, "He was rough." She smoothed her apron. "Rough with me. Rough with love. He didn't talk to me very nicely. So, one day in May, I just rode away."

"Ever hear from him?"

"No. He was probably happy to be rid of me. Now he doesn't have to think, doesn't have to act like a human being."

"Animals. They're all around us."

"Yeah. I don't miss him. I wish I could have my own place. Doris and Dusty have been so good to me."

"I can see your sister in you, you in her."

Dusty and Abram came out on the porch and sat. Dusty had a guitar and cigar. "Hey, you two!" he shouted down to them.

He played. He used a finger-picking style, dancing between three or four chords. The cigar was clamped at the edge of his mouth, and it glowed now and then, the chord choices his sweet interpretation of the night.

"He's good."

"Yes. And the only songs he plays are ones he just makes up." She looked over at Dusty. "Can't play but one or two that aren't his own."

"That's interesting. Creative."

Rosetta wanted to get back to learning Carter's world. She knew that when Doris came outside, they would be called up to the porch, into the light.

"Do you miss it? Back home?"

"Not really. And it's not like I don't think about it. I do. Every day. But, in a way, I'm like you—I don't feel like I was talked to nicely. It got so bad that I just decided to leave."

"And take Abram to New York?"

"Yeah. I guess in a way he was my reason. I don't *think* I'm exploiting him or using him as my excuse. I would have left with or without him." He paused. "I just got sick of being associated with people who don't respect human dignity. I... I had to get out of there."

"Does Abram know how to read and write?"

"I've been trying to teach him on the road. Funny, I used to give a little class after lunch on the farm. Abram usually chose to sleep. Ironic! But he's capable. I sure hope there's something good for him up north, somethin' that makes him feel worthy."

"It's a rough start, ain't it... to live your first decades as a slave."

"Oh, God, yes! Can't even imagine." He sighed deeply, then looked her straight in the eye. "I just wanna break that chain. It ain't right. The men with all the power wanna keep that power. But they're forgettin' that we're all men, here. And women."

"Will you be comin' back this way? On the way back down?"

"That depends on what we find in New York! I've never been. So, who knows what we'll find when we get there."

She grew quiet. And he nervously searched for the thread of the conversation. "Ever been north?"

"Never." She wrapped her arms around herself. "No farther north than Tennessee."

"You cold, Miss?" He came halfway to his feet. "You wanting the fire, inside?"

"Maybe in a minute." She looked into her lap. "If you have Sunday off, maybe would you like to walk to the lake? Take a paddle in the rowboat?"

"Hey, you two!" Doris waved them up.

He leaned in. "Oh, Rosetta, that sounds lovely. I would love to."

They walked up the steps to the porch. Doris made sure everyone had a seat and a drink. Carter breathed deeply, taking in the company of former strangers, getting used to feeling like a family component.

Feels like somethin' picked me up from someplace rough and dropped me, soft-like, into this world. And yet these strangers... they seem to have lived inside of me forever. And it's only now that their faces are coming into view.

And I love them.

The Water's Surface

sunday morning came like a good dream...
wordless but meaningful, appealing
to the heart side of the mind

The plan was for Dusty and Abram to run errands in town, and for Rosetta to show Carter around the pond. But the morning was overcast with low clouds and drizzle, so after breakfast, the men used the time to evaluate their project status. They stood inside the barn, the only light coming from the big door and two small windows.

"I think the doorway will go *here*." Dusty gestured, keeping one hand raised as he envisioned the opening.

"Will there be an actual door?" Carter asked.

"I dunno. What do you think, men?"

Abram offered, "Maybe you don't need one. Maybe a doorway that's always open will let more light into the barn."

"Yeah. Ya know, I like that idea. I was lying in bed last night, devising a slider of some sort." He stood back, hands on hips. "But I think you're right. A doorway that's always open."

Of course, all of this would need to be run by the Missus.

They exited the barn. "So, we'll use the slab wood as siding." Dusty pointed to the stack of boards that were rounded on one side—the part of the tree just inside the layer of bark.

"We'll need to come up with a plan for the windows."

Carter thought about it, then asked, "How much glass are you able to get your hands on?"

"Well, not sure. Will have to see what they have today."

"Because," Carter added, "if you'd like, I wouldn't mind making the side windows."

Dusty confessed that he was nervous about getting the glass properly sized. But Carter said he would take charge of that. "I think we can score it with a chisel—scratch against a straight edge, and then snap it over a board."

"Is that how they do it?" Dusty inquired.

"Yeah, I saw a man do it in Georgia once. He was making a window out of stained glass. He would score it with a little scratchin' tool, and then tap the glass until it cracked. It was incredible because it would break exactly on the line."

"Okay, then. You'll be our glass man!"

The three hitched Dusty's horse to the wagon. Carter saddled up Tara, not because Tara was required, but because Carter thought the exercise would do her good.

By the time they were ready, the wind had fissured the clouds and the sun found its way through the cracks, hinting at what was to come.

Carter grabbed his water canteen and made his way to the house. Rosetta came out to meet him. She wore her bonnet, but was dressed for hiking. She looked tall and strong. Doris came just halfway out the door and waved to them.

"Have fun, you two!"

Carter was a gentleman. "Would you like to come with us?" He knew that she had to stay with the children, but he offered, anyway.

And she led him past the barn. "It's about a quarter mile. I think you'll find it quite lovely."

"I'm sure I will."

She found the trailhead, flanked on each side by downed logs long grown over with moss and ivy. The path was worn down by the family and at least one horse.

"How often do you come out here?"

"Oh, once a week. More in the summer. Kids like to swim. I used to swim when I was younger. I'm a little scared of snakes." She pondered for a moment. "Not sure when I developed my fear of them."

"That's okay." He touched her shoulder as they walked. "That's called wisdom."

She laughed, and he had no idea how his very first touch sent a shot of current through her.

As the trail finished, they ducked to clear a birch branch that had snapped, impeding them. Carter's back brushed against it and cold raindrops held since this morning fell on them. "Oh! That's cold! Sorry. I'll clear that on the way back."

The path opened like two hands touching and coming apart. They stood on the sand, the pond spread before them. "Nice!" Carter thought it looked more like a lake. It looked to be a quarter mile long and an eighth across. Steep, pine-covered hills climbed up and away on two sides, and there was an interesting curve at the far end. There was even an island in the middle.

"This is beautiful, Rosetta!"

She beamed, and they walked toward the rowboat, flipped belly-up in the sand. Carter added, "That looks like an interesting cove up there. Have you been?"

"Oh, yes. I could probably navigate this in the dark. It's nice just hugging the coast. So picturesque."

"And the island?"

"Yeah. Pretty. Sometimes, I like being out there, in the middle of it all, but away from everything."

Carter turned the boat over and dusted the sand off his hands. They each grabbed an oar and fit it into an oarlock. Rosetta continued, "I always said I was gonna sleep overnight on the island. Never have."

"That sounds like a nice adventure. If you need a bodyguard, I'm your man!"

"I'll have to remember that."

Rosetta got in and sat at the boat's stern. Carter pushed off from shore, then leapt into the bow, falling not-so-gracefully into the craft. She laughed. She laughed a lot. He stepped over the front seat and sat in rowing position, facing aft, facing Rosetta, and the strokes began.

"So, what would you like to see today? Around the island?"

"Yes, let's do that. Around the island!"

It felt funny steering backward to someplace new, but facing the woman, distracted. It felt peculiar venturing forward in reverse, but he put his trust in her vision, content to be blind for a while.

And she... she got to see it all—the destination and the man who was taking her there. And she smiled. And she guided him right or left. And she held her bonnet so the wind wouldn't take it.

And she could have passed for an Edwardian lady from England —such was her sweet, refined presence—had it not been for the rugged hiking attire. White gloves and parasol were all that were missing, really. *But I much prefer her this way.*

And on the shore, the waves met boulders of red and copper, remnants of the glacier that carved the little lake and left the island as a gift. *Planned, or afterthought?*

"Want to go ashore, here?" Carter asked, intentionally vague.

"Love to." They approached a little section posing as a port, and Carter parked the oars. He grabbed a branch that had fingertips in the water. He pulled and the boat nosed ashore.

He hopped out, then grabbed the boat by the bow. Rosetta still sat aft, so it was easy to pull the craft up onto the bank. Then he offered his hand and she came forward, both hands on the gunnels—the boat sides—then took his hand with both of her own.

And now they occupied a place apart from all others, as detached and self-sustaining as a new planet. Finally together. Truly alone.

And they ventured, never thinking to look back at the mainland, pretending that this was all there was.

And the wind loved this place, obvious by the way it played in the canopy. And as they walked, its most beautiful music serenaded, touching a place no one had touched in a long time.

The path went right up the backbone of their little world, and they were gentle with its sensitive spine. Carter took Rosetta's hand when tree roots impeded, letting go only when he had to.

Until the last time.

That time, her grasp told him that it was fine to just hang on. And he looked back at her, maybe to ensure that she was real, maybe to show that he was happy with this.

And when they came to the end, as far north as they could go, they stood side by side and watched the constant waves, their fingers becoming friends.

And he offered his other hand. And she placed hers there. And they just stared. Not moving, but not afraid. Hungry, but not starved. Enthralled, to be sure, but holding time so it stood still.

"I remember how I felt the first time I saw you."

"You do?"

"Yes. Because I feel the same right now." He added, "Just so very fortunate."

And he set free her hands. And his went to her face, her cheeks, her cheekbones. And when she saw his mouth moving to hers, she grabbed at his waistcoat—not out of passion, but to steady herself when she closed her eyes.

And she felt herself falling into that sweet, familiar unknown, where we close our eyes in order to be lost. And when he kissed her more deeply, she could taste the onion from this morning's potatoes, and she loved it even more this time 'round—the flavor and her newfound hunger.

And he cradled her face, her head, and one hand went to the back of her neck and allowed him to step closer and tilt her face up to him. And the music above them was replaced by music inside, and it was glorious, it was simple, the kind everyone wants to feel on a Sunday morning.

"You are beautiful," he declared, but only in a whisper. And she gave no verbal response, but pulled him in for another taste. And he felt her body against his, and his arms went around her waist, and she gave a whimper of approval, so feminine and so powerful.

And she wished that she had brought a picnic blanket, that they might recline and relieve their feet. And she felt he read her mind when he offered, "Would you like to sit?" He pulled off his jacket and scanned the area for a dry, comfortable place.

She sat on his coat—a place where pine needles congregated—but only after verifying that he was all right with it. He sat on a low stump, checking for sap, briefly puzzling at who might have felled the tree.

He liked how she looked, sitting there. Young, a breeze knowing her, even way out here. She looked up at him and pulled a wisp of hair from her eyes. She wished his coat were twice as big.

"How far from your last home, Rosetta?"

She looked off as if calculating, as if she could see the place in the distance. "Two days ride. Maybe three."

"Do you miss it?"

"Yes! It's terrible to love a place but have to move against your will."

He pulled some bark off the stump, smelled it. The pine signature made his mouth water. If she hadn't been here, he would have pulled his knife and carved a shape, a likeness.

"Nice of your sister. But I hate that you had to flee."

126

"Everything happens for a reason." Her declaration ended with a content smile, and she stretched her arms in front of her. "Things could be worse."

Carter had a hundred questions, but felt he didn't yet deserve answers. Still, it was hard to get an accurate picture of events, a clear picture of her.

"When I found out that I was with child, he became angry. And to this day, I don't understand. I... he drank. And came home drunk, and we didn't have much of anything to eat. There were nights when I felt like I was starving."

Carter was all eyes, ears too.

"I decided—if he behaved like this before the baby, then things would only get worse. Talking did no good."

"One night, he pushed me. I went right out the front door."

"Jeez."

"I had a baby to protect. And lots of time to consider things." She looked out across the water, again. "I left at sundown, when I knew he would be drinking somewhere, when I thought darkness would finally be on *my* side."

She looked off, her face numbed by the distress of years, her eyes sweet and child-like, deserving none of this. "Didn't matter," she forced out. "In the end, I mean. Baby..." She cleared her throat. "Lost baby."

Newness

they were aware of the world's soft intensities—
the flutter of leaves and hearts
the constant, predictable wave action and their breaths
unexpected breezes and the rush of adrenaline

He never dreamed that on his journey he would encounter someone who made him ponder his own path. He was focused, driven! He had a timeline and destination! It seemed inconceivable that a woman could interrupt his mission, could make him question all of that.

But for now, Sunday morn, his spirit lived in his heart region and he let his mind fill up with scents and music and moving pictures. He was ruled by the place scoffed at—but so deeply desired—by every living creature.

"I didn't see you coming to me," she said, her voice surprising him.

He smiled and pulled her closer, rocking her on the shore of a tiny island, one so small that it appeared on no official map, only in sketches and memories.

"I know you have to continue." She looked out at the waves. "I know you have an important place to be."

Clarity

nothing intensifies longing
like the start of love

A friend once warned her that love at first sight was fiction, that true love takes years. And yet experience taught her the opposite—that years brought only pain and that moments are for taking, for leaping.

She trusted her instincts. She knew from experience what love looked like, lust too. And that it was all right to play the part of the fool now and then. Not always. Not when hearts were vulnerable. But sometimes one deserved to step inside a beautiful piece of music, inside a beautiful story, even if the future held no promises.

She had known Carter Monroe for days. She admired his manner. She witnessed how he worked, how he spoke, and how he regarded people. He had loving, worldly qualities. And he had a bravery about him, a sincerity.

"Did you grow up with sisters?"

"I did. A couple." He added, "If you count slave sisters, who—in my heart—I do."

She was intrigued by his talent for communication, for sharing. He was open and caring. He wasn't afraid to linger, tracing her skin with his fingers. He was emotionally available, even if he would soon leave her world.

They rowed back across the pond, she facing the mainland, he watching their tiny island grow smaller.

And as drunk and dizzy as he felt, she appeared strong, able, in perspective. But he didn't realize that she would go to her room and write, scribble, pen poetry with a fever. And he would carve a pair of birds joined at the wing, and he would puzzle over how to make a single mouthpiece, one music from two songbirds.

Dusty and Abram returned with the sheets of glass. Dusty had a lightness to his step, so Carter surmised that he had worked a deal.

"We're gonna make the biggest darn windows east of the Mississippi!"

Carter helped them get it all unloaded. They placed lumber between the sheets of glass for support.

"We even got you a new tool, Mister Glass Cutter!" Dusty presented Carter with the cutting tool. It looked small, especially in relation to the task at hand.

"Great!" Carter could feel the pressure to succeed, though he'd never worked glass in his life. *But if I'm careful, and go one step at a time...*

They had some time before supper, so the men planned out tomorrow's work. When they were satisfied and had all the tools and materials situated, Dusty asked, "So, how was the pond?"

"Oh, it's nice over there. Very beautiful."

"She's a nice girl, that Rosetta."

"Very beautiful," he repeated.

They supped, and everyone seemed content tonight. "What did you do today, Doris?" Carter asked.

"Oh, I did some darning, and some reading, and I took a walk out to Bonnie's place." Then she added, "We exchange goods and services. She's real good with cloth, that one." She was on her feet to collect the dishes before Carter could inquire precisely what was traded.

Carter announced, though, that he was going to wash the dishes tonight. "After all, it's Sunday evening and the women deserve a night off." Surprisingly, they took him up on his offer. Rosetta dried, and it was exquisite to feel her hip bump into his once or twice. He had all he could do to focus, to not break a dish, to not just grab her by the shoulders and love her.

"I loved today."

"I did, too. Thank you."

"I can still taste you," she whispered.

Carter exhaled through pursed lips. His head swam, and he steadied himself against the sink. He looked to see if anyone was in the living area, within earshot.

"I don't know where you learned to kiss like that, but you have a beautiful mouth, Miss."

Measured

we grow as attached
to unexpected treasures
as to lifelong dreams
because beauty is in the sheer discovery

That night, the buggy and white horse returned. Carter watched the dark figure walk to the house. Just as before, the man waited, was welcomed inside.

"Who out there, Master Carter?"

"Oh, it's no one. It's…"

"It's a night doctor, ain't it?"

"What?"

"It's a night doctor!"

"Quiet, quiet. It's… I don't know who it is."

"I gotta get outta here, Master Carter!"

"What'sa matter?"

"I'm tellin' ya—it's one of them night doctors."

Carter muddled it. "What the hell is that?"

"They watch for slaves who escape."

"What? No."

"And when they catch 'em, they do experiments on 'em."

"Who the hell told you that?"

"Everybody told me that—because it's the truth!"

"Are they… human?" Abram had his eyes on the door. Carter clarified. "Are they people?"

"I don't know. It don't matter! They do experiments!"

They waited. And in a few minutes, the buggy turned around and trotted down the drive, gone. Carter kept it simple. "See?" He was tired, and he closed his eyes to relieve their burning. And when they woke up, it was barely daylight.

They said good morning to the family, and studied their faces for hints of sabotage, for clues of betrayal. Carter noticed every nuance, every downward glance, every unspoken signal. But if this were a setup, they were mighty fine players.

Dusty teased him. "I sure hope those dishes didn't make your hands too soft to cut glass!"

"Dusty!" Doris protested. "He's gonna do just fine!"

"And," Rosetta added, "that was a very gentlemanly thing to do, Carter Monroe."

They ate. And the men went to their work area. And they measured for the first window. Carter clarified how wide they wanted the wood frame to be, then subtracted from the overall length and width of the opening. When he had the glass dimensions, he wrote them down, then measured and calculated again.

"You always this careful?"

Carter looked at Dusty, but the wheels in his mind were turning. "Just had a thought." He walked to the outside of the structure. "If we make tall windows—six feet each—if you break one of these, it's gonna be a bear to replace."

He touched a spot halfway up the opening. "But if we make two three-foot windows, it would be much easier to replace a broken one." Dusty rubbed his chin, and Carter added, "And I don't think you'd lose any daylight."

Dusty clapped his hands together. "I like it. Good call, Carter."

When it came time to score the glass, Carter clamped a straightedge to the pane, and everyone gathered around to watch the process. It actually took longer to tap the glass after it was scored. Carter made sure it had cracked all the way through before he attempted to break the glass. Abram and Dusty helped, each adding their weight at the same time, and the first cut was a success.

Carter cleaned up the shards that didn't come off cleanly—they were minor and would never be detected once they were in their new frame.

Abram sawed the wood for the window frame, and Dusty created a dado joint along each length—the glass would ride in the dado. And after they had successfully created and installed the first window, the rest of the window components were created *en masse*. Then the assembly could happen in a line and each man could perfect his portion of the process.

By lunchtime, four windows were installed. The women brought food out, and were gleeful at the progress. They stepped inside the barn so that they could envision the completed room, and it was lovely to see their smiles, to hear the female perspective, to reap the real rewards of the planning and hard work.

They set the food on the boards, the ones that rested on the saw horses inside the structure. The ladies stood inside and ate. The men reached through the future window frames and took a biscuit, a plate of beans. "Wish we had some honey for ya, fellas."

But it was perfect as is. "Plenty of sweetness already, ladies—thank you!"

It felt nice to see Rosetta's face. Yesterday was lovely, the perfect Sunday, the perfect pace and unfolding of a dream, emotions in slow motion. He watched her eat and felt the meaning of words like "compatibility."

"What's so funny?" Rosetta surprised him.

"Hmm?" He stopped chewing and looked at her.

"You were a thousand miles away and smiling!"

Carter felt all eyes upon him. "Just happy." He bit his biscuit, and talked through it. "Jus'appy."

The men finished off every remnant of food from every plate and washed it down with sun tea. While they finished, Doris fingered the new wood, the boards that were becoming her new room. She imagined tables of herbs and looked up to see how the upper windows would bless the space with daylight.

Carter saw this, saw how she and Dusty got along, how she wished for a room and he granted it, how they cooperated—wish fulfillment and gratitude. He once thought he and Sarah Jane enjoyed this, and could not say if their failure was because of him or her. But the web of their lives seemed highly complex. Doris and Dusty's seemed quaint and simple.

Of course! They all do from the outside! If you're standing outside of a room, if you're not invested, it's easy to be aloof, to be floating. But once you're inside, you become a component of that room, enmeshed, adding your own complexity, contributing or withholding.

In the next few days, the men finished the project. The windows let new life into the barn, and planting tables graced the periphery of the herb room. The side windows were made to slide up and down a few inches, letting in the breeze.

But the freshness was bittersweet and everyone tip-toed, wondering when the travelers would decide that it was time to go. The kids saw their mom comforting Rosetta more than once that day.

Abram was also keenly aware that a decision was forthcoming. "Are we leaving today?"

"Today?" Carter seemed genuinely off-guard.

"We're finished with the project, ain't we?"

Leaving

there is comfort in the weeping
celebration in sorrow's sacred tears

Thursday, the leaving day, was preceded by a sleepless night. And the sunlight was unsympathetic. Its presence was almost insulting, too showy for their reverence. Every family member gave bleary-eyed hugs. Doris gave food for the journey. Dusty was grateful for the work. And Rosetta managed to survive the good-bye, but not without silent tears, each salty path a tribute to the beauty they had found.

He whispered during their last embrace, "I will write you when I arrive, okay? You are right inside, here." He grabbed his shirt, right at chest level.

He let Abram ride the first leg of the journey. Tara seemed eager to be moving again. Abram, too, both high-stepping. And when they were at the edge of the property, Carter turned back to see the adults still in farewell formation. The kids were running circles around them, an image photographed in his memory.

Then he hustled to catch up with the horse.

And when he looked to his right, his eye caught a glimpse of the dragonfly that had landed on his shoulder. And he almost flicked it away, but wished it would stay. And for nearly a mile, it did.

"Do you think Doris gave us jelly?"

"Hmmm?" Carter looked up. "I didn't look inside." But when he peeked, two little jars lay swaddled in a soft towel, preserved like twin babes.

"They had good jelly," Abram reminisced.

Carter looked at his shoulder and saw that the dragonfly had flown. *Hmm... didn't even see it go.* Such is silence, the slipping away.

It felt natural to be back upon the road it. Still, the first hours dragged—they were still full of food and new friends. It took a good long while for the road to relearn them, to become one again.

Carter stayed on foot all day, refusing the horse, needing to expend his excess energy on something. The saddle would have produced idle thoughts, doubts. It would have been too easy to wheel the horse in the other direction, to make a run for it, to make an instant life with Rosetta.

And it would be sweet. And it would be whole.

Then why the migration? Why the conflict?

He reasoned with his heart, explaining that the road would not be forever, that New York was the mission and the mission needed to happen. Something great called him there, and the first bit of testing should not derail that calling.

Get there. Then decide.

When sunset loomed, Carter wasn't hungry. He'd just as soon travel through the night, walk until he dropped, anything but darkness and a head full of thoughts! But they found a spot on a bare hill and made a fire. They employed the trail routine, but it felt strange not to wash for supper, not to groom for the women.

They unwrapped the food that came from Doris's kitchen—fried chicken, yellow beans, bread. Carter quietly blessed his portion. He ate it only because he was absolutely famished.

"Still delicious, isn't it?"

"Mmmm," Abram agreed.

"Can taste every herb and spice." He pictured the light in that house, the sources of warmth—fire and hearts, women and children, the love within the walls. And it left a lump in his throat. And if he were alone, this is the part where he'd have wept. And he saved one of the chicken bones, dried it by the fire, thought about making it into a necklace, an amulet, a token of future affection.

They slept, and woke to light precipitation. And they moved their feet in the direction of their dream, though Carter was finding it hard to venture farther from the heart he left behind. *That's what trudging is. Mindless, heartless.*

And the *mindless* mechanism worked—they made good time for several days, snapping back into a pace that carried them close to thirty-five miles per day.

And at night, Carter fell to sleep wishing that Rosetta would visit him in his dreams. But on the fifth night, it was Doris who would surprise him, who walked up to him with a basket of folded fabric and a beautiful smile. He had no idea what it was for, but in that moment realized how handsome she was, how elegant and whole. His dream whispered into his bad ear—though the reason was unclear—that she could bring him a beautiful life.

He was mildly uncomfortable to have dreamt of another man's wife, but the feeling that remained was one of sweetness, innocence. It felt natural, as if she'd been whispering all along. It just took this long for his ear to register.

And in the morning, he went to his clothing pack and dug down deep, finding the two nightshirts that she had made or traded for. He regarded the stitching, the pattern, but was most pleased when he simply buried his face in them and smelled the loveliness of that family. And it wasn't until he unfolded the first shirt that he saw the note.

A little warmth for your nights on the road.
So happy that the road brought you to us.
Much love, Doris, Rosetta, Dusty

And they wore them the next night. And Carter kept his on under his clothes the whole next day. He wanted to be close to that family smell as long as possible, not realizing until it was too late that the extended wearing actually hastened the covering of their scent with his own.

The Flow of the Scribe

and the miles accumulated
so the vistas and the valleys
bittersweet the distance and proximity

Carter sighed a lot these days. Abram commented on it. And if Abram noticed... well, that was something. Rosetta—as delicate as she was—refused to let his passion rest. If anything, her presence inside of him grew. She set him free but would not let him go.

I need to write her. I need to connect. And if I write ten letters in ten nights, I shall choose the best and post that to her.

But the note he wrote on the first night said all he wanted to say. It came from his heart and could not be improved. He simply spoke to her.

Dearest Rosetta,

Your name is a song... I say it as I travel, and the sun comes out. I say it as I lie beneath stars, and find you next to me. I think it before I open my eyes to the morn, and the day is beautiful.

I pray that you are well. The impression you have left on me is sweet, and new, and powerful. We two are no strangers to love. And we are old enough to be wise, honest, and realistic. It is true that my feet carry me away from you, yet there is a connection so tender between us, and my presumptuous heart guesses that you may feel it as well.

Whether you do or do not, it is an honor to know you, to feel this, and to share it with you.

In mid-summer, I shall be in the hills and lakes of New York. I try to picture what that looks like. And, somehow, the picture becomes real when I envision you in the scene. There you are, in your bonnet, untying your apron, smiling at me. And the trees around our little house sway in time, for they know the beauty of our love. Every living thing celebrates this thing we share.

I don't know how you came to me... you are under a star so bright! I cannot fathom what I did to deserve you. But neither shall I let my lack of understanding impede me. All I know is that I shall reach my destination.

And on my journey and after I arrive, I shall love you in my heart. I believe in the time we had, in the steps that led me to you, in the stars that are still moving together. You, sweet Rosetta, make me believe in this... the best feeling I have ever held in my heart.

Please give my best to Doris, Dusty, and the children. And know that you are thought of every day. And even in the quiet (especially in the quiet) I am loving you.

Have faith, my darling,
Carter

When the letter was dry, he folded it and tucked it in the little leather satchel that his sister made for him. He checked the map for the next city big enough to have a post office, then put everything away and came inside the tent.

He fell to sleep before he knew that sleep was near. And that was fine, for his dreaming mind recorded a single image of her—*standing in the doorway and watching him return.* And that single frame produced a feeling sweet enough to revive his weariness, a pleasure deep enough to hold him through his next days of climbing.

And when they approached the border of Kentucky, the travelers hugged in celebration, making more real the crossing.

But when they stepped out of Tennessee, Carter felt a pain in his throat. He worried that she would sense him leaving her state, her realm, her circle of love. His faith was strong, but he was frightened by prospects unseen. He feared men and movements and makings of his own creation.

So that night, he dedicated to her a new ritual, one that was clean of herbal remedy, one that required focus rather than illusion, one that celebrated a connection to something great.

They sat up late by the fire, both of them watching the images dance. It was nice to have nothing to do. Carter worked on a splinter in the heel of his hand.

"There," he said, spitting it out. "That's the last of the slivers from Tennessee."

He laid it on a stone at the fire's edge and could not recall which part of the sunroom they were working on when the thing pierced him. He sighed. *Was that chapter ages ago or just days?* It was melting into him as sweet chapters do, but still right there on his skin, hard to let it go.

ß reath of Kentucky

sad, this Kentucky road
prints that in the dust remain but a day
wind and rain swearing, declaring that we were never here

Carter's morning came early, before the light. Not because of cold or thirst or noise. He'd simply rested well and felt recharged.

He wasn't conscious more than a couple seconds when he remembered the dream.

Rosetta stepped from behind the velvet curtain
with the ease of a thousand performances
all sequins and lashes
a full evening dress and half curtsey

she met and dared every eye
save those in the balcony where Carter sat, now dizzy and
aware of the precipice, the shortness of the railing

He rose quietly and fetched the bow and arrow. A *good morning to give Abram a hot breakfast.* He left a note just inside the tent. *Abram, please make a fire.*

He had his choice of critters—raccoon, quail, rabbit. The latter seemed like the best choice, and he blessed the thing and its family while it was still warm.

When he returned to camp, there was no fire, so he woke Abram and asked him to strike the tent. "I brought us some breakfast."

He gathered a small pile of pine needles, some kindling, and spied a downed branch. He nicked his flint until sparks rained down on the needles and caught, white smoke their sign of surrender. He broke up the kindling and criss-crossed them to make an up-draft.

"How 'bout fetchin' that downed branch for me, Abram?"

Abram saw where he was pointing. "And can you break it into two or three pieces for me?"

Abram strapped the tent together, dancing a little, then *ran* to the branch. He dragged it into their clearing, stomped on it in an exaggerated fashion, then ran eight steps to the edge of the brush and relieved himself.

When he returned with the firewood, Carter was smiling. "Sorry! I didn't know you had to go!"

Carter pet the animal between his eyes, then set free its sweet soul. The meat came out easily and he skewered it. It was still warm when it hit the fire, the sizzle rising and both men salivating at the sound.

Carter cleaned the pelt and let it dry next to the fire. He was replenishing his accumulation now, having given a month's worth to Doris, Dusty, and Rosetta.

Never expected to meet them. Not expecting to meet anyone quite like them up ahead.

They tore into the meat and, like kids, burned their mouths, impatient for the cooling. If they had rabbit for breakfast seven days running, it's likely they would burn themselves each morning.

And maybe it was intentional.

Every day around noon, on horseback or on foot, their tongues would play inside their mouths and rediscover the burnt roofs and taste buds. And they would remember the breakfast that now powered them. And it would be enough to carry them to supper.

Something, Sometime

Dear Rosetta,

I hope this finds you well, happy.

We are currently in Kentucky, and crossing the line from your sweet state caused more than a little angst! Leaving you was difficult, but feeling the distance unroll is excruciating. Often, I find myself watching my own feet on the dusty road, not sure if they are my own—they just keep moving forward.

And I tell myself that the new land will bring something good. And I have more than a little faith. And trust. And stamina.

Tonight, by the fire, I curse myself for spending a single afternoon out of your sight! For taking my eyes off of you once.

But alas... all of these things are sweet proof—proof that a beautiful fire burns, proof that there is still magic in this world.

I have to thank you for making the magic inside of this heart. You are beautiful, and missed, and loved.

Sweet Rosetta,

Carter

When the letter was dry, he folded it and tucked it in the little leather satchel. He pulled out his map and compass to determine the next city in their journey. He had intentionally avoided population centers; but, for Rosetta, he would make exceptions, break rules, challenge the natural laws.

It sounds like someone is playing the Fool.

He'd never really played that part, before. Everything before was logical. Even relationships were measured and calculated for merit, for purpose, for projected longevity.

Maybe it's time I do change my approach. God knows my previous calculations didn't end up accurate! Maybe it's time to let my horses run.

Truly, Fully

Dear Rosetta,

I dreamed last night that inside a booth I stood, talking into a box that carried my voice all the way to Tennessee. All the way to you.

And when I paused, I could hear your voice returning to me, slow at first, like water finding its way through rocks and races. And when it found me, drenched me, I could literally feel your words rain over me. And so sweet was your water, your every word like music.

And I could detect that sweet, little dialect that I'd never heard until your town, your place, amidst your people.

When I woke, the hair on my arms was still at attention. Just as when I was near you.

And this morning as Abram and I traveled, I could think of nothing else but our dream conversation. And as my thoughts evolved, I decided that—as lovely as talking into magic boxes would be—I would rather just have you near me. Truly, fully.

By the time Abram and I get to New York, your life and mine will be new. But I pray that the changes bring us nearer, for the mere thought of you causes a sweet tsunami to wash over my (typically peaceful) Pacific region.

(Did I just ink that? Apologies—I am weary!)

But you… you are so sweetly thought of, Dear Rosetta~

Carter Monroe

When the letter was dry, he folded it and tucked it in the little leather satchel. He looked into the fire, and closed his eyes to see her. And when he closed them tighter, they burned.

146

Abram slept in the tent behind him. Tara slept standing, head dropped. Carter sat between them—the carrier and the carried—but felt alone, felt the weight of the trek. He smiled at the way Abram envisioned the map, how north was up, a climb, and how south could be an easy descent. Tonight, Carter felt that Abram was right, that north was indeed a tough climb, made more difficult by what was back at base camp. Her.

He climbed into the tent and fell to sleep in seconds. At some point he dreamed of her, or at least dreamed that he talked about her. And he woke, he smiled, a funny phrase still on his lips. He'd expressed to a dream-stranger how he felt about Rosetta—out of character, but funny nonetheless.

"I would love to nuzzle her puzzle."

He had no idea where the words came from, and was quite certain he would not repeat them to her in his next love letter. And only he knew that the words were true, albeit lacking in the sacredness that he felt.

Low and Childlike

we trust and we move on
sometimes moving on too quickly

When they came to town, Carter was up and Abram walked at his side. It was late afternoon, and somewhere meat was grilling. And after days on the trail, the thought of a table and chair was intoxicating.

But it was the Post Office they sought, and they walked past the food and drink, the table and chairs. Abram wiped his nose and peeked sideways through the doorway, catching a glimpse of a waiter, two ladies at a table, and wafting smoke. His glance was not lost on Carter.

"That look good to you?"

"What?" His eyes were wide.

"The dinner place. Look good to you?"

"Oh. Yeah." He added, low and childlike, "Fancy!"

Carter dismounted and took out his little leather satchel, then walked inside. Abram watered Tara, then sat on the boardwalk and looked up the street. Inside, Carter inquired about envelopes, stamps, paper. He decided to send each letter separately. *So worth it.*

When he was finished, he talked to the postal clerk about the sign advertising Morse Messaging.

"Well, you write your message, here. And, for a fee, we'll run it over to the Morse transmitter at the train station. He'll transmit your message over the wires." When Carter scratched his head, the man continued. "The Morse operator at the recipient's town takes the message right to the house."

"Do you mean, so..." He stammered. "Does my handwriting get ...traced?"

"Ah… the Morse operator *here* converts your text into the Morse alphabet. He taps out the message using dots and dashes. When it gets to the other end, the receiver *there* converts it back to text."

Carter ran his fingers through his hair. "When did they come up with *this*?"

At that moment, he was too stunned to make the connection between the Morse and his dream—talking into the long-distance box. But his mind was racing, imagining a day when the Morse operator would no longer be required, when a family would learn this code and send their own messages.

"Thanks for posting my letters."

"You bet, sir."

Carter walked to the door, but turned. "Say, can you recommend someplace to have a bite to eat, spend the night?"

The clerk rubbed his chin. "Well, the Holler Back is nice. They'll get ya settled in. And can they do chicken! A quarter mile outta town."

"You reckon they'll have a problem with my man?"

The clerk leaned against the counter and craned his neck to get a better look at the "man" to whom Carter referred. When he righted himself, he looked Carter dead in the eye, letting the silence ask the questions and strangle the answers.

"You don't mean…"

Carter meant exactly that. But his eye went to the letters in the clerk's hand, and he feared for their safekeeping. So he lied, "Oh, the accommodations would be for me."

"Ah, of course. The Holler Back. Tell them Earl sent ya."

Carter walked out onto the boardwalk. The sun was low now, cutting right down the middle of Main Street, just like the glacier that shaped this town, that cleaved the valley between two perfect mountain rises.

Carter mounted Tara, and they walked. At their first opportunity, they slipped behind the row of buildings and turned one hundred eighty degrees. They continued until they found the backdoor of the "fancy" place that Abram saw.

The back door was open. Two stairs came down to a broken, empty chair. A dog was occupied with a greasy pan. A trash bin—a massive box with wheels and a hitch—sat leaking, dreaming of its prior life in the apple orchard. And kitchen sounds came from inside —barked orders, sizzling meat, metal tongs on iron grates.

Carter came down, then fiddled with his saddle bag. Abram watched, curious, but didn't ask aloud.

It was only a couple minutes before a kitchen hand came out with a load of trash. He spied the pair that loitered out back, hesitated, then dumped his load.

"You like tobacco, son?"

The young man wiped grease off his left hand before answering. "Reckon."

"I got a stash of it, right from Mississippi, if you can get us a couple plates." Carter presented it, holding it at his waist in hopes that a slow reveal would increase its mystique, its appeal.

"Wait."

With one hand, he took the can back inside. He was out of sight for a good ten minutes, so long that Carter began to suspect failure. But the boy returned as agreed, carrying two generous plates of hot food—sweet potatoes, peas, and steak of some sort. Carter was grateful for the quantity and for the trust. He set the pouch of tobacco down on the step, then accepted the two plates.

The boy watched them for just a moment. Carter thanked him with his eyes, and noticed the boy's eyes—green and young, but incredibly overtired. They had bags beneath them, like he hadn't slept well a day in his life.

He took the pouch of smoke and went back to his work. It wasn't until then that Carter noticed that his right hand was unable to leave his side, his right shoulder in a permanent shrug. And even with his first taste of the delicious steak, Carter felt a wicked stab of pity, right in his chest.

The men sat on the ground, up against the building, and ate without knife or fork. They ate steak the way it was intended to be eaten—held with the hands, torn with the incisors, wrestled greedily with the jaws.

But the potatoes and the peas—they made the meal. Three different foods on a plate was extraordinary. Three foods on a plate formed a circle of love and care. And as they filled themselves, another sunset found them, warned that they had but minutes to find shelter—someplace outside of the circle of love and care.

And the last remaining bites—though still delicious—were taken with a level of resignation, as if the meal had been stolen, wolfed down and unreal, merely consumed.

They stacked the two plates on the bottom step, and as they loaded up, Carter looked one last time to catch a glimpse of the boy. But he was a ghost, from another dimension, and one encounter was all Carter got.

And as Carter turned, a single gust of wind blew upside his head, flipping the hat off his head. *Somethin' mysterious about that boy. He knows something. Maybe he doesn't even realize that he knows something, but he's gonna make a mark. Just hope it's with an angel and not a devil.*

They both felt like walking, so Carter led Tara by the reins.

And back on Main Street, colors were going dim. But whites knew it was their time to shine.

The ruffles of a blouse as she exits a carriage.

The man's collar as he calls to a friend.

The barber shaking the hair out of a sheet.

For these few moments, there is magic like no other time in the day. For less than five minutes, the world floats in a trance of gold. Strangers could meet during these moments and fall into a love that lasts forever.

They kept walking, and the ruffles and the collar and the sheet lived on without another thought, all flirty and wispy-animated behind their backs.

"We're in the holler, right now."

"The holler?"

"For some reason, they call a valley a holler, here."

And in a few minutes, they approached the Holler Back, and Carter had Abram hold Tara. "Work on getting this knot out." He knew it was impossible. It was leather dongle, thin and pulled tight. But he needed to keep Abram occupied—on the outside of the horse.

Then he called "Hello" to the host inside.

The innkeeper came out with a lantern, greeted him, and took his money in exchange for a single cabin for the night. "Lamp and matches next to the bed, men."

He headed back to his abode. With his back to them, he waved. "Tea and cornbread in the mornin'." And just before he stepped inside, "Eggs, too."

Carter was pretty sure the man had not seen past the horse, Abram's face. *If people are not blind to color, then—damn—I'll help make them so.*

They came inside and found the matches. Carter lit the lamp and woke the sleepy walls, rousted the picture frames, revealed the tiny bed. The space was barely large enough to hold them, but it was warm in here.

They undressed and climbed under the covers. The frame sagged, registering the strain to such a degree that Carter laughed, expecting the thing to snap. They sighed, exhaling the sum of the day—the miles and all they had seen, the months behind and those ahead.

Even when each lay on his side at the very edge of the bed, upper thighs and shoulders met and fit and stayed there. There was simply no escape and no use complaining about it.

"Good-night, Master Carter."

Carter had no idea where that came from. Of all the nights that they had shared a night space, this was the first time Abram had bid him good-night, and for the reason Carter was at a loss.

"Good-night, Abram. Sleep well."

"That meat was good."

Ah... so that's where his mind is. "I'm glad you liked it. You are the one who found the place. So thank you."

"I didn't know you could pay without using money."

"Well, sometimes you have to be creative. If you have something to trade, it's worth a try."

They slept, colliding throughout the night. Carter dreamed of his sister.

And when he woke at dawn, he went to the window and watched a couple birds flitting through the bushes, finding berries. He thought of her, the last remnant of his immediate family, the little cleat which kept him moored to the South. And when that little cleat gave way, it was time to sail or forever drift.

And now he was in Kentucky, heading for New York, sad to lose her, regretting the things he could have done for her, guilty for the brother he could have been.

And now she's a bird. Or the breeze. And whether she's singing in my ear or blowing on the back of my neck, I will always appreciate the touch.

It would be tricky getting out of here without the innkeeper seeing Abram. Sure, Carter could handle things, but he didn't need the confrontation.

Then again, the thought of those eggs sounded mighty inviting. So he woke Abram and had him walk Tara to the edge of the property under cover of dawn. Then he fetched his mess kit and walked back to the inn and waited until he could smell breakfast.

"Good morning! Say that was a fine little cabin— thank you."

"Well, good. Glad you enjoyed your stay."

"Say, my brother and I are all saddled up. Do you suppose I could have the eggs in my pan so we could get on the trail?"

Reid looked on him with some surprise. "Yer in a hurry, ain't ya!"

"We're just running a little behind is all."

"Well, sure. Here." He scooped a generous mound of scrambled eggs into Carter's pan. "And a couple Johnny cakes fer ya." Then he whispered, "Wish I had some butter fer ya!"

"Reid, this is perfect—thank you, again!" He sealed the thing shut, then trotted down the drive to where Abram waited. They walked a hundred yards, then stopped and tore into the hot breakfast.

"We're gonna remember this place! Ya know, in case we ever come back through here!"

Abram looked up from his breakfast, eyes dark and sleepy, and smiled. "Yeah."

This Kentucky road had been good to them, had fed them, had let them pass safely between its hills. *Another host, gracious and unexpected.*

The Secret Signal

to those so inclined
thunder calls

When it rained, they came together. After the tools were brought in to dry, so the laundry from the line, they met in the very place that ended seven lives.

Between kisses, lips on her neck, he would ask, "Do you think we are being sacrilegious? Dishonorable?"

And she would take one step back, her eyes on his but darker than those he'd known just moments ago. "Actually, Carter," she said, peeling down her wet top, "we're helping them live on."

And he would think, *Never have I seen skin so delicious.* And he loved everything about her. And no one in the world had made him feel these things.

And she would wrap around him like he was her savior. To hold him less tightly would be to lose him to the world, and she could not afford to lose anything more.

And they would try for silence, lips and biting, the breaths and nails, the scooting of the bed. And she commended him for his bravery, his insistence on tasting. And his reward was the arching of her back, when her eyes went to the ceiling, to the black gills of the place, but they saw only heaven. *Gertie.*

And those months lasted forever, until she ran. Sans note. Sans explanation. And his attempts at survival led him to the barber where he fell into a painting of the sea, the cradle of water, dreams of the complete, nautical escape.

Zuko and Pops

to have felt sun on the face for so long
felt somewhat gluttonous
but one senses when one should give back

When they came up behind the old man—crouching, hands on his knees—they thought he was catching his breath. They hadn't seen the man on the ground, so low did he lie. As they approached, Carter touched his pistol, just to be safe. No telling what had just occurred.

The old man stood. "Can you help? We got no money."

Carter halted Tara. That's when he saw the blood on the younger man's pants. "What happened?"

"He got tore up climbin' over a fence." The man held out his hands, palms up. "We was starvin', sir. Hungry is all."

Carter dismounted and took a look. It looked as though the younger man had taken a large, sharp piece of fencing in the front of his thigh.

"Wood?"

"Yeah."

"Do you think you got it all out?"

"Yeah, I do."

"When did this happen?"

"This morn."

"Okay. I'm gonna pour some alcohol on it, just to make sure it's clean. Gonna sting, but it'll kill the germs." Then he turned to the old man, "Anyone comin' after you for this?"

"Naw, we wanted a chicken, but the dog was after us. Didn't see no peoples."

Carter went to it, pouring from the new bottle of bourbon, then bandaged the man up with the sleeve from an extra shirt.

"Can ya get up?"

156

The man did. He didn't appear to have lost a whole lot of blood, but he was unsteady.

"You men eaten today?"

"No sir," Zuko and Pops answered in unison. So Carter found them something from the saddle bag. Jerked beef. After he gave it to them, he and Abram joined.

Turns out they were also heading north, so off they ventured, Zuko up on Tara. When Carter asked how far they aimed to travel, they had no idea, and that concerned him—for everyone's safety.

"Well, where are you comin' from?"

The men looked sideways at each other. Obviously, they were concerned that Carter could be rounding up slaves. But Carter was also careful. Traveling with two was challenging. Four would be at least twice as difficult.

So, for now, they just walked. And at the end of the day, they found a safe place to camp. Abram made a fire and Carter went off with bow and arrow to find food. Sunset was a good time to find rabbit, and he bagged two. He also found a pheasant, which would be a nice change of pace.

He cooked the bird on a spit and the rabbits in a large skillet. When the rabbit was minutes from being done, Carter stirred in some rice, which boiled in the rabbit juice and made the whole thing more substantial.

"That must be what heaven smells like," Pops pronounced.

And they went to it. And Carter knew what it felt like to go hungry, and every man deserved to feel fed. He was happy that his preparation skills were appreciated.

"So, Pops," Carter called. "Where you gonna end your journey? Where do you wanna be in a month?"

"Oh, I dunno." He looked into the fire, then back at Carter. "Someplace where I can work with wood."

Carter sat up. "You a builder?"

"I like to work with rough lumber. Size it. Worked in a mill for a while. I liked that work."

"What about you, Zuko?"

"I dunno. I might like to herd cattle. Something like that."

"So, you like to work in the saddle?" Carter probed.

"Yeah. I like to work in the saddle."

After a pause, Pops asked, "You gonna break out that bottle, again, Mister Carter?"

Carter met his glance. Pops was dead serious. Uncomfortably so.

"Well, first of all, that bottle's gotta get someplace." Then he finished, "Besides, Abram and I gotta get up early, hit the trail. Miles and miles to go tomorrow. Ain't that right, Abram?"

"That's right," he said dryly.

When they got ready for bed, Carter gave his blanket to Zuko and Pops. "You guys stay close to the fire, now. Extra logs right there." Without fanfare, he brought the saddlebags and Tara's bridle inside the tent.

And he slept lightly. Every snapping twig or pop from the fire caused him to peek out from the tent, then curse his paranoia.

He woke when the dawn was still grey, foggy. Abram slept, his mouth agape, his hands placed under his head, warm, safe. Carter exited the tent and got dressed. Tara looked back at him. The two guests were still asleep, huddled by the fire pit, which had long grown cold. The extra firewood sat where they had left it.

Carter grabbed a couple leaves of tobacco, then tucked his pistol in his belt. He quietly took the men's shoes and hid them behind the tent. Then he walked into the woods to find a place to relieve himself. He squatted with his back to a tree and looked overhead. Looking up always made it easier. Something about the force of nature.

And just as he finished cleaning up, he heard Abram.

"No! No! Master Carter!"

Carter drew his pistol and ran back to camp. When he got there, Zuko was up on Tara and Pops was trying to untie the knotted lead rope that Carter had tied especially for them, wetted and shrunk with last night's urine, now hard as a fist.

If Carter had brought his bow, he might have placed an arrow in Zuko's right ear. But these two were going nowhere. Still, he drew a bead on the men.

"On the horse. Hands up." Zuko did as he was told. "Pops, get over here."

"No!"

"Pops! Get the hell over here!"

"You gonna shoot me?"

"Sure as hell!"

Pops was still fighting the knot, so Carter walked over to him. When Pops saw him, his legs came apart and the bourbon bottle fell from between his knees. Carter saw this and brought the butt down on Pops, and the man went down in a heap.

"Dad!" Zuko came down off the horse and knelt on the ground. "You sonofabitch!" he spat at Carter.

Carter put the pistol in his left hand and produced his hunting knife. If Zuko made a quick move, Carter preferred to use the blade. At the same time, he checked the immediate area to see if they had stolen anything else. Miraculously, they decided against the bridle, the rifle, and the saddlebags and took only the liquor.

Carter backed away a few paces, then called to Abram. "Get their shoes for them. Behind the tent." Abram did this and tossed them, startling Tara, who knocked Zuko down.

"Abram, break down the tent." Carter turned to the two visitors. "You two clowns can walk the hell outta here. You've been fed. Now get."

When the two got to the road, they had a small argument about which way to go. So Carter whistled to them. When they looked up, he pointed south, and they went there.

When it was time to ride, both Carter and Abram were up on Tara. "I'm thinkin' we need to put some distance between them and us." So they rode at a light canter for a mile or two, then walked.

All day, Carter puzzled over how Zuko and Pops could have betrayed them. *Not only were they fed and cared for, they could have enjoyed that for longer-term!*

In the end, Carter chalked it up to the fact that the men grew up on desperation and hunger, and suffered from a lack of love.

And he sent a wish into the ether that they would one day be filled, whole.

Days Worthwhile

Dear Carter Monroe (I love writing your name!),

We are so enjoying the sun room. It's as if the sun didn't know that the barn existed, but now it smiles upon our new herb gardens. It smiles when we sit down to read or visit.

Doris and Dusty are very grateful. Sometimes, I see them admiring where you joined two beams, how you hammered a peg, or how you created a window. Sometimes, the look in their eyes is of wonder — I honestly think that they are bewildered that you and Abram crossed our path, came to stay, and granted us so many gifts!

But we are also missing you very much!

Danny Roots stopped by this weekend. His eyes were wide when he saw the beautiful work you did. He wasn't sure whether to believe his eyes! He had nothing but good things to say about you. He got a new horse — Bon Bon.

I often think about the lovely day we spent rowing, enjoying the island, discovering each other. Funny, too... so much left to discover. So much unknown! And so many things — stories, feelings, and such — left unsaid.

Nights, I think about this place called New York. It scares me when I think that all of it — the whole thing — is bustling and busy, with no room to be alone.

And then there is peace.

So, when New York scares me, I remember that there must be portions of it that are tranquil, where one can hear one's thoughts, where one can focus on a dream.

But do you know the best part of my imagination?

I love when I picture you walking into New York and how everything will change! New York will stop to take notice! Because Carter Monroe is a man unlike any they have seen!

My friend… I have known men. I grew up alongside them. I have worked with them. I have loved them.

I am not perfect. You are not perfect. But our imperfections have taught us. I know this because I feel we are still learning, always learning, improving.

My little fire is about to go out, so I will bid thee good-night. I hope that you are warm and fed and happy tonight. And if I cross your mind now and then… well, it just makes a day worthwhile.

Thinking of you, especially at every half moon. Sweetness and love and safe travels to you, dear Carter.

Rosetta

With tenderness, she folded and kissed the letter, breathing in something beyond the pulp, giving off something that might be realized by the recipient. She paused without thinking, simply picturing him.

She finally parted with it, tucking it into its envelope. She copied the address onto the front.

The Methodist Church

Scotch Hill, Pennsylvania

Attention: Carter Monroe

Places, Everyone!

London, Campton, Sandy Hook, Kentucky
Clay, Locust Knob, Fisher Summit, WV
Point Marion, Painter Rock Hill, Scotch Hill, PA

i should like to live on every hill
to leave my soul, to build a stone structure and live here
and yet leave to wandering my feet

Strange, this road, this journey. Odd to move across the planet like a snail, predator and prey, wondrous and insignificant.

And yet, no matter the state, the hills that lined up to the horizon were like the faces of women—each so utterly unique, and no two facing the sun in quite the same way. *And how easy and right it would be to stop and live upon any one of them.*

But the mission moved them, the dream that they could stand somewhere as the same people but have things be different. They had ventured so far that they no longer talked about the distance behind or in front of them.

Still, Carter tried to impart to Abram one piece of hope every day. "When you get to New York, I need you to do something for me, Abram."

Abram spoke from atop the horse, "What, ain't you comin'?"

"Huh? Oh, yeah… I'm comin'!"

"Because you said 'when *you* get to New York' instead of 'we'."

"Okay. When *we* get to New York, there's something I need you to do."

Abram just stared, the horse moving him along.

"When you are on the street, I want you to get in the habit of looking men in the eye. Because then men will respect you. If you don't make eye contact, they will think they can treat you like a dog! But when you make eye contact, they have to…"

A shot rang out, and the ball of lead lead hit a tree trunk just to their right.

"GO LEFT!" Carter yelled, using Tara for cover. When they hit the woods, Carter hoped Abram would stop, wait for him, but he kept going. So Carter dropped, flat, then lifted his head just enough to survey through dead weeds that blew. *Shhhhh.*

He waited for movement, his heart like a team of horses and his mouth like cotton. *Nothing.* He could feel the wet ground soaking into his pant legs, his elbows, but he dared not shift his weight. He retraced what they had seen in the last hour.

Kentucky. Just let me leave in peace.

He wondered what Abram's instincts would have him do. He would likely not flank the shooter and attack. But, hopefully, he would have the rifle in his hands by now.

Not a sound. Not a move.

Five minutes passed. The situation had swung from lethal to ridiculous. He decided it was time for closure. He stood, then immediately dropped again to his belly. *God, nothin'.*

He watched for another minute, then stood, then ran the way Abram went. It was easy to track him—the grass was high and Tara carved a wide path. After fifty yards he slowed, in case the hunter was also tracking the man and horse. When he saw no movement, he continued on the run.

He ran for a quarter mile. He crossed a stream and found hoof prints on the opposite bank. The hill was steep, and Carter cursed the path they took but was impressed that Abram scaled such steepness.

He was also impressed that Abram had made a gradual arc back toward the road.

And, sure enough, he came to another spot where they crossed the stream, and now it looked like they would beat him back to the road.

Damn!

Now he worried. Abram on horseback, alone, on the road at high noon was not something Carter wished for. And he ran until he tasted blood in his throat. And he rested, hands on knees, until he caught his breath. And then he ran some more.

When he was nearly at the peak of a hill, his instincts told him to move with care, and he slowed. Listened. Stopped. He observed, especially to his right. When he saw nothing, he moved to the summit, where he practically ran right into Tara's flanks.

The horse stood, head down, nosing for grass, riderless. Carter's first thought was that Abram was thrown. Then he wondered if Abram was using Tara as a trap, and he dropped, flat again.

Abram might be drawing a bead on me right now!

So he waited. He listened, but could hear nothing above the sound of wind through the canopy of leaves. *Birch. Noisy.* After a minute, he called. "Abram."

Not a sound. "Abram, it's Carter! Comin' out."

He stood and immediately moved to Tara, took the rifle out of the holster, and positioned himself so he could see ninety degrees at a time. Then he studied Tara. The reins were over her head, touching the ground. *Good sign. Probably done voluntarily.*

He thought about where Abram would go. *Dismount from the left, and move away.* He returned to the horse and grabbed the pistol that was still tucked in its place. The bow and arrow were still there. *Why hadn't Abram grabbed a weapon?*

He left Tara to graze, moving off to the left. He alternated wide surveillance with close inspection—head down for footprints, head up for a body hiding behind trees. He stayed within sight of the horse, making an arc, calling in a near-whisper for his traveling companion.

He looked back down the hill, toward the stream, trying to think like Abram. It made no sense for him to go deeper in the woods. *But why would he leave Tara?*

The thought occurred to him that Abram could have been scared to be seen on horseback, but wanted to get back to the road. So, Carter took one more scan. When he saw nothing, he turned back to Tara.

He pivoted, then froze.

Two men were inspecting his horse, his pack, his saddlebags. Carter held his breath to calm the electrical storm in his chest. Coming to one knee now. Folding now, slow as a shadow. Inconspicuous as a mosaic. One with the forest.

He could see them sneering but could not hear their voices.

His left eye closed and his right looked down the barrel, the bead on the temple of the man who held the rifle.

A mosquito found his good ear and went in, its irritating sound now frantic and high-pitched. And Carter moved his jaw side to side to shake the insect, trying to maintain focus.

Now the man with the rifle used its barrel to move Tara's tail to the right, pretending to insert it there, calling to the other man with a "Pssst!"

And with one eye closed, and on one knee, ignoring the bug and its blood meal, Carter was decisive.

And when thunder filled the woods, even the birch leaves were silenced, and both bad men went down—one reflexively, one for good.

And Carter stood and pulled his pistol and trained it on the man whose knees buckled. And from thirty feet, the man's eyes were wide on Carter, and his face wore the blowback of his blood cousin, and he fumbled for a button, or a snap, or a holster. And Carter considered Tara's proximity and nothing else and fired low and the fumbling ended.

The man's eyes were wide, looking at Carter but past him, and breaths came in pants, his mouth forming an "O." Carter went to his knees and grabbed the man by his lapels and brought his face to his.

"Where is the black man?"

Only the eyes. Only that mouth, the panting.

Carter shook him. *"WHERE IS THE NEGRO?"*

But he heard none of this and his right eye flickered and then both went out.

And when the sounds of nature returned, Carter was still on his knees, heavy. He looked up and clicked his tongue to Tara, who had bolted at the last shot but waited, ears up, on high alert.

In a flash of brilliance or stupidity, Carter took the first man's rifle and laid it so it aimed at the second man's wound. Carter deduced that this was the gun that had been fired earlier; at least one bullet would be missed. *There. A mystery and a clue.*

Then he found the pistol that had caused the fumble, considered taking it, but placed it in its owner's hand.

Then he went to Tara, who now had a leg through her reins. Carter flexed the beast's knee and pulled the leg back through the leather. Then he mounted her and cantered for the road. As he approached the line between wood and road, he slowed, watching for Abram.

Then he stopped. His head scanned like a turret, full right, then full left. He tried to recall the color of Abram's shirt. *Brownish. Greenish. Dark.* He looked full right, again, hoping to see Abram reaching the edge of the wood.

He turned full left, seeing nothing. As he pondered, as his mind caught up with his body, he coughed, choking up something that tasted remotely like breakfast but more like poison. And he wretched, heaving onto his left pant leg, diaphragm spasming.

And when his eyes cleared, and after he spit, he moved into the road.

If Abram was ahead, Carter had to find him, fast. He spurred Tara and galloped for three quarters of a mile. He slowed to a walk, looked ahead as far as he could see, then yelled. "Abram!"

He turned around and cantered back to the spot and past it, just in case. Nothing. He turned around again, this time trotting, hoping to cover as much ground as possible, but not so fast that he would miss a clue.

But when he got back as far north as he had been, he stopped, and turned left, into the woods again. Nothing moved. The day carried on like nothing had happened, breezily nonchalant. And he felt like throwing up again.

The resilience of days. The vulnerability of men.

Carter dismounted, then walked Tara straight back into the woods, perpendicular to the road. He tied her within in a thicker stand of trees. He held the rifle and walked until he was mere feet from the road. He found a dry spot and sat. Hopefully, Abram would know to travel north, to continue the mission, but to do it safely, within the bosom of the trees.

The Nature of Men

every day
a thousand angles and refractions
a thousand beams from which to select the worthy

He waited and watched, and he cursed men. Men acted in a way that demanded action, a response. Men had their own natural laws, and inaction meant failure, death, atrophy, de-evolution.

Carter reached in his pack and found a short piece of jerked beef. *Three states, and still it sustains us. Us.* As he tore off a piece, he looked down the length of woods, waiting for a snap of twig, hoping for a flash Abram's face.

Damn. What if he's injured, back in the woods?

For now, he reasoned, this was the smartest place to put himself.

He chewed to keep his mind off those he had just hunted. Some would find it sad or sick that he was able to eat after what he did. But —as was his custom when taking an animal for food—he had not looked at the faces more than necessary. *Besides, those two did not deserve the customary blessing.*

Still, his mind went to their homes. They would not return for dinner. And people would worry. And then it would be dark. And in the morning, they would be found. And there would be more questions than answers. And people would... *There!* A flash of movement.

There. South and deeper in the woods. Carter waited, and it showed itself again. He fingered the rifle, but didn't pick it up. Tara noticed it, too, and she went on alert. Carter patted her neck. "It's okay, girl."

Tara whinnied and the man stopped and focused on the horse, some one hundred yards away. Then the two men locked on each other.

When Abram met up with them, Carter said, "Tara recognized you before I did. What the hell happened?"

"I was ridin' down the steepest hill, and Tara put her head down. I went right over. I was still holdin' onto the reins!"

"Well, ya did great—we both survived!"

"Who was it shot at us?"

"Don't know," Carter lied. "But let's ride outta here."

They both mounted up, Carter in back, holding the rifle. They did an easy canter for a mile or two, then slowed to a walk. And as soon as it was feasible, they pulled off the road and traveled parallel, through the woods and fields. *No sense gettin' spotted, if we can help it. Let's just be invisible for a while.*

When night fell, Carter stayed outside the tent, in the shadow nearest the fire, rifle at the ready. He couldn't sleep, haunted by the spirits of the two who had pursued him and failed. And in his mind, he ran through the events from every possible angle, always concluding the way it actually did.

They didn't have to do that to her. And from the rear, no less! Bastards. They put me in this position—not me!

Still, the weight was enormous. Every now and then, Tara would turn in the darkness, gaze at him, curious of his sleeping choice, concerned.

With Someone in Mind

the fairest of lands
and sweetest of wines
fail to ensnare the consecrated
for their eye is on the next world

When he first started the job, Carter slept in the barn. He had everything a man could want—a desk, a water pump and washbowl, a little bed. There was a large, kindling box to hold his clothes, his gear.

It was the perfect setup.

He could come and go as he pleased. To get to his room, he didn't have to walk through the house, didn't have to be cordial to anyone in the hall. And in the night, if the stars called to him, he could open the big door and walk naked beneath them.

The horses lived there as well. Carter loved the equine smells. *Like a beautiful, damp summer night.* Besides, he was good about mucking out the stall, breaking out a new bale of straw. And he enjoyed the night sounds that the horses made.

He reckoned that they enjoyed him, as well.

They greeted him when he walked in. He had a connection to the animal world. And maybe it was because he lived as close to that world as possible, eating when they ate, scratching parts they could not reach, thinking like they thought.

Over time, though, Sarah Jane suggested that he move inside.

Immediately, he realized how he would miss life out here. But Sarah Jane was beautiful. And it had really been a long, long time since he'd been with a woman. And he thought that maybe it was the healthy thing to do. So he agreed, on a trial basis.

He cried the first night they made love.

If he'd been asked the reason, he'd say she was a medicine woman. She'd found his pain and dragged it sideways through his tightest portal. In one night, she'd worn his soul down to zero, then built it anew. She put him through a session as strenuous as any he'd registered in the fields or farm.

And when he stood to find his clothes and return to the barn, his bare feet slapped the wood floor with sweet uncoordination, head bowed and shoulders slumped forward. He pulled the hair back from his eyes and held it as if drugged, bewildered.

"Why don't you stay?"

In the darkness, he looked at her upon the bed, her pedestal. He could see her outline but not her details, the details he'd just moments ago explored and loved exquisitely, the ones he'd lovingly ravaged. Even in darkness, she radiated—not light, not color; but a certain power that he'd never experienced before.

Again, the medicine woman.

"If I... I can't. I need to..." The feet kept slapping until he discovered his britches. And he picked up the pile of clothes and hugged them to his chest, standings sideways, half here and half departed.

There was barely a moon out there, just a half. It was bright enough to find and light his backside, leaving his face and chest in darkness.

It was the beam of moonlight that caused Sarah Jane to rise, to walk in a trance of her own. He felt her coming to him, one hand on his shoulder and the other tracing in the moonlight with her hand.

And then her nails. "You are... lovely."

He smiled aloud, pulling his clothes tighter against him, against his shudders. Such words he had never heard.

172

And she let her hand go over him, and over him again, admiring his smoothness like curved marble. And her fingers went between the curves, flirting, causing him to exhale and hold his breath at a distance, not daring to let it back in.

And he never should have stayed.

Because everything changed, then. Because he was weak. Because he wasn't thinking clearly. Because everything, everything just felt so good.

And he was tired. And it's likely that had he left he would have fallen on the stairs. But another part of his mind whispered that he *belonged* there.

Once you stay
you know you can never leave
unless you leave

And when he climbed back up onto the high bed, he was filled with a richness, a wholeness. She was more than he'd imagined, deeper.

As he drifted, he regarded her as a missing component from his childhood, running in slow, blurry motion through a meadow. Happy, and he was unable to take his eyes from her.

She wants me to stay. That… that means something.

She moved onto her back and he propped up on his elbow, adoring her with his hand. He stayed. And before he realized it, sleep had injected him and provided a soft landing. His face was pressed against her shoulder, and when she moved, he moved to stay there— needing his lips, his nose, his forehead against her bare skin.

And when he woke in the middle of the night, he tried to study her face. In it, he saw a masculinity, a competence, capability. But at the same time, he saw the most beautiful, most feminine of profiles— divine softness, not of this world, her inner world occupying a plane he did not completely fathom.

But in that moment, he understood the way that instinct worked, the way attraction operates, the ease with which a beautiful species procreates, the formula for joy.

And when morning descended, and when their door was opened, the help were in a state of obvious nonchalance, dusting clean railings, carrying objects of irrelevance, eager to confirm their suspicions.

"Good morning, Master Carter, sir."

"Ah, good morning, Nettie."

"And isn't it just a *fine* morning, sir!"

And at lunchtime, he told the field help that there would be no class today. "I just need to lie down for a while."

And when she came to find him, he was sprawled at a forty-five degree angle on his barn bunk.

And in that moment, she sensed that she would never quite have him, never quite reach and hold him. He was a barn animal. *Sure, he can be entrusted to come into the house for a visit; but he will never quite be comfortable inside.*

She inhaled and looked around, taking in the beams and webs, the dust and dirty shafts of light. She failed to see the attraction.

Fittings

blur the lines, people
the ones that divide you dimensionally
and rejoice in the new palette

"I am going to wear this," she declared.

Carter looked up from the bed.

"Would you like to place it on me?" She held it out to him.

He exhaled. "What... what does it mean?"

"It's just a symbol! Jesus!"

He was learning how quickly she could shift from tranquility to wrath. And she made him feel anxious.

"I *know* it's a symbol!" He calmed a bit. "Are we ready for that?"

She grabbed it back from him and walked to her bureau. "It was my mother's! And I just thought it would be nice!"

He refused to engage her. He sat on the corner of the mattress and watched her in the mirror. He closed his mouth so she would not hear him sigh, not know that he felt the four walls closing in on him.

"I thought you liked me! I thought you might..."

"I *do* like you," he interrupted. "But isn't that the ring you wore with Shane?"

Her reflection looked downward, silent. The floor squeaked when she shifted her weight. And then her voice sounded like a girl much younger. "Does that matter, now?"

He was confused. *Does she think we are marrying?*

"Do you think we are marrying?" he heard himself ask.

"Are we not engaged, already? Really?"

He stood and walked to her. Instead of holding her from behind, he stood against the wall, in front of her. "I am your straw boss, Sarah Jane. I get the crop up and out of the ground for you, picked, and then to market."

"But you can be more than that!"

When he didn't speak, she turned, nearly bending at the waist to deliver, "Don't you aspire to be *more* than that someday?" When he shrugged, she erupted, "You just wanna be somebody's nigger slave?"

He felt himself sucking in his cheeks, biting. Felt a fire in the center of his forehead, and he stormed out, down the hall, down the stairs. He wanted to slam the door to the outside, but Nettie was there to hold it for him.

Her eyes were concerned, so he just smiled as he passed her. "Nettie."

"Master Carter."

He went to the barn. And if Logan did not have Tara pulling a plow, he would have mounted the horse and ridden into the uplands, bareback. Tara knew where Carter preferred to ride—just high enough to see the valley, the next peak, north.

Sarah Jane knew it, too. And she would be here in a moment to intercept him. So he walked out into the rows of tobacco, close enough to hear the help.

They were laughing while they worked. He stood a couple rows away, where he could barely see them as they picked, as they filled their baskets. He heard Harrison, then deduced that he was imitating Carter.

"Now I want y'all to work on yer books today. Me? I'm going to be catchin' up on my sleep, y'all." He tried to stay in character, but he laughed, and they all joined in. "If I could just *find* that ol' Sandman!" And he did a jig-dance, shaking his shoulders, causing everyone to 'bout double over with delight.

Carter tucked his lips in to keep from laughing, himself. In a moment, he crossed the last couple of rows until he reached them. Harrison was caught by surprise.

"Master Carter!"

"Mr. Harrison." Then he added, "How's the pickin'?"

"Oh, Master Carter. It's gwine jes' fine!"

"Good. Good." And when he turned away, he mimicked Harrison's jig-dance, but subtly, just enough so that they recognized it.

He went on to check on Logan and Tara, turnin' a field over. "Going well?" he shouted.

"Oh, yes, sir."

"Looks good, Logan."

That night—any night that he smoked—he imagined the future, a better world.

And he imagined the farm, how this place would be run under his rule. Each hand would be called "sir." Everyone would eat and sleep in the house. Everyone would share in the work, share in the wealth, and everyone would eat from the same plate and service.

When there is inclusion, there are no more colors. We are one. And, for God's sake, let us blend! When races mix, there is even less division, distinction. New colors are to be celebrated!

He wanted that day to come—very badly, he did. But a part of him sensed, knew that it would not be in his lifetime. And he was ashamed.

He pulled on the pipe and held the smoke inside. He closed his eyes and felt the star beams raining down like fingers and nails on his scalp. Tickled. Soothed.

Sarah Jane had really set him off. And he had no intention of making up to her. But the stars massaged him and whispered but a single word. *Compassion.*

He imagined her as a little girl.

She was sobbing, silk ribbon still in her hair, tears down the dress that she'd put on just for him. All she needed was love. Not a pony. Not a necklace. Just love. And he could never break the heart of a little girl.

And now he was depressed. *Thank you, stars. Just the dose of guilt that I needed.*

He loaded up the pipe and lit it again. *No girls, this time! Something… something… imaginative!*

One day, we'll have our own, personal trains. And they'll require no tracks. And candles that never melt will light our nights.

He walked a city street, the darkness lit by the inventions of man. Hooves and carriage wheels clicked on bricks and cobblestones. And above that, a singer, a woman. Her song was carried, somehow, down the street and he moved closer to see how it was that her voice was projecting.

Even from this distance, she was a vision. Body of sweet cream. Hair of chocolate, spilling everywhere, but deliciously.

As he stepped closer, her dress and face became clearer. She sang in English, but in a dialect he could not place. "I long to sit and talk with you by the shore" sounded so rich and sweet and alluring. "I lawng to sit and tawk with you by the shoowa."

And he was lost, floating, blessedly mesmerized, adoring her.

And she sang into a tube, a fixture that connected like capillaries to several cone-shaped devices — "enunciators" was the word he mouthed. And they propelled her voice out into the night.

And she moved as if the song was in the very heart of her. And though it was the device and mechanism that brought him here, it was the singer who mesmerized him.

And between songs, she spoke to the crowd, and her voice was so loving that he placed his palm flat against his chest. And someone shouted out a request, and she pointed in his direction, handling him with grace.

"Why, yes. Thank you, Darling!"

And when the next song started, three men emerged from the shadows and accompanied her, dressed in matching coats and ties. They served at her pleasure and she was their queen.

He relit the herb, trying to get back to her, to hear just one more song, to see that face.

And when the last song was finished, a huckster sold wooden boxes that held her voice, that played her song—a music box that required no winding.

And Carter bought one and put it against his good ear and heard her as if she were still right in front of him. And in his mind he watched those lips, the way her hands moved, her beautiful bare arms.

And he wanted to open it, learn how it operated. But something told him to simply enjoy it like a normal person would.

And he turned his head, and he saw her walking down the stairs from the stage. She was wrapped in a shawl, now, and he knew that he could love her. And his lips moved with that very thought. "I would love you so good."

And the tallest of the backing vocalists took her hand. And before she vanished, she looked straight at Carter, as if she'd heard his declaration. And his heart froze. And both knew that that single look would forever hold them, enfold them.

The Concept of Liquid Fractions

your name is a curse
that becomes a song
when the right singer plays it

Abram put the stopper back in the canteen and licked his lips. Carter looked up from the map. "How much of that do we have left?"

Abram pulled the cap back out and closed one eye. "It's pert near full."

Carter returned to the map, measuring a day's travel with thumb and finger. "It's got to last us another day. Maybe two."

Abram weighed the options. "Okay. So, we drink half of it today and the other three quarters tomorrow."

Carter had all he could do to keep from bustin' out laughin'. He would eventually clarify what a quarter meant, but he couldn't do it with a straight face, not right now. He did want to write down this conversation—it was too precious to leave to the wind.

He stowed the map, but not before sifting through his little book of papers. When he came upon one in particular, he smiled, then looked at Abram.

"Hey."

Abram turned, but did not speak. He watched Carter walk over with the paper, heard the thing rustle in his hands, even noticed that one corner had been smudged and folded.

"When you came to Miss Sarah Jane's place, did they introduce you as Abram or as Buck?"

Abram's eyes went to the ground, as if he were hearing a word form another lifetime. He blinked. "Sometimes, to some people, I was Buck."

"It says here that you were born with the name Abram, the first born of father Anan and mother Akua."

Abram's eyes were still cast down, as if he were watching a play on a stage in the interior of his mind, as if he were concentrating, memorizing a part.

He repeated it, quieter. "Akua."

Carter sniffed deeply. "They called you Buck because it was easy to remember."

Carter insisted on giving each of the help their own choice—original name or new name. He was surprised that more than half actually wanted their new names. And nights, when he smoked and pondered, he wondered what he himself would have chosen. *To assimilate and start a new life? Or to stay connected to the one remnant of home, heritage.*

In the end, he decided that both were brave. Both were worthy. Neither was more right than the other. *We all have reasons too deep to articulate.*

"Do you remember your parents?"

Carter watched as Abram carefully organized his thoughts.

"I remember Mama."

He went deeper into his experience. "I am twelve. My last memory of my Mama is nails and wood. A can of paint. A bird and cross."

The moon rose and then seemed to just hang there and orbit no farther. Half lit, stuck, waiting for them to finish their conversation. But Carter changed the subject.

"I think we are halfway to New York, now."

"That is good. I feel it—the halfway mark."

Dreams and Realities

so much to be learned
traveling roads and chapters, passengers and compatriots
hunger and laughter appropriately bold
yet how subtly the insecurities unfold

Everything she owned fit in that bag—the one the family lent her, the "overnighter." A spare top that Miss Kathryn handed down. Two pairs of summer things, a pair of warm things. Five socks. Various coins in a snap purse. A brush for her hair and salt rag for her teeth.

She'd been standing there, bag in hand, for close to half an hour, but in her glory.

I get to go someplace! A journey far away!

And at the sound of horse hooves, Kathryn emerged from the Kinsman residence. Her feet hit the bottom step precisely as the horses came to a halt.

The footman took their bags and secured them to the top of the coach. Tahira watched as her overnighter was tied. She questioned the haste with which the footman made the knot, but she held it. Besides, it was time for good-byes.

And those were equally hasty. The family stood in the sun, smiling, and the servants were grouped to the right. She and Kathryn were helped up the two steps, sat opposite one another, and waved through the coach window.

The horses were wheeled. The hundred-eighty degree turn made the women dizzy, and they regained their bearings only when the turn was finished. So eager were the horses that Kathryn was pinned against her seat back. Tahira held the hand strap to keep from coming out of hers. And at the safest opportunity, Kathryn invited her to come sit with her so she didn't have to ride backward.

"That would make me positively nauseous!"

And when they were finally finished with the main roads of the city, Tahira realized that she had been smiling so intently that her cheeks hurt.

Out the window, the buildings thinned out and fields and trees and countryside filled their vista. But the road also thinned, and its state of disrepair was quickly evident. Every so often, a wheel would hit a pothole with a thunderous, bone-jarring result. At first, the women laughed at this. But then it become uncomfortable and they gathered their dresses into heaps beneath them for padding.

Kathryn untied her bonnet and shook out her hair. Tahira observed this and smiled—she had always marveled at Miss Kathryn's locks of gold.

"Go ahead," Kathryn motioned to Tahira. And the girl did the same with her bonnet. "No one will see us out here!"

They covered forty miles a day, west through Massachusetts, south into New York, and farther south into Pennsylvania. "I almost wish we could slow down to see the countryside in person!"

"Yes," Tahira agreed.

"It's a shame to whisk through it at such a pace!"

They bedded down each night in pre-designated cities and towns, inns that expected them ahead of time. And at each stop, the driver collected and surrendered letters, parcels, and various goods as personal and professional favors.

During one leg of the journey, a small piano was hoisted and lashed to the back of the coach. It may have been the women's imagination, but it seemed as though the front of the coach was elevated, unsafe. They were happy when it was offloaded at the next stop, a church in Troy, New York.

At another stop, two men came aboard, but they traveled up top. The coach operator understood and enforced the trust vested in him by the Kinsmans. And when the men stepped down to leave, the footman held his hand on the door.

"Won't be but a moment, please, ladies."

And the women leaned closer for a look at the men. The footman tried to reassure them further. "Quite a lovely night, isn't it?" The shorter man paid the coach operator, then led the taller man away in handcuffs. When they were on the boardwalk, the footman opened the door.

"Hotel Hanna, ladies!"

And they walked arm in arm, and the footmen brought their bags inside, and the women washed up for supper. And each night, the two enjoyed the waiter assigned exclusively to their table. And Kathryn would order wine with her meal. And both would have dessert. And Tahira marveled at the luxury of ordering from a menu, of getting up from the table and not having to carry dishes or clean up.

And they would return to their room and unbutton their outfits and laugh about the width of the maître d'hôtel or the waiter's faux pas. And, again, it felt glorious to be out in the world and allowed to be silly.

And they would play cards. And Kathryn would voice the need for a cigar and would threaten to go looking for one, and Tahira would find her—in Kathryn's own words—positively naughty. And in three weeks, not once did they finish a card game. A hand here, a hand there, but never to completion. Yet Kathryn had never laughed so hard, not at any of the county tournaments she had entered over the years.

And they would blow out the lamp, and one of them would giggle. And she would giggle so long that she could no longer explain the reason. And the other would join in. And just when they felt in control, Kathryn would pass wind, and Tahira would comment— marvel, really—at how Kathryn managed to accomplish even *that* in a pretty way.

Only night sighs remained—the cyclical surrender to sleep. Then the start of dreams, when the shape of all things changed.

Tahira woke to cries within the first hour, consumed with fear, filled with pity and compassion for her employer. For at this hour the tortures of the subconscious hunted Kathryn. Relentless. And for all her power and fortune, hiding was her only defense, cowardice her only strategy.

Kathryn was running, chased. And she would call out, softly at first, "No... don't take him. Just... *please!* God, let him stay with me. I promise... *I promise.*"

Then the whispering, the frantic negotiation with her captors, her private villains. And she would play all parts—the merciful and pitiless—every role in her concentric monologue.

"If we do..." she would say in a deep, manly voice, then trail off.

"Run. Run!"

"No, *you're* the fool!"

And then quiet. And then, on the nights when it was really bad, she would cry out, a voice that made Tahira's blood run cold. And Tahira would say "Shhhhh... Shhhhh! It's okay. Oooo-kay! I've got ya. I've got ya."

And even in partial subconsciousness, Kathryn would reply sheepishly. "Yes. Okay. Yes."

And Tahira would lie there, facing the dark ceiling, and think about the line that was drawn between reality and sleep. She would ponder how Kathryn could rule her waking hours with such confidence, only to suffer at the hands of nocturnal cruelty only she could know.

And at the end of the first week, when they were hours into their daily journey, Tahira asked her about the dreams. And Kathryn—for whatever reason—would skirt the question. "I think it was a mad dog. Or maybe a tiger. I'm pretty sure it was a tiger."

And she would divert Tahira's attention. "Oh, just look at that sky! Isn't that lovely! Boston just doesn't show the sun the way they do here."

And Tahira would look at the sky, but wonder about the place inside of us where all truths live. And she wondered if everyone, self included, was blind to that place. And even if they tried really hard, maybe the things that occupied that place were just too hard to decipher, reconcile.

This Shall Be My Home

a thousand beds this night shall move
a hundred more shall burn
'tis night that taught the lost to cry
and sea captains to yearn

The last leg of the journey was so long that when it came time to stand and exit the carriage, Tahira nearly went to her knees. When the footman opened the door, she followed Kathryn down the two steps, finally touching down in Pennsylvania.

It was an hour before sunset, and the low rays turned her perspective and new residence to gold.

Kathryn's sister, Claire, and son of seventeen came out to greet them. Kathryn introduced Tahira, and Claire gave her a hug. "So nice to finally meet you. I hope you like it, here, Tahira. And this is Chauncey—he's the man of the house, for now!"

Everyone made their way up the stone steps. "Oh, and the ride was positively endless!" Kathryn stated.

They all came inside. The family found seats in the living room and Tahira was introduced to Flo, the head of the house staff. The two spoke quietly, then disappeared to other parts of the house.

The divide between the Massachusetts women—which for three weeks had all but been erased—was abruptly apparent once again. It was the first time in nearly three weeks that Tahira had been more than a breath away from Kathryn, and she was stunned by the abruptness.

But Flo was nice enough. She sensed Tahira's plight, her fears, so she ceased with the formality. "Tell me, Tahira. How is Boston?"

"Oh, well, it's a nice place." She thought before speaking further. "A very busy city."

"But what about your people? Who did you leave behind?"

"Oh, cousins, mostly."

"Where might your mama and daddy be?"

"Oh, they are in the South."

Flo put an arm around Tahira and started to walk again. "I think you will find it nice, here. Scary at first, as all new places are. But we're all here to help one another."

They walked into the kitchen, and Flo introduced Ann and Penny. "Ann is our baker. She's responsible for the delicious smells around here! And Penny is the one who *procures*—she and Penny exchanged smiles when she said the word—the food from the farm and in town."

"You from all the way Boston town?" Ann asked.

Tahira stepped forward. "Uh, yes."

"That place huge!"

"Oh, so you know Boston?"

"My brother stay there. I go'd there for one summer. Shit, that place crazy!"

Penny chimed in. "They didn't know what to *make* of you, girl!" After the laughter ceased, Penny turned to Flo. "How long Miss Kathryn stayin'?"

Flo answered quietly, as if it were a secret. "Couple of months."

Ann turned back into the conversation, facing Tahira. "So what you gonna do around here?"

Flo cut in. "Tahira will be helping all of us out. She'll be under my wing for a time."

"She know how to bake?" Ann asked incredulously, as if Tahira weren't there.

"She'll be helping us *all* out." Ann and Penny were silenced. It was clear that Flo was in charge, here. And to take the edge off, she added, "That an apple pie in there?"

"It is." Ann replied, refocused and soothed. Then she smiled, "We got some cinnamon!"

Flo escorted Tahira to the dining room and explained where people sat, their habits and preferences. "Tonight, you can help me serve up supper. It's nice and calm on a Sunday night."

They wore white gloves. Flo dished the food onto the family's plates, Tahira cleared. And it felt very strange to be formal once again with Miss Kathryn. But she smiled to herself—the trip from Boston was an adventure that she would not soon forget. And the two of them shared stories, laughs, and the splendid slowness of time.

Later, Tahira washed dishes in the big sink. And when she finished, she and Flo talked. In just a few hours, Flo had come into Tahira's life and assumed the role of a close, loving aunt.

"Flo, why am I here? Did someone leave?"

Flo looked up from her handiwork, exhaling. "Well, between you and me..." she hesitated, forming her thoughts, "our kitchen help ran off with our stable hand."

"Oh."

"And Lord knows where they ended up."

"Okay."

Flo looked off, her brow furrowed. Then she looked back at Tahira and spoke low. "I guess when love comes, it don't ask questions, does it?" Then she added, "But it sure put this family in a bind."

Tahira learned that—after the stable hand left and there was no one to maintain the barn—Claire had no choice but to send the horses to her brother.

Tahira's mind went to the son, the seventeen-year old, and Flo seemed to read her. "Chauncey could do it, but he had a misfortune in his younger days and won't go near the horses."

The servants were quartered in the rear of the house, windowless, attached but separate. Tahira shared a bed with Flo. Ann and Penny shared a bed in the same room. A bed sheet hung from the ceiling to give the impression of two separate bedrooms.

"It's a nice bed," Tahira noticed as she climbed up.

"It ought to be—it used to belong to the Missus and her husband!"

Tahira asked carefully, "Where is the Master?"

"Oh, he's out on business. Gone for weeks." Then she changed the subject. "Laundry day tomorrow. Bed sheets. Gonna be busy, so sleep tight, girl."

"Night, Flo." Tahira whispered, "And thank you."

She thought about Kathryn. A part of her expected her traveling companion to come find her, ensure Tahira was good with everything. But that didn't happen.

And it felt strangely quiet, inland. Even after three weeks, she missed the sounds of the Charles River Basin. She missed looking out from her hilltop, across to the Boston Navy Yard. She tried to put herself there, but fell to sleep before her intended setting was realized.

She dreamed of the former bed owners. She dreamed of the former stable hand. She saw him and his lover running, hiding, laughing. At this, she might have laughed aloud, for she partially woke herself. But then she dreamed of Chauncey, the possibilities of his childhood misfortune.

She saw him open the barn door and a stack of pies come down around him, hot, crusty. As the dream ended, she breathed in and smelled cinnamon.

When she woke, she was alone. With no window, she could not tell the time of night or day. But a light crept in from the adjacent room. She lay there for several minutes, but heard not a sound. So, she slipped out from the big bed at peeked outside the door.

Flo sat by the lamp, doing her handiwork. Her head was tilted. She was focused on her work, but her mind was someplace else. She was in another time, puzzling over events that had already or would soon occur.

Tahira backed up quietly, then climbed back under the covers. Her own body heat had waited for her. And she fell back to sleep as if she had not gotten up, as if Flo and her handiwork were just a dream, as if she had only just rolled over.

$\int$outhern Connections

there is nothing in the world
quite like the verbal interplay
be it productive or disastrous
that occurs between sisters

When the knock on the door came, Penny thought it might be the meat man. But it was a man with a letter, and she took it, turned it over, then over again, then asked. "I supposed to pay you?"

"No, ma'am. The stamp, there, says it's already been paid for."

She thanked him and closed the door, fingering the stamp like it was magical. She brought it to Miss Claire. "Just came to the door, Miss."

Claire took it and thanked her. Kathryn put down her book. Claire studied the return address. "Well, I'll be. I believe it's from our cousin Doris in Tennessee."

She went to her writing desk and found the letter opener, then deftly slit the thing. She read aloud.

Dear Cousin Claire,

Best wishes from Tennessee! I hope that this finds you and your family well and joyful. Things here are just fine. I wanted to ask a favor and tell you a story at the same time. So, here goes:

A week ago, a friend of ours was stranded on the road. Two gentlemen —Carter Monroe and his man, Abram —helped our dear friend and brought him to our place.

Not only were they gracious to our friend, they also helped Dusty build a new sunroom addition on our barn. They stayed for about a week, and we enjoyed the two of them ever so much.

They are traveling to New York. I mentioned that I had kin in Pennsylvania, and they offered to provide similar help to you and your family in exchange for—at this point, Claire looked over the paper at her sister, then back—*in exchange for simple bedding and a meal.*

I can't promise that they will make their way through your fair city, but I asked them to stop and say hello if they were nearby.

She paused again, with sincerity, noting, "Well, isn't that just sweet."

Dusty, sister Rosetta, and the children all send their love. And I pray that all aspects of your life are bountiful. Take care, sweet cousin.

With affection,

Doris

The room was quiet for several moments. Claire brought the paper to her nose and sniffed it, as if doing so would render additional information.

Kathryn finally asked, "So how does that set with you—having two strange men staying?"

Claire looked out the window, but was looking past everything she saw. "Well, I suppose there *are* things that a man could help with." She held the letter up, again. "She doesn't really say if he is upstanding."

Kathryn contested her. "Well, he did rescue their friend who was stranded. And they slept there for over a week. So the two must be decent fellows, wouldn't you say?"

Claire ignored this, calling, "Flo? Flo!"

Flo appeared in the doorway. "Miss?"

"Flo, could you please bring Miss Kathryn a glass of... something. And I suppose I will have one as well, if it's not too much trouble."

"Yes, Miss."

When the drink arrived, Claire sipped hers, then held the glass against her cheek.

192

"You all right, Sister?"

Claire said, "Just... suddenly... is it warm?"

"I think it's fine." She mused to herself. *Why Claire Kinsman. If I didn't know better, I would say that you're nervous about having a handy man come to visit.* And then she just came out with the words.

Claire's eyes widened and went to Kathryn, but she kept the glass to her face and said nothing in retort.

She stood. "Let's make a list! Not a long list, because we would be disheartened if they failed to show. But a *prioritized* list so that they can get straight to work."

She continued, "And do you think we should draw up an arrangement? Number of days work and number of meals, that sort of thing? Or maybe this Mr. Monroe can start our Chauncey on a little apprenticeship. Would you mind writing while I..."

"Claire!"

Claire stopped, wide-eyed, as if surprised to discover that another person occupied the room.

"Dear Claire!" Kathryn relieved her of her list. "You are all a-flutter about nothin'! Let's just set on this for a while. We'll make our list—and it will be a fine little list—all in good time."

Kathryn was elated to discover that Wednesday Lunch with the ladies was still a practiced ritual, and she had Tahira take extra time putting up her hair. Claire called upstairs to her. "They're here, Sister! Sister?"

"Momentarily!"

When she came outside and saw Claire, Mrs. Klingbeil, and Mrs. Farnham, she was happy that she'd put in the extra effort. The three looked rather extravagant—ruffles and brooches, hats and perfume, and soft leather gloves to hold the reins. "Ladies!"

She climbed in, met the two neighbors, and off they trotted, up into town.

Over lunch, they shared the gossip that was newsworthy. They discussed their men. Kathryn volunteered just enough information to stay in the conversation, revealing surface facts without delving into actual fears and feelings.

"Oh, and," Claire slowly let on, "it appears we may soon have house guests."

"Really?" Mrs. Klingbeil inquired.

Claire sipped her tea, and slowly—to build the suspense. Then she reached for the sugar bowl and pretended to be deeply interested in its contents.

"Oh, do tell!" added Mrs. Farnham, growing impatient.

"Well, we had a letter this week from a cousin in Tennessee." She sipped again. "It appears that a couple of handy men—who aided them in building a sunroom—may be traveling north, through *our* fair city."

"Good heavens! Are they kin?"

When Claire hesitated, the two women looked to sister Kathryn, who leaned in and laid a glove on Mrs. Farnham's forearm. "Well, they're *someone's* kin!"

And at that, they laughed and sipped, imaginations running wild, pinkies extended. The waiter noticed the raising of four teacups and brought a fresh pot.

"Oh, please. Just half for me—it's far too warm today!"

Brothers in West Virginia

Kelly,

We are halfway through West Virginia. Just two more states until our destination is realized. Each state, though, tempts me to stay, to surrender my pack and burn my marching orders!

The citizens of West Virginia are the most hospitable I have experienced —it's quite like being in a separate, landlocked country. When I step into Pennsylvania, I shall be looking back over my shoulder. It will be hard to leave such landscapes, such promise.

You should come up to New York! Of course, I have yet to lay my eyes upon the place, but have had months to ponder and dream. And you are the closest thing to a brother I have ever had.

Think it over! We could sail together, join the merchants that sail Lake Ontario. Imagine docking in a Canadian port, then sweeping Canadian women off their feet!

I would be honored to post some funds for your travel. And we would enjoy the life we've always wanted.

The air is different here. Changeable, exciting! The flora is so different in the north. The grass is cool and thin. The sounds are different. The birds are small, much more expressive.

Think it over. And write to me at my ultimate destination—The Hotel Carlson, Rochester, New York.

Take good care. Say hello to all.
Carter Monroe

The Clock and Rocker

always there is time to foster
and always there is time

It wasn't often that Flo got to enjoy this chair, the rocker. But the ladies were out tonight. Only Chauncey and the servants were at home. She intentionally tried *not* to rock with the beat of the clock, but the pairing seemed to occur naturally, as if the chair needed to prove that it, too, was crafted for keeping time.

Most of the room lay in darkness, save for the fire reflected in Flo's eyes. The flames were too dim for her handiwork. *Too tired, anyway.* Long done crackling, it behaved like a good dog—low and quiet.

When the knock came on the front door, she pulled off her blanket. Her eyes went to the clock. *The ladies already?*

She opened the door and laid eyes on them, confused. She blinked and held the knob tightly, moving her body so that the lamp from the foyer went past her and lit them.

"Can I help you?"

Carter took off his hat. "Evening, ma'am. Kinsman residence?"

She cocked her head, studying them further. "It is. Who's askin'?"

"It's Carter Monroe, and Abram, from Mississippi way. Dusty and Doris had sent a letter..."

"Yes! Mr. Monroe and Mr. Abram. Yes!" She turned her head to the house and called, "Tahira!" Then she returned to them. "Do you have horses that need 'tending to?"

"Just one horse, ma'am."

"I'm afraid we, uh, lost our stable hand, but I can show you to the barn." She lifted the lamp and came outside. "I'm afraid Mrs. Kinsman is out in town with her sister. Should be back in an hour or two."

She led them to the barn, showed them the water pump. "You say you come all the way from Mississippi?"

Carter lifted the left stirrup and unhitched Tara's girth strap. "Oh, yes, ma'am."

"Pennsylvania your destination?" Her eyes drifted to Abram as she asked this, so he answered.

"New York, ma'am."

While Carter took the bit from Tara's mouth, Abram brought down the saddle and blanket. He hoisted them over the stall door, hung them there. Tara flexed her jaw, happy to be free of all these things.

The men turned when they heard water being pumped into a bucket, and Tahira didn't look up until it was nearly full. And though both men had adequate time to react, to help her carry the thing, they both locked on the girl and just blinked.

Finally, Abram offered to take it, but she carried it into the stall. Tara didn't give her a second glance—her nose went into the coolness.

Carter licked his own lips. He held his hand out to Flo. "I didn't catch your name, ma'am."

"Florence. Friends call me Flo. And this is Tahira." Flo led the way back to the front of the house. Carter carried the men's things.

She led them to the kitchen and had them sit. Both men moved slowly, legs too tired to support them, but bones refusing to bend and let them down. Flo set a cloth on the table and unwrapped it before them. Bread. Tahira started coffee, then disappeared into another room. The men tore into the bread, then realized it was dry and regretted biting off such large pieces. With Flo's back turned, Abram removed his piece, then bit it in half.

The room felt surreal. The change from outdoors to indoors still felt sudden, and sleep tugged at them, beckoning like eager whores. Not even the pan of food that Flo had going could hold them, and Carter nodded. Another minute and he could easily be on the floor.

But Flo emptied the pan onto two plates and brought them over. Potatoes and bacon, a corner of green beans, leftovers from supper. And the sight of it revived them. And when they finished, the coffee came, and it relit their internal furnaces, and they chatted with Flo through that cup and another.

"Miss Claire and Miss Kathryn should be home soon."

Carter swallowed. "Miss Kathryn?"

"Sister. Visitin' from Boston."

Carter said, "Boston, Massachusetts," for Abram's benefit.

But the men simply could not stay up any later. Flo commented that she was losing them, so with a lamp she sent them out the back kitchen door to the stable boy's quarters. And they washed up. And they went way out back to take care of things. And they blew out the lamp and shared a bed. And for a minute they smelled the dust of the place. But after a bit, the dust was no longer detected, in their minds turning into clouds, stars, galaxies.

Claire and Kathryn came home. They walked in laughing, tipsy, stooping to slap their knees. And as soon as Flo had a chance to butt in, she announced, "The men from Mississippi arrived this evening, ma'am."

The room went dead-quiet, as if the ladies were listening to see if the men were upstairs. Kathryn pointed to the ceiling. Flo corrected her. "Stable."

And with that knowledge, the two instantly sobered up. And their minds went from frivolity to sobriety, from silliness to lady-likeness. In a moment, they were heading up the stairs, closing their door. Flo heard the pitter-patter of their bare feet, then silly laughter, then bed springs.

She put another log on the fire and returned to the rocker, hers again. And in a while she found the rhythm. The fire caught the log, and she thought of the girl who ran away with the stable hand.

If she were mine, maybe I coulda kept her.

198

She'd been Flo's for eight years, came when she was just eight, never knew a washcloth or shoes until Flo saw to it. Never had a dry bed until Flo believed she could. Never knew why a woman's body did what it did until Flo explained it.

Maybe I taught her too much. Too well. She took it with her—everything I showed her, she took with her.

And as her lids grew heavy, she pulled her arms in tighter against her, imagining a daughter from that belly, pretending she had the power to see to this, too.

The ladies upstairs whispered. Sisters, sharing the same mind. Understanding without needing to speak, but speaking nonetheless. And they envisioned the men who came from so far away. And they wondered what drove them. And they wished they could be men and make such bold decisions, carry guns, eat on the trail.

The men slept without dreaming, worn out. And the coffee made Carter get up in the night. And before he made it back to bed, he met Abram in the darkness, and they startled each other, cursed, then laughed about it. They returned to sleep so soundly that neither remembered getting up.

Flo came to bed so late that when she crawled in, the concern in Tahira's voiced was touched with sweetness. "Here, Flo. Have the warm side."

Flo kissed her forehead. And Tahira whispered, "I love you." And Flo wasn't sure if the girl was awake or asleep, but she loved it. She needed it.

Everybody Falls

we bring skills
and we break things

The sun came up before anyone woke in the house or stirred in the barn. And when they did, all were anxious to discover what the host and the house guests were like.

Ann and Penny fixed breakfast, and it was the smell of food that called everyone together. Carter trimmed his beard, washed his hair in the barn and held the door for Abram.

It felt amazing to meet relatives of Doris and Rosetta. "Oh, I can definitely see the similarity!" And it felt nice to have men in the house, their presence larger than life. And everyone sat at the long table—hostess, guests, servants. Carter loved that it was this way. Only the women knew that it rarely occurred.

"How long before you men will be pushing on?"

"Well, our schedule is pretty flexible. We've made good time." Flo handed the plate of pancakes his way, and he added, "Do you have any projects or repairs that need doing?"

Claire set down her teacup. "Well, we do have a short list, if you're interested."

Carter looked to Abram, then to the family. "Well, let's take a look, see where we can help!"

He thought that Abram might be irritated. In Tennessee, he was anxious to get back on the road; but the man seemed energized and happy today.

After breakfast, Claire fetched the list—it appeared to be on multiple sheets. And she walked as she read aloud, leading them as if on some kind of tour.

"Front door doesn't close easily. See? Scrapes at the bottom of this side." She took just a couple of steps. "This porch beam scares me." She shook it. "Maybe it can be tightened up?"

She walked to the south side of the house. "In summer, this window gets so hot that it melts anything on the kitchen counter." Then to the rear of the house. "I wonder if we can have a little sitting area, here. Here or back on the side I just showed you."

She headed to the barn, but with the wave of her hand added one more detail. "And if the new sitting area could be shaded, that would be good," as if she were *accustomed* to moving men with simply a wave.

She continued. "When we have things to put up in the loft, we're pulling on ropes and…" she looked at the men, "it's just really hard to hold the rope while the person in the loft is untying the item."

She walked to the water pump. "We'd like a way to carry more than one bucket at a time. But," she added, "easily." It was fine that she felt Carter and Abram were stocked with magic solutions, as if they had a lock on the natural laws.

"Okay. Sounds good," Carter announced, rubbing his palms. And all eyes went to him. "And can we use the expertise of Master Chauncey?"

Chauncey blushed, took his hands out of his pockets, and shifted his feet. His mom spoke for him. "Oh, he would like that!"

Carter turned to him. "You look like you swing a mean hammer!"

They started on the front door, the easiest fix. The three men opened and closed the thing several times to see where the cause of the binding lay. Carter explained, "We may need to *plane* some wood off from this part of the door, where it's rubbing." He demonstrated with his hand what planing meant. "But I have an idea to try first."

He had Chauncey fetch a sheet of scrap paper and a driver. They traced the rough outline of the hinge and the screw locations.

"Okay, Chauncey, you've got the hard job. We'll hold the door. You unscrew the top hinge."

He hesitated, unsure which way to unscrew, so Carter called, "Left-loose. Right-tight." When the boy had the three screws removed, Carter folded the paper so that it was four sheets thick and in the shape of the hinge. He held this in the space previously occupied by the hinge.

Four sheets, he realized, might be too thick. So he removed one and absently handed it to Abram.

He used one of the screws to drill through the three marks on the paper. "Okay, Chauncey. Let's get those screws back into the hinge."

"And now we pray." They retested the door, which now had just enough width added to the top that the bottom no longer dragged. Carter exclaimed, "Now, look at that! Just like new!"

He had Chauncey tighten the screws in the bottom hinge, just to pull that half of the door in a little more. "Tell me... left-loose and..."

"Right-tight," Chauncey replied.

Abram announced, "One project down!"

Carter replied, "We won't tell the ladies how easy that one was!"

They moved to the south side of the house. "So, let's sum up the issue here. Abram?"

"Too much sun and heat."

"Right. *And...* she would like a sitting area in the back or right here. So, let's take a moment and picture some options."

Chauncey spoke up. "In town, some stores have awnings."

"That's exactly what I was thinking!" Carter scratched his beard. "But if we combine the next two projects, I wonder if we could do something... a little more... Mediterranean."

He continued walking around the area, visualizing. "Chauncey, do you want to bring two outdoor chairs from the back of the house?"

They arranged the chairs in a place conducive to lounging, but placed out of the way of horses coming down the drive, to the barn.

"Here's what I'm picturing. Tell me if I'm crazy."

Abram joked, "You're crazy," and pulled his lips inside his mouth, perfectly content with himself.

Carter placed Chauncey and Abram eight feet from the house, eight feet apart. Then he walked to the house. "We attach a board above the window, flat against the house.

"We send two boards out *from* the house, to support beams where you two are standing. Then, we send boards across those two boards... like dominoes. Maybe twelve of them."

He turned to face the men. "We can plant some wisteria and string it through the boards. And it will not only block direct sunlight from penetrating the window, it will diffuse the light below, so you get a nice, partial shade to sit in."

"Where are we gonna get boards around here?" Abram asked.

"Well, we'll need to scout around, check the barn. Chauncey, do you know of a lumber mill nearby?"

"Hmmm... Mom might."

"Know of any barns that are falling down?"

"Oh, yeah! A tree fell on one this winter. Cut it right in two." It was within walking distance, and Chauncey led them there.

"Hi, Nick," Chauncey shouted from the road. The young man looked up from his hoeing, waved. He fetched his father, and Carter explained their project.

"Yeah, we're not gonna rebuild. Will probably sell off the wood." They poked around, and Carter saw what they needed.

"What would you say is a fair price for those two beams and eighteen of these boards?"

Nick's dad took off his hat. "Oh, I dunno. Maybe five."

Carter was semi-committal. "Okay. Yeah, okay." He was thinking ahead. If I come back with ten dollars, could we use your wagon to get the wood down the road?"

"Oh, sure. Good, then."

Carter walked back to the house and saddled up Tara. Abram and Chauncey stayed behind, working loose their boards, stacking them. They tried wiggling loose the beams, but it was hard going.

Carter told them to dig around it. "Just on this half. Deep as you can." Then he hitched the wagon to the horse.

When they'd loosened the earth around the beam, Carter threw a rope around it, then tied the other end to the back of the wagon. He led Tara, who lifted a front hoof and pulled. The post didn't budge, and the horse brought her hoof back down. Carter gave a little clicking sound, and Tara tried again. This time, the thing gave way, and Carter gave the horse a "Yeeeaaaw!" to move the wagon out of the fall zone.

The beam shook the ground when it landed, mere feet from the end of the wagon. Carter exhaled deeply, looking around for Nick's dad, happy that he missed the close call.

"Okay, there's *one!*"

They did the same for the second, which came down easier, and with less thunder. The beams and boards were too long to fit on the wagon, and too heavy to safely hang off the end, so they loaded them diagonally.

They men walked while Tara pulled the load back home. They unloaded the lumber in the drive, and Carter ask Chauncey if they had a shovel.

"We do!"

"How 'bout a pick?"

"Hmmm... we don't have one of those. Nick's dad has one."

Carter fetched his wallet. "Do you want to take Tara and the wagon back? And give Nick's dad eleven dollars if we can borrow the pick for a day?"

Carter noticed Chauncey grab himself, his privates, and Carter asked, "What?"

The young man stammered. "Yeah, I don't... can't ride."

"Really. Did you fall?"

Chauncey sighed. "Well, I fell once, and pulled off a rider."

"Oh. He okay?"

"No. It was… bad. She was bad."

Carter understood the boy's plight. "Abram, wanna go with Chauncey?"

They got the horse and wagon wheeled around, and off they went. Carter laid out a couple boards on the ground for length, then went at the two holes for the upright beams. The shovel Chauncey fetched him was a sad excuse for a tool—rusted, loose. Somehow, it had been bent sideways and Carter wondered how they managed that feat.

When Abram and Chauncey got to Nick's, they unhitched the wagon and talked with Nick for a while. "Are you the new stable boy?" Nick asked the visitor.

"No. Just in town for a while." But his mind flirted with the idea.

"You going to Canada, then?"

"New York."

Abram rode Tara, and Chauncey walked. "You should get back on, someday."

Chauncey looked up at the man, the sun in his eyes, but he didn't speak.

"Everybody falls," Abram offered.

Abram didn't realize—and Chauncey didn't share—that the fallen girl still lay paralyzed some nine months later. Nor that Chauncey's dad was in Philadelphia for precisely that reason—to financially assist in her care at the best of hospitals. And that the guilt that the boy and family endured was great, deep.

When they got back home, Carter had taken off his shirt. He was leaning on the shovel. "Whew! I got down to the gravel layer! Glad you got the pick, men."

"Nick's dad wouldn't take the extra dollar. He said you could just use the pick."

Carter let Abram have a go at the thing. He swung it eight times or so, then Chauncey used the shovel to bring out the loose stuff. "We'll save the gravel. That'll actually help keep our upright in place," Carter explained.

Tahira brought out a wooden tray and three cups of cold drink. "Mmm… this is delicious!"

She smiled. "It's a mixture—part tea and part lemonade." She stood in the middle of the three men, waiting until they were finished. Carter explained how the pergola was going to look when it was done.

She smiled, cocking her head so she could envision the structure. Her smile was interesting—shy, but generous. She seemed delicate, but totally comfortable among them. "Are you gonna use nails, or some sort of pegging?"

Carter was pleasantly surprised by her inquiry. "Oh! Well, mostly pegging, because that is stronger than a nail. But we may drive a nail here and there."

She collected their cups and walked back into the house. The three men watched for a moment, each appreciating a different aspect of her.

"Chauncey, you ready to give it a go on the pickaxe?"

The young man worked on the other hole while Abram stood by with the shovel. Carter started laying out the best of the boards. "Some of these are pretty warped." So he stacked them, hoping it would get them all a little flatter, a little more consistent with one another. Then he went looking around in the barn.

When he came out, he was up on Tara. "You know, guys... Tahira made a good point. We're gonna need some pegging. I'm gonna have a look around in town." Tara pawed at the ground, eager to go someplace. "If you finish the two holes," he handed down a saw he found in the barn, "how 'bout sawing off those five longest boards so they're all the same length."

He rode off at a trot. "Back in an hour!"

He'd made a point of noticing the offerings of the town on the ride in. It had been dark, but some things don't need light to reveal themselves—piano music, clinking glasses, laughter. Church bells and sweet, milled pine.

And that's where he steered. He rode past the steam saw, the lumbermen and stacks of boards, the saw dust. And two doors down was a woodworker's shop.

He stopped there, and was happy to learn that the man knew the Kinsman family, had a drill to lend for a couple days, and had a penchant for southern whisky. The man was surprised to learn that a bottle made it all the way from Mississippi without popping its cork.

And when he learned that Carter was going next door for some pegs, he said "I've got some pegs you can have."

So, Carter rode out of town with what he needed, having spent not a nickel in coin or currency. When he got back to the Kinsman residence, Abram and Chauncey were seated on the uncut boards, recuperating, laughing. Carter smiled at how animated and alive Abram seemed. *I never saw that laugh—not in all these months! It's like he just grew teeth!*

"Did you finish *both* holes *already?"*

"We did!"

Carter dropped the sack of wooden pegs at their feet, then came down off Tara, drill and bit in hand. "Now *this* will put muscle in your arm, right Abram?"

Chauncey had never seen one, and he marveled at the design, the smooth, wood shoulder knob and blackened steel. And when Carter marked the board that would attach above the kitchen window, the young man got his chance.

"Drill bit to the wood. Shoulder against the knob. Good. Now slowly crank." And the board surrendered only what was demanded, a perfect circle, straight out the other side.

"Fun? Just seven more to go!"

Within the Folds

show me
but don't tell
your words are too intense

put it down on paper
that I may experience
your inside pictures

The men had been here for a couple days. And today, Tahira could not get the lunch dishes done fast enough! She excused herself and went to the only private place she knew. She latched the door, sat, then pulled the paper from her sock.

He'd handed it to her before he stood from the table.

And it's not like she didn't already know that he had feelings for her—she just didn't expect him to offer it in front of people!

So here she sat, trying not breathe too deeply in this place, but also very aware of the racing of her breath and heart.

It was folded thrice, then corner to corner.

I lik you. Come north wish me.
Abram

She read it twice more, never realizing that it was in the shape of a door hinge. She folded it, then placed it someplace more loving than her sock. And when she walked through the house, Flo made no bones about watching her. Her eyes panned while the girl moved. Tahira sensed this and looked up at her.

Flo was doing something with her tongue, mouth open, head tilted back, skeptical, judging.

As in a dream she walked, tentative, the love note all that hid her nakedness—its creases and folds, its revealing double-entendre, words that scarcely covered her.

And never could a doorway come soon enough, and she walked through it, and turned right for no reason, just to be angling, cornering, throwing guilt off her trail.

Death and Grooming Choices

there is a reason
man and beast speak in unique tongues
by design we must seek another path to understanding

After dinner, when the sun knew that its end was near and conjured colors it had reserved for a special time, Carter brushed Tara, focusing on her mane, forelock, and tail.

And he could hear the help washing the dishes, the laughter and the clanking plates, the kitchen window like a megaphone directed straight at the barn, the stall. He smiled at Tahira—he'd never heard her so animated, but he loved it.

And lately, each time he was close to completing this regimen, each time he stood behind Tara and re-earned her trust, combing her tail, respecting her most vulnerable side, his mind-pictures went to the men he killed.

And there was nauseating conflict. Compassion and logic. Plaintiffs and defendants. Split-second decisiveness and endless pondering

It was a predictable cycle. It rendered the same judgement each time. After several moments, his sense of guilt would crumble, broken down and washed away by waves of redemption, a nod to his protective nature.

I would have killed any man who did that to an animal. Any animal. Any man.

Even so, he thought about those who raised the men and those who loved them. These people would forever deal with the puzzle, going to their own graves without a solution.

As heavy as my heart and as true my compassion, I would do the same thing today, this very minute.

And when the tail was pristine, the epitome of fineness, he spanked her left flank and came 'round the side of her, and she half turned to watch him approach, her eyes sweet as a lover.

Man and beast breathed deep the new peace, the tranquility they had created just then—moments that bridged eons. Understanding that blurred species. They operated in wholly separate evolutionary tracks, but tracks that traveled in parallel.

They had reached a point—the apex of a relationship—where trust required no spoken confirmation. Trust was simply known and worn and shared, a blanket. And words—no matter how thoughtfully woven—had no place in this tapestry.

The Rustle of a Cotton Sleeve

righteous perspectives
the greater good and the lesser of two evils
so go the levels of freedom

It was one of the first moments they were alone. Finally.

"Do you realize that we are both bringing someone to a new world?" she asked.

He *had* thought about that. And he'd considered the differences. He was bringing a slave to freedom. She was bringing a servant from one house of employ to another.

"Is Tahira free?" he asked in return. He actually *heard* her breath stop, indignant.

"What?" Her reaction, he thought, only amplified her sense of privilege.

"Is she free? Can she leave here under her own free will and find a place to…"

"To *survive*?" she cut in. "A place to live, and be fed? To have some sense of *dignity* in this world?"

Carter was taken aback. She'd made a point. *Damn her.* He exhaled deeply. It had been a long time since he'd been in a battle of wits, and he hadn't missed sniping, the unmerciful stabs.

"You're right—it would probably take years, maybe generations of assistance."

"At least!" she assured him.

"So, what are you doing to steer her in that direction? Can she read and write?"

Kathryn half-stood. "Would you like me to fetch her and give you a demonstration? Is that… would that satisfy you?"

213

"I know she's a smart girl. And if you've had a hand in that, then thank you! Thank you on behalf of..." he didn't know how to finish. He was tired and waved his hand. "...all mankind."

He didn't intend for it to sound sarcastic. But that last sentence gave her the fuel to stand full upright.

"Ya know, *you* don't have a lock on all that is good and just and righteous, sir! You're no different than I am! You just happen to be a man! You're more mobile, more equipped—but so what!"

She paced a three-foot square, then continued. "I was simply making a point that we are *both* trying to do something good in this God-awful world." Now it was she who felt tired. Her voice was no longer in battle. "I... I was exploring the notion that you and I... had something in common."

She sighed, sat, both hands through her hair. "That's all." A weaker woman would have cried, here.

"I'm sorry," he said, near whispered. "I'm a self-righteous bastard. This is documented."

She'd brought her hands down and was staring off. "Do you want to walk outside?"

They walked down the driveway, gravel crunching underfoot. Past the two posts that would eventually hold the new pergola but now stood naked, pointless.

And the moon was low. And it was dropping. And it seemed to pull everything on earth with it. Shoulders, eyelids, breath. Even the spin of the world was hereby required to slow.

And when they got to the road, they turned left, away from town. And the crickets alternated their singing and their waiting. And when a response did not come, they sang again, eternally patient, hopeful.

"So simple," he said. He felt her look at him while she walked. "The crickets. Such a simple life, eh?"

She looked ahead in the darkness, but he could sense her smile. "I suppose. But you don't live that close to the ground. You don't *know* what they endure." She laughed a little, pondered. "They might have incredibly complex relationships!"

Now he liked her. Now he appreciated her mind, where it went, what it considered. "Look, I'm sorry that I offended you back there. I... I just feel sensitive to the plight of the Negro."

He heard her reaching—the rustling of a cotton sleeve—and her hand was on his shoulder. She surprised him further, her grip.

And he stopped walking. But the hand stayed there. And he was so fatigued that his head practically fell. And the moon was not helping, nor this hand. This woman's hand.

It would be so easy to turn into her. And she waited, surprised at his resolve. Her thumb said so—it was massaging his deltoid and someplace much, much deeper, making sure he felt her, *heard* her.

And he turned into her.

And she brought her other hand up, both now admiring his width, completing a circuit, an electric lockset. And he could have done a hundred things. But when he moved, he simply wrapped her in his arms and brought her close.

But his mouth passed hers and his chin went to her shoulder, a simple hug. And whispered. "This world is so hard. And only a handful get to feel anything like this, tonight." And he rubbed her back. And he loved the femininity and strength. "Thank you."

"You're thanking me?" she whispered

He sighed. "Just... for making me feel human. Again."

She could smell the work he had done today—the digging and the riding, the drilling and hammering. On other men, she'd found it offensive. But this... this smelled manly, and in a beautiful way.

And what was it about his comment, about the ability for one to make another feel human? *Maybe it's the simplicity. He has an advantage over other men because he and I have no expectations. This is all he needs to bring, and be. And then he will walk away.* She smiled, and he heard it on her lips.

"What's that?"

She explained, still holding onto him. "We make each other feel human again because this is all we bring. Simple."

"Like the crickets, after all."

"Like the crickets," she echoed.

He pulled away and smiled. "A few minutes ago, we were locking horns!"

"Silly," she admitted.

"Know what's nice?"

She looked up at him.

"When people are at the brink of war, so close to their deepest emotions and beliefs, it's a huge relief when they realize they are fighting for the same... the same damn thing."

"Yeah." She was quiet. "Nice."

"It's horrible when people *start* with love, then move to war." Almost whispering, "I've had that."

"I have had that, as well. And you're right—this is better."

She would have loved a kiss, and he felt himself going that way. But instead, they rocked each other once more and that was enough. Enough to sleep on, dream on.

And she would thank him hours later, telepathically. *He could have easily taken me, had me. Of course, I'm disappointed! But I appreciate that he considers someone other than himself. He thinks ahead. By not taking, he has given.*

And, of course, when Claire woke and discovered she had returned, she wanted to know every little detail. And when Kathryn stared at the ceiling, searching for the words to describe what happened, Claire thought she was holding out on her!

"Come *on!*"

"No, it's hard to explain." She adjusted her pillow and rubbed her forehead. "He's every bit as deep as he is strong. He's as thoughtful as he is capable."

Claire moved in closer, head actually placed on Kathryn's arm. "Yeah?" And when seconds passed, she repeated it. "Yeah?"

"So, we had an hour. Picture it—with any other man... in the darkness? In the moonlight? Wouldn't you think he would just take whatever he possibly could?"

"Oh, yes!" Claire thought the story was heading in that very direction, and she pulled the extra pillow between her thighs.

Kathryn sighed. "Well, he gave me so much more. And... we didn't even kiss!"

"You *what*, now?"

"No, we talked about... I dunno, some deep stuff. We kinda fought, actually. And then we walked. And we talked about... crickets."

"Crickets. *Crickets!*"

"We listened." Kathryn was in a trance, now, as if recalling a dream. "We listened to the world. And it felt like we were above it, looking down. And I'm pretty sure I made the first move—I grabbed his shoulder."

"Oh!"

"Yeah. Strong! And he held me, just rocked me. Just rubbed my back. So... simple."

Claire rubbed her sister's arm, the one she was using as a pillow. "I bet he's awake right now. I bet he's thinking about you."

Kathryn sniffed. Her smile felt warm. "I don't know."

They fell back to sleep, just like that, sister on sister. Both dreaming of the same man. Kathryn remained in her trance. New memories. Ancient desires. Thigh pillows.

$he Said Yes

her portrait
mostly naked but wistfully draped
is twice as alluring revealing half the prize

When the men got back from town, Chauncey tore through the house. He found his mom and Kathryn upstairs. They were attending to a ledger of sorts. Without looking up, Claire asked, "How did it go, Hon?"

He was completely out of breath. "Oh, good."

"Got what you needed to finish the projects?"

He gulped. "Yup."

Aunt Kathryn detected his brevity and looked up at him. "Everything okay, Doll?"

He stepped closer. "Carter and Abram... they got into a huge argument."

"About?"

"About... being a slave. Freedom. About freedom."

Kathryn felt the stab of their conversation a couple nights ago. *Easily buried, easily exhumed.*

"Abram is going to ask if he can stay on. As a stable man."

Claire set down her work and took off her spectacles. "Really, now. And Carter, of course, wants him to continue north with him." She looked off. "Yes. Sure."

Chauncey was whispering now. "Carter was mad. Asked Abram if he wanted to be a slave forever—he and his children."

"Oh, dear. Well..."

"That's when Abram threw down the supplies—right there in the street! He picked 'em up, but then he stormed off. We caught up to him on Tara. And he was still seething. He said, 'I'm already *your* slave!' to Carter."

"Shhh…" Claire reminded him.

Kathryn tried to soothe everyone. "Well, sorry you had to see that, Chauncey."

The lad returned to the yard. Abram was nowhere to be seen. So Chauncey had the honor of driving wooden pegs into the pergola project. They ran the two *stringers*, long, thick boards from above the kitchen window out to their corresponding, upright beams. Carter held the work while Chauncey drove pegs into each.

"That was the hard part, son!" He messed up Chauncey's hair, congratulating him. "We have our rectangle—now we add boards from one stringer to the other, lined up like dominoes."

These overhead boards were thinner, and the pegs went in easily. "Still fun! Satisfyin'." And when they had half of them up and attached, the women came to the kitchen window and admired the new shade.

"What do you think?" Carter called. His smile gave away no hint of his battle with Abram.

"Very nice!" Claire expressed. Both women were beaming. And by suppertime, the two men had the project completed.

"All except for some kind of climbing plant. You can help your mom with that, right?"

"Sure."

"You did a great job, here, Mr. Kinsman. You've got a great work ethic."

"Thanks!"

"You…" Carter wagged his finger at him, "you're gonna go far in this life."

Carter washed up at the water pump, drenching his entire head, drying off with a towel. He went into the barn to find Abram, who was lying down.

"You comin' for supper?"

"Yeah."

"Hey." Abram still hadn't made eye contact. "Hey!" Now he looked. "You do whatever you need to do. You're a man. I... if you don't want to go on to New York, that's entirely your call."

At the table, stress was evident. Abram was still, eyes not meeting anyone else's. He was still smarting from this afternoon. But Carter was in high spirits. "This has to be the best dinner I have *ever* tasted! Thank you! Delicious!"

Claire gave credit to Ann and Penny. Carter was *this close* to suggesting they open a restaurant, but did not want to offend Kathryn. But he was nothing if not talkative.

"Got some news for you folks." He cleared his throat. "Abram, here, is considering stayin' on to work for y'all, if you need the help."

"Oh! Well!" Claire played like she was surprised by the news. She wiped her mouth with her napkin, surprised that Carter brought it up at the family table. Kathryn, too, and her smile said that she liked it that way.

Carter continued, "I tell ya—I've been blessed to have traveled with him this far, and to have worked with him, lived with him."

"Well," Claire started, "when Peter returns, he'll have the horses and carriage. So we *could* use an extra hand. That is, if you would like it, Abram."

"Oh, yes, ma'am."

They had coffee and apple cobbler for dessert. And Carter felt full, excited, sad, content. He leaned back in his chair and stared at the edge of the table, the mitre, the care that someone took in crafting it.

When he returned from his daydream, he looked up and saw Kathryn's smile. He smiled, looking back down, nodding. He never, ever expected Abram to make this particular choice.

Kathryn read this. "This is quite a surprise."

Carter smiled, acknowledging her, admiring her insight. She'd been right. But rather than flaunt it, she winked at him, put him at ease.

"Half moon, tonight," he said. "Want to go see?"

She said yes.

And they walked under the pergola, where Kathryn whirled 'round one of the uprights a couple times. Then they headed out to the road. And there it was, this thing suspended in the heavens, almost perfectly halved by darkness, tugging at them once again, pulling even the song from the crickets.

"You gonna be okay, goin' on ahead? All alone?"

Carter gave a little laugh, then exhaled. "Ya know, I wanted to take Abram to a new world. And I guess in a way I've done that, right?"

"What about you? Does New York still call to you?"

"Crazy, but I once saw a painting—a ship on one of the Great Lakes. I wanted to feel that, to feel what it's like to ride the waves. A sailor. Maybe it was the style that the artist used, but I was pulled to it like a magnet."

"And who would Carter Monroe be if not magnetized?"

He totally surprised her when he reached for her hand. And it felt good, just walking in the moonlight, just holding hands.

And their fingers played, never settling down.

They walked in silence for a while, just enjoying everything out there and everything inside, their connectivity—to the world and each other.

"When will you return to Boston?"

"Oh, before the snow." She kicked at the earth a little. He let the silence ask the question. "Not real excited," she replied. "But there's a house there, a family." She looked off and spoke in a near whisper, "Of sorts."

He gripped her hand tighter. "It'll be good."

"Yeah."

If not for Rosetta, he would have kissed her. Married or not, she was the most naturally cultured, born-beautiful woman he'd ever seen. He wanted to be the one to hold *her* by the shoulders tonight.

And he'd observed them, those shoulders. And he knew just how his hands would fit around them. And he was torn. The last couple days had been a lesson to him—to be focused, driven, but not inflexible. To be a machine, but with human heart. And for these, she was the reason.

So he turned and faced her. And took her other hand. And felt his boot touch the toe of her shoe.

"I could so easily fall into you, Kathryn. I... just love how smart, and easy-going, and beautiful you are."

"Oh. Thank you."

"You are married. And I have someone waiting for me. And, in the last couple days, I've pretended that you weren't and that I didn't!"

She laughed a little, a little nervously. "I know."

He pulled her hands out to her sides, straight out from her shoulders, and they compared wingspans, then smiles. And he couldn't help but slowly let go of those hands and move his to the sides of her face.

And in the darkness he could still see that face. And he let his hands move back, into her hair, and it felt surprisingly coarse, as if from a meadow. *Appropriate.*

And he stepped closer, and brought her in, and his hands found her back, and worked it. And she was the easiest thing he'd worked all day. And his were the strongest hands she'd ever had on her. And that simple fact brought a tear that she blinked away—the realization that she'd never have this.

"I wish you could stay."

Claire waited up for her, probed gently, then held her sister as she wept for love that was walking away, unfinished.

And Carter lay in his bunk, next to Abram, who snored tonight. *That's a first.* And he faced away from his bedmate, and bit hard into his finger, as if that would stop the ache in his throat.

And he saw himself walking into the house, finding the staircase, deducing the correct room, knocking. And he'd find her mouth and everything about this fantasy made perfect sense tonight.

And then there's tomorrow.

And in his mind he played a game of chess with his alter ego.

She doesn't love her man. That's clear!

- She's not the only one who has someone.

You don't know if Rosetta will ever come!

- Don't I have to believe in something? Do something honorable?

What about the coming war?

- War? What about it?

Thousands will die. More will hunger to bring death.

- Yeah?

All that hate, all that killing. The world will feel it. Nature will bleed. Something bad is coming. You should do your part to bring love. You should make someone feel beautiful.

- Really, now!

You know it would make her happy.

- It would be... incomplete!

She knows that! And still she wants it. It means something!

- If... how... I would scare the devil out of the poor thing!

Well, you're just full of excuses, aren't you?

He fell asleep before he could think of a response. And when he woke around three, he touched his chest and felt magic there. He felt blessed. He felt reasonable, and practical, and in control.

In the darkness, he rolled off the bed, walked barefoot to the barn door, and pulled it aside. Low, low, at the end of the drive, the moon lay. Low enough to be cradled by the trees.

Cradled. He whispered the word aloud and climbed back into bed. And when he woke the room was grey. And he shuddered—the cold and the sudden primal desire to mate.

"Did you go somewhere last night?" Abram would later ask.
"Huh? Oh. Tummy," he lied.

Words on Paper

poetic
to see my grande design for emancipation
unraveled by the slave i sought to free

After breakfast, Carter set Abram and Chauncey to a task, then saddled up Tara. "I'll be back around lunch, men. And remember: precise chiseling will save work at assembly time."

As he rode down the drive, the tap-tapping of their chisels started, and he strained to hear for as long as he could. Only certain, assertive taps made it to his good ear, and when he turned his head askew, more found him.

He sighed. His flaw, his defect. He opened wide his jaw, then moved it side to side, hoping to open the broken pathway.

And he wondered what it looked like in there. *Is it clogged, stopped up? Is it broken? Damn!*

And he rehearsed his Yankee accent aloud as he rode. "Gud morning. More-ning. Ing, ing, ing. Gud morning. I need a document. Thaynk yu. Yu. Yu. Thaynk yu. Ay-brum. Ay-brum Wood. Wood. Woodchuck. Wood-pecker." He smiled and Tara cleared her nostrils at his ridiculousness.

If I sound like Johnny Reb, he's gonna peg me for a spy.

By the time he got to town, the sky was a bright grey, the air charged with electricity. It caused God's creatures to move with haste. And off to the west, a stand of Quaking Aspen turned up their leaves, the white undersides surrendering to the promise of rain. But the rain played fickle and would commit only impulsively.

Outside the printer's shop, he tied Tara and stepped up on the boardwalk. The man's front door had a little window shaped like a diamond, but the glass was loose and it rattled when Carter opened and closed the door.

Strauss was bent over his task, and he looked up from his press and plates and fonts. His eyes met Carter's, but he offered no smile. He waited, locked on the face as if doing so would eventually register the stranger's identity.

"Morning," Carter began. "I understand you might be able to assist me with a document."

Strauss stood and peered over his glasses. His hair was wet and parted at the crown, his mustache black as the ink of his trade. His front was protected by an apron, his left hand by a glove.

He spoke in a monotone. "What sort of document?" He spoke so low that Carter was forced to read his lips.

"Freeman's papers," Carter replied, just as low.

Strauss cleared his throat and shot a look at the front window. His eyes signaled that something in the room had suddenly changed. He moved so that his face was no more than a breath from Carter's.

"Do you have thirty dollars?"

Carter puffed his cheeks and looked at the gloved left hand. "I have twenty-six." He looked up at Strauss. "And some tobacco from Mississippi."

Strauss's eyes never left Carter, but his good hand moved under the counter and felt around. Carter froze, good ear cocked slightly, dismayed that his next moment may depend only on his hearing.

Strauss came up with a pencil. *Without looking. Not bad.* But he was less impressive when fetching a piece of paper. "You'd think I'd have paper and ink coming out my ears."

When he was situated, he ran through questions and answers. "Slave's name?"

"Ay-brum Wood." When Carter began spelling, Strauss raised his gloved hand to stop him.

"Age?"

Carter looked down, calculating. "Twenty-four."

"Color?"

"Brown."

"Height?"

"Five and nine."

"Any scars? Markings?"

Carter drew in the air, the backs of four fingers making a graceful sweep, like a dancer.

"Whipping?"

"Yuh."

"On his back."

"Yuh."

"Are you going to the sea?"

Carter cocked that ear again. "I'm sorry?"

"Where will the man reside? At a seaport, per chance?"

"Uh, no. He'll reside here." Strauss looked up at him, so Carter clarified. "Pennsylvania."

Strauss walked to the other side of his press, looking for a certain something. He spoke while he did this. "I have..." he opened and closed a drawer. "...a nice stamp for sailors. 'Seaman's Protection.' But if you're not going to a port town..." he found what he sought. "...that won't help you, now."

Carter took the opportunity to look around a bit more. Slots and cubbies, Wanted posters and horse sales, and a clock—a Regulator, similar to the one in Claire's home— the likes of which Carter had never seen before he set foot in Pennsylvania.

"Here we are."

Strauss showed him an example of a Great American Eagle. "Here's the ticket. This will impress anyone." He set down the paper. "Now, if you can pay me this morning, I can have this ready for you by, oh, tomorrow morning."

"That would be fine."

"Would that work for you?"

Carter repeated the answer already given. "That would be just fine, sir."

He left the printer shop and Tara came to attention; but Carter walked down the boardwalk, slowly, hands in his pockets, just feeling the morning. He came to a bench and sat to watch the activity, the scurrying. Tara pretended to ignore him, back to her dream of green pastures, oats.

He thought about the pace he'd traveled, the driven compulsion which nothing could interrupt. He never expected to stop in Pennsylvania, never intended to build a pergola, a sunroom. *Funny, the times I stopped were the best of times.*

And now he would travel on, solo. His mission had changed, in a sense, but he was still determined to reach his own personal utopia.

When he returned to the house, Chauncey and Abram were dismayed to learn that he had brought back nothing from town.

"Were you expecting sweets?"

"You were gone long enough!" Chauncey chided.

Carter just smiled and continued into the barn. He unbridled and unsaddled Tara, who took a long pull from her water bucket. And he watched, stared, listened. Soon, he would leave, alone. And he would miss the next occurrences at this house and ride into the unknown.

He stood there a long time, leaning on the stall door, pondering the simple decisions, the ones that changed everything in a life and rippled outward, impacting everyone within range of the waves.

Walking Away

we are surrounded by our isolation
in the company of solitude

Pulling out of Scotch Hill was brutal. This family had appeared to him when he was dog-tired, beaten down, and today he was leaving. He stayed in the barn as long as he possibly could, steadying himself.

They congregated under the pergola—the one that magically appeared while he was here. Claire had expected only an awning, but that would never do. She got a place to sit, a place to string trumpet vines, an extension of inside out, outside in.

He hugged each of them—Claire and Chauncey. Flo, Ann, Tahira, and Penny. Abram. Carter whispered during his embrace, "Now you shall write your own story."

And Kathryn.

She donned her mask, disguising the sadness—lips pulled tight, eyes squinted that both might remain under her control. But Carter threw his arms around her, somehow finding his way up and under that mask. And the sweet kiss on her neck was one of sorrow and gratitude that could be expressed no other way.

And everyone laughed when Tara pawed the ground, impatient for her master. And Kathryn wasn't the only one who laughed through tears.

He pulled himself up into the saddle, and somehow it felt good to be here, again. And Claire handed up a sack of food. "For your lunch."

And the horse hooves made the most satisfying sound on the gravel drive. And Carter looked back, and waved, and with his mind took a final ambrotype. Then he looked up the road and called Tara to a trot.

And they watched him through the trees as he rode, frames of man and horse flickering, face becoming puzzle pieces, less and less apparent until he was but a blur, then shadow, then memory.

The help went inside to start the morning cleaning. Abram and Chauncey went to the barn. And Kathryn fell against her sister and wept. So fond of his face had they grown, too the laughter and the muscle. So easy and powerful was his presence that it was nearly unfathomable that he would leave.

"Want to walk some?"

Kathryn shook her head and dabbed her handkerchief. And Claire kept her arm around her while they walked down the drive. And they turned the corner onto the road, and followed his path, just because.

And before they got to town, Kathryn suggested they turn around. "If he's getting supplies, I couldn't bear seeing him again."

And they walked back home, but at a slower pace, arm-in-arm.

And when they came inside, they just sat, eyes downward, having lost the energy to raise them. And his departure made their own lives dismal, rudderless, hopeless.

And Carter, having traveled just two miles from their home, found himself missing the beauty that a houseful of women imparted. They had treated him so! Simple conversation, mutual respect, admiration.

He was envious of the former slave he left behind, for Abram would continue to experience all the things that Carter was now missing. And every mile underfoot made that more apparent.

Traveling Thoughts

ironic, this journey's purpose: to escape people, to evade
yet in the sweetest chapters i stood surrounded
captivated by characters beyond imagination

The air of Pennsylvania and, finally, New York was like a song. It entered his lungs and spread like a chorus, the notes able to quench thirsty veins and arteries, imparting a familiar, mellow buzz in his temples.

So much greenery. Such longing, lush hills. *I could stop anywhere, here, and be perfectly content.* And maybe it was fear talking—the fear of pushing all the way through to his destination, of *becoming* a sailor, of failing or even succeeding.

He was beyond weary. He became his weariness.

And for no reason, he would crest a hill and tears would come. And he would stop and dismount, admire a valley of white pine, the wind teasing its softest needles and then running up the opposite hill.

And he leaned into Tara and felt the warmth of her neck. And his eyes pooled, and he tried not to blink. And they spilled over. And he wasn't sure if it was for the old stories, buried deep but alive again, or for stories born just weeks ago.

He was never so close to his inner voice as in these days... days when he spoke not a word, save to his horse.

And nights, when he had no one to protect, he felt unprotected. He slept lightly, and woke confused in the darkness, forgetting his orientation, his direction. And he lay back down on his bare arm and nuzzled it, kissing his biceps and whispering. *Rosetta. Kathryn.*

Mornings were too quiet, just a fire to keep him company, to treat himself to warm food. And hot tea for as long as it lasted. At lunch he would rest Tara in the shade of an apple orchard and they would feast. Then night again, nights lined up like train cars. The silhouettes of silent strangers taking him like so much scenery, revealing nothing in return.

And he would lie close to the fire and say it out loud: *Ontario. Lake Ontario.* And he imagined it as a small ocean. And he wished Tara would lie beside him, like a dog would. And he would untether her, but she knew not how to give him what he required, and she was confused to be free of the rope.

On a day that he estimated as a Tuesday, he rode through Italy, New York. It was not on his map, but he was now convinced that the best finds are those not yet documented.

And he went down the middle of the most exquisite valley and felt it cradle him, fill his spirit. And he stopped for a burial, a hillside of mourners. He tied Tara to the fence and took off his hat and joined them. And when an eye met his, he gave the slightest nod, lips tight, pained.

And when they lowered Elizzie, her sister wailed. And her husband put his fist to his mouth, the horror of finding her dead still etched. When Carter saw this, his hand went to his face, shielding his own. And he mourned with them, mourned the girl he did not know but loved, having been here.

And he wondered what she was seeing, if she accepted his presence, trusted his sincerity.

And he helped to bury her—this resting soul, a woman he never met. And he leaned on the shovel when the survivors came to thank him. He respected their sacred pain but selfishly hungered for their eyes on him, any eyes, any form of human connection.

He stayed until everyone had left, sat watching the shadows on the opposite bank of the valley. *No matter where I go, this pain, these stories.*

He was conscious of his breathing and inhaled the air that Elizzie once expelled, the air of Plato, the air of Jesus.

He called it a day long before sundown, and rested for the night in Italy Valley. He felt strong enough to travel farther, he just felt compelled to lie down here, to live among these spirits.

Another two or three days in the saddle.

And, for reasons he did not understand, he felt himself slowing, as if these last few days on the freedom trail were to be savored, as if he mourned its ending.

And, as if she understood it as well—the diminishing of opportunities—Tara walked to the fire that night, sniffed the ground, then buckled her knees and lay down—out of reach, but incredibly near him.

Checking In

humorous that my best traveling days
were those that found me stationary

Carter rode up to the Hotel Carlson. He pulled his right foot out of the stirrup and tried to swing his leg over the saddle, but it felt like two hundred pounds of thigh. He leaned forward and just rolled off Tara's back. When he hit the ground, he held onto the saddle, steadying himself.

Tara looked back over her left shoulder, and Carter patted her neck. "I'm good, girl."

He heard footsteps on the gravel. "Good afternoon, sir."

The stablehand came up and gently took the reins and gave Tara a little click-click sound. "Can I give her a nice wipe-down? Some water and oats?"

Carter stared for a second, surprised at the level of service, but more surprised to see a Negro in a servant's role. "Uh, sure." His head was foggy from the trail. "Let me just... let me just get my gear untied."

He untied his bedroll, his packs, took his rifle out of the holster. The man asked, "And what is your name, sir?"

"Monroe. Carter Monroe."

"I will see that she's taken good care of, Mister Monroe." And he led Tara away.

"Say!" Carter said, stopping the man. "Let me... can I ask you something?"

"Of course, sir."

"I just came from Mississippi."

"Sir!" His eyes were wide. "Are you visiting?"

"No, I hope to stay, live in the North." Carter shifted his weight. "Question... are you... a slave? A servant?"

"No, sir. This is my job."

"Your job."

"That's right, sir."

"You're paid for this work, then. Yes?"

"Yes, sir!" And off he and Tara went. Carter watched long enough to notice Tara scraping the fronts of her hooves, weary from the journey.

Carter stepped up onto the porch and dropped his gear.

Then he pushed open the beveled glass door that rang a little bell. As he stepped inside and strode up to the front desk, the innkeeper looked up from his reading glasses.

"Afternoon, sir!"

"Good afternoon. Might you have a room for the next week or so?"

"Ah, certainly, sir." The man peered past Carter. "Will anyone be joining you?"

"Just me." Then he added, "Horse."

Carter signed the visitor's log, paid for the first night, and took the key and towel from his host. Rowdiness and cigar smoke came from the bar.

The man rang a little bell. "I'll have your gear brought up to you."

"Thank you." He headed for the stairs.

"Oh! Mr. Monroe, I believe..." he turned to the cubbies behind him, "you have a letter here. Ah." He studied the postmark, then look over his glasses. "Here it is."

Mississippi. The Wood house. *I swear, he writes like an old woman.*

Another man brought Carter's gear upstairs.

Room 404 was cozy and comfortable. Bed with a metal headboard. Window that overlooked the Erie Canal. Carter had to stand on his tiptoes to see down to the water, but it was worth it. He unlocked the latch and pushed it open, smelling the afternoon, breathing in this New York.

He watched a small team of mules pulling a barge piled high with burlap sacks. A man led the beasts, who seemed to pull the load quite effortlessly. He watched until they were almost around the bend. *The assess of the asses of...*

He was so fatigued that his mind was being silly, finding the humor in things that were only remotely funny. He poured water from the pitcher into the basin, some into a glass. Then he just stared, deciding which to do first—drink or use the washcloth. Finally, he dropped the cloth in the basin and, while it sank, he sipped. He hadn't had a glass to his lips in several states and it tasted magical.

He wrung out the washcloth and brought it to his face. It was so comforting, so soothing that it brought tears to his eyes. He hung the cloth over the edge of the basin, then plopped down on the bed—boots and all—and closed his eyes for a while. He could not believe that his walking was over, that he had arrived.

And he just needed to quietly listen for a while. He kicked off the first boot.

He was asleep in seconds, but rolled over on his side so he could feel the pillow on his face. The bed felt so incredibly comfortable, and he drifted back to sleep, and dreamed.

A woman walks in and pulls off Carter's boots. He is vaguely aware of the sound of pouring water. She discovers the letter near the basin and uses two hands to bring it to her face. It's as if she can't read. Instead, she studies the script, traces it like it's intricate art.

She's the color of Danny Root's Palomino. She's blonde and big-boned. Her hair is pulled back and tied, her dress a blue plaid.

And now she's behind him, up against him, lying close, warm. And again the tears come. The beauty of finally being in the place of his dream feels overwhelming. Being here is surreal. So, the hand on his shoulder, the love he'd been missing.

When he woke, it was dark and the cold was coming in through his little window. But his first thought was one of mild panic. *Tara.* Then he remembered that she was taken care of. He stood and went to the basin again, realizing that he was still wearing one boot. He washed his face again, sipped more water.

He contemplated his next step—not for the week, not even for tomorrow, but for now, tonight. He held Kelly's letter in one hand, drumming it against the other. He was excited to read Kelly, but wanted to delay the surprise. He spoke aloud, "I gotta get somethin' to eat."

He took his key and walked downstairs. Still the cigar smoke and sound of card playing, and now a guitar and banjo.

"What are my dinner choices in this town, friend?"

"Well, sir, we do a real nice steak, right here. Got some fish caught today in Lake Ontario, too. But if you feel like walking, you can't miss —uptown or downtown—some great places in either direction, Main Street, walking distance."

"What's your favorite?"

"Me? I like uptown. Little place called McCarthy's. Right side of the street. Yellow building. Can't miss it."

Carter pulled open the beveled glass door that rang a little bell and walked out into the night. He stood for just a second, getting his bearings, taking in this new place in its nighttime dress. He walked back behind the inn, down the little gravel drive, to check on Tara.

He met a couple of the hands—one carrying water and one leaning back against the wall, his chair on two legs. He stood when he saw Carter.

"Evening, sir."

"Evening. Don't get up, friend. I just wanted to check on my horse."

The man put his fingers to his mouth, as if he should know Carter's name and his horse. Carter helped him out. "Carter Monroe. Quarter Horse."

"Oh, yes," the man said as he walked.

Tara came right up to the little half-door and nickered, her movements telegraphed by the sound of soft, dry straw.

"Hey, girl."

She'd been brushed, combed. And Carter patted her. It felt strange to be separated, even though it had been just a couple of hours. And he whispered, "I'll come see you before bunk."

Carter thanked the stablehand and started for the door. "Say, can you recommend a place to get a good meal?"

"Well, sir..." he hesitated. "I usually eat at home." He added, "Here."

"Inside? The restaurant?"

"Well, Cook brings us our meals. Out here."

"I see." Carter paused. "Well, very good, then. So, do you live right here?" He pointed at the ground, hoping to learn if the men had an actual room or lived in the barn.

"We have a guest house, right out back."

"Oh. Nice." He headed for the door, again. "What time do you close up the barn?"

"Just as soon as you leave, sir." He laughed. Carter laughed back and started walking, knowing that Tara was in good hands, despite his promise to return and kiss her good-night.

Brothers in New York

Hello, dear Carter.

This is Kelly's mom, Dot.

It is with heavy heart that I write to inform you that we lost Kelly just last month. He went to the doctor because he had man trouble, urinating. Couldn't. Well, they found a growth that seemed too dangerous to remove, and it quickly spread.

Carter, he was in such terrible pain. And I didn't want him to have to suffer any longer. It was a terrible, terrible decision, but one Sunday when I was at church, Kelly walked into the spirit world.

The quiet here has been agonizing. I feel like my light has been blown out. You know that he was always full of life. And he always appreciated your friendship!

I am enclosing a letter that he wrote to you. He wrote it before yours arrived. He always knew that you would write. I believe he knows it, still.

I hope that you are enjoying your new life, Carter. Please carry Kelly with you. I know that he would have loved any place where you were. You were always as close as his own two brothers.

I would love to hear from you sometime. Please know that you are thought of, loved.

Sincerely,

Dottie Wood

Carter sat on the edge of the bed, bent at the waist, cursing himself for drinking the bottle of wine with dinner. *I was celebratin'! And all the while... God damn!*

The responsibility of reading page two sickened him. Peeling down a corner of Dottie's letter was like lifting a sheet at the morgue —silent, surreal. *Yeah. That's him.* Even Kelly's handwriting was dead, now. Only echoes remained.

Well, hey there, Carter. What do ya know?

Guess you heard that I was taken by this thing inside me.

Right now, I'm thinking more about where I been, and all I've seen. It's a lot! And even though I haven't traveled more than forty or so miles from home (thanks to you!), I can't complain. I think I've been blessed in small and huge ways.

This week, ya know what I did? I walked behind the little barn and snipped somethin' sweet from one of our bushes—a couple of buds, and crushed them into my little pipe. Sat there in nothin' but my bathrobe and socks, and that stuff never tasted better.

I always admired you 'cause you came from a land far away. You had no idea what you would find here, but you came! I never done that. Not in my whole life.

And the pipe blew out. Felt like a cold spirit found me there, in our secret place. We thought no one would ever find us there.

So, please… say a prayer, and end it with a smile. Because I have had a good life, golden. Toast me and carry on.

Ya done good, Monroe. Keep going. Make a family. Make more like you. Show them Yanks how we do it in the Southland. (And kiss one for me!)

I'll hold the door open for ya.

Kelly Wood

Mourning Ride

despite our known fragility
the shock is profound
when death walks in, uninvited

He was at the barn door before the help arrived, so he sat on the bench and listened to the world waking up. It would be heavenly to ride today, to ride with no destination in mind, to travel where the horse led without the burden of mileage or direction.

When Stuart came up the path from the guesthouse, he was surprised to see Carter.

"And how was your supper last night?"

"Oh, it was fine." Carter added, "You have a lovely town."

"Ah, thank you, sir."

Carter saddled and bridled Tara, who seemed rested and eager for the morning light. And they rode down the path, past the guesthouse, to the canal towpath. Carter looked both ways, then chose north, toward Rochester.

And they just walked. And the cinders and hooves made a beautiful sound, peaceful and steady. They encountered fisherman. And a small barge of flour. And a makeshift raft that carried a young man and his possessions—a red chest of drawers, a yellow dog, a washbasin and pitcher. Carter stopped to watch and both tipped their hats as the craft passed.

He patted Tara's neck so hard it echoed off the opposite bank. It felt like ages since they had ridden, wonderful to watch the steam rise like ghosts from the surface of this manmade river. Even Tara was upbeat, her head bobbing with energy.

Up ahead, a bridge spanned the waterway, and they stopped to watch the traffic overhead. Carriages and men on horseback alternated turns crossing the one-laner, each trotting to keep those in line from growing impatient. Carter smiled at the bustle, at the notion of people with places to go. He was glad to be outside of that bustle for a while longer. He would need to return to the world of work, to the mechanism that drove an engine of prosperity.

As he passed under the bridge, he heard wind chimes play in the breeze. From the same residence came woodsmoke of bacon or fish. It nudged his hunger and the chimes reminded him of Kelly Wood's place, of Kelly, of the letter that sat on the bureau back in his hotel room.

He leaned forward, so far that his face was in Tara's mane. He hugged the horse's neck, giving comfort to receive comfort. And he played What If's... *What if I'd known that he was sick? What if I'd invited him to come to New York? What if I'd stayed?*

But apart from knowing how to reset a dislocated bone or applying direct pressure, Carter knew not the ways of internal medicine. There would have been nothing that he could have provided Kelly.

Still, he felt helpless for not even *knowing* Kelly was stricken. And as he rode on, the thought of his friend suffering made him lean in again.

When they came to a second bridge, Carter steered them up the bank and onto the crossroad. They were immediately swept up in the traffic to what looked like the center of town. Mercantile, library, post office. Barber shop, butcher, livery stable. He could be in any city, north or south, right now. Subtleties were all that differentiated them.

The pace was unique! Carter felt like people were more focused on *getting there,* on making good time. They were friendly enough here, but they didn't dilly-dally.

The greetings were also similar. People shouted and laughed, but more rapid-fire, direct. Gone was the slow curve of the southern vocal note. The northern version felt clipped, to the point.

Still, when Carter tied Tara out front of the Red Pony and came inside, he was greeted with enthusiasm. And when he returned a greeting, heads turned.

He ordered eggs and toast, something called hash browns, and coffee; and was happy to learn that the Northerners had a handle on taste. He met the eye of every patron that entered, and in his first full day in this area, he decided that he had chosen well.

He met people. He learned more about the Great Lake called Ontario. At the barber shop, he happened upon Micah St. Paul, who's dad supervised pier operations in Rochester. During a shave, they talked about dock, delivery, and shipboard opportunities.

Micah was interested to learn that Carter supervised a farm, knew a little about construction, and had traveled a great distance to make a dream happen up north.

"When you get up there, you ask for Montel St. Paul, got that? I'll talk to him at dinner tonight. I think he can use a man like you."

When Carter and Tara headed back along the canal, their pace was southern-casual, but the rider felt a great sense of satisfaction. At one point, they spent an hour in a park—Tara grazing and Carter daydreaming. For a while, he considered the canal work possibilities.

But I've come so far! I've steered here with the intention of working on one of the big lakes. I gotta check that opportunity out.

Carter led Tara the rest of the way, not so much to give the horse a break as to simply let the beast look upon him for a spell. And—as if she wanted to be more on the man's level—Tara walked with head hung low. A couple times, Carter stopped and turned and just loved the horse.

It was a beautiful day, and it felt incredible to take the time to love Tara. Giving the love felt as good as getting it.

244

Put to Good Use

from tobacco farmer to ship's mate
through occupations and adventures
we make our way in this world

Carter caught the morning coach to Rochester, then a transfer that took him up Lake Avenue, just six miles farther north to Charlotte. On the way, two people politely corrected his pronunciation.

"Up here, we call it *Char-LOTTE,* unlike the fine city in Carolina." And during that six-mile trek, Carter rehearsed it under his breath.

Rochester was one of the busiest cities he had experienced. But as they made their way north, the density thinned. And he watched with great anticipation as they approached the lake. And when they came over the crest of the final hill, there it was—Ontario!

To Carter, it looked like an ocean. The lighthouse made him think so, that and the sheer dimension of the water. The far side vanished at the horizon. *It might as well be an ocean!*

The coach pulled into a cargo marshaling area in front of the port authority. And when he stepped out, the air was so crisp and pure that he swore he could detect salt.

Micah had directed him to an office on the second floor, and he immediately went there. He had to wait but a minute or two, and then was summoned inside where the secretary introduced him to Mr. St. Paul.

"Mr. Monroe, nice to meet you. My son told me that he met you—yesterday was it?"

"It was. Thank you for seeing me, Mr. St. Paul."

"Pleasure. Come. Sit."

They talked about Carter's trek, about Carter's experience on the farm, and about the kind of work that Carter had envisioned.

"I've always wanted to work aboard a ship. The cargo or its route don't much matter to me—I'm just looking for hard, steady work, and a little adventure."

"Well, we're always looking for men who've got muscle in the arm." He paused and made sure Carter was eye to eye with him on this next point. "But we also want someone who's got smarts, who can lead men, who can see a process and improve it."

"Ah, that's perfect. I've done that all my life. That's what I love."

St. Paul explained that Carter might be away from home for nights at a time, running cargo between Rochester and Toronto. "We may have some larger operations in the future. They are building a series of locks on the canals that will connect Lake Ontario with the Atlantic, but that's a ways off."

"You said 'Atlantic' and my hair stood on end!"

"Oh, yeah? You wanna be an old salt, do ya?"

For now, Carter was assigned as a Boatswain's Mate aboard the cargo ship *Northern Star*. They would export flour, grain, sugar, and timber. On the return trip, they would import paper pulp, food, and spirits.

St. Paul asked him to find a place in town, get situated, and report to work the following Wednesday. And when Carter stood to leave, they shook hands. And St. Paul gripped it tightly, checking the bond, reading the soul of the man.

"You stop at Miss Slater's desk on your way out. She's got an advance for you—that way, you can get situated with your new place, get set up. She can recommend some nearby accommodations."

"Why, thank you, sir."

"And we'll see you Wednesday. Bring your coat and work gloves."

Carter spent the next hour studying the comings and goings at the port. Ships docked and ships got underway. Wagons loaded and unloaded, all with a fair amount of precision. Horses whinnied. Men yelled and whistled. Smokestacks puffed and horns tooted their nautical intentions.

He turned and absorbed the inland view. *So, this is my new city!* He pictured the hard days of traveling, the cold nights, the lean weeks. And he pictured Rosetta. He would write her tonight. He would tell her of his progress, but would remain careful to ensure that the new career would work out.

I just want to be established. I want to make sure I can provide something good, whole. He smiled. *But damn—I am excited at the prospect of inviting her up here!*

He wandered. He walked main streets and side streets. He tried to encounter as many people as he could. He investigated the housing that Miss Slater had recommended and ended up returning to the first one, on Pierrepont Avenue. He checked out the stable situation and liked what he saw.

He haggled just a bit with the landlord, then signed the paperwork and placed a deposit for the first month.

To thank the man for his consideration, Carter invited him to lunch. At this, Mr. Silva was surprised. And he led the way to The Pelican, where they ate fried haddock from a basket. They dipped it into a tartar sauce, a new experience for Carter. And they washed it down with draught beer from a local brewery. They sat back, full, comfortable with one another. Carter paid the bill and they walked back to the Shore Road. Carter kept his neck craned, taking in every aspect of this new world, life, life setting.

"Carter, you need anything, just give a shout. I'm right downstairs."

He slowly turned his new key in the lock. The deadbolt retracted from the wall with a satisfying click. He locked it again, just to feel the inner mechanisms, the alignment of key and lock pins. He did this several times, as if rehearsing, as if authenticating his identity over and over.

Things closed to me are opening today.

Finally, he pulled down the door lever, and sunshine met him inside. His boots echoed in his room, and when he stepped lightly, the floors creaked. He would need to save for a bed, for a table and chairs.

These things would come in time. For now, he was excited just to have four walls!

At four o'clock, he caught the coach back down Lake Avenue, then the transfer from Rochester. Fellow passengers nodded after a hard day's work, but Carter's eyes were out the window, taking in everything new.

Later, he rode Tara up into town. His intent was to try a new place to eat; but when he rode by McCarthy's, a sidewalk sandwich board read "Chicken and Dumplings" and he returned there.

He was seated at a little table by the front window, and enjoyed watching Tara during his supper. He marveled at how far the beast had come. He appreciated the sticky situations from which the horse extracted him and Abram. And he wondered what she was feeling, thinking of her new surroundings.

He wondered how Tara would fare while he was out on the lake. He would need to make arrangements. But the thought of losing Tara —even though it was for just days at a time—hung like a dark cloud.

Tomorrow, he would conclude his time at the Hotel Carlson and make the trip into Rochester, Charlotte. *Char-LOTTE.* He would carry everything he owned.

$ea Duty

we need to discover
where we are valued, worthy, a contributor
for decades, it's what defines us

She'd arrived during the night, while he slept in his new residence just two streets inland. Somehow, she'd slipped into her berth—bow out, ready for a new sortie—without waking him.

And the first time he laid eyes on the *Northern Star,* he felt a shot of cold across his shoulders, ice in his chest. He'd never been this close to a ship of this size, and his mind was dubious, thought his eyes exaggerated.

And steam came from the pier, shots of it intermittently escaping through relief valves. Cranes pivoted on her deck, men and ropes straining to get her cargo down onto solid ground. Whistles signaled once when a crate landed, twice when the ropes were free. And horses nodded and pawed in anticipation, exhaling steam of their own, glad to be part of this action.

All the while, Carter was making his way to her, seabag in hand, gloves at the ready.

He climbed the gangplank to the quarterdeck, leaving the land behind. And the moment he set foot on her deck, he felt the motion of earth's water. And the guard eyed him with authority.

Carter held out his paperwork. "Reporting for duty, sir."

The man took it, turned away slightly, and spat overboard. "Okay, yer gonna have to go aft to First Division."

Carter knew what aft meant, and his eyes went that way, to the stern of the ship. But he had no idea what First Division meant. "Is that the Boatswain's Mates division?"

The man eyed him as if to say, *You still here?* "Of course!"

It may have been Carter's first day aboard, but it was not his first encounter with a first-class ass. And he knew something about taking the high road. "Thank you, Shipmate."

But to prove he was not above pettiness, he leaned in, employing *reverse psychology* decades before it was even coined. "Enjoy your quarterdeck watch. Yer a better man than I am—I could never just stand there for four hours!"

He hoisted his seabag and walked aft, walked like he knew where he was going. *All I need to do is get there.* When he got all the way aft, there was no one around; but he heard voices, so he climbed a ladder from the main deck to the 01 Level.

At last, a makeshift desk, men talking, smoking. When no one looked at him, he spoke up, "Sir." Heads turned and made no bones about sizing him up. Before they could finish, he barked, "Carter Monroe, Boatswain's Mate."

Godfrey waved his hand, wanting his paperwork. He peered at the page, one eye squinting to avoid his own cigar smoke. He finally looked up at his newest sailor. "You get seasick?"

Carter lied, "Actually, I prefer rough seas."

Godfrey removed his cigar, studying the new man's eyes. "Where you from? You a reb?"

"Born in Pennsylvania," he lied. "That's as far south as I've been, Chief."

"Chief" caused Godfrey to be taken aback. And he yelled, "KINCAID!"

A man rolled up to them. He moved like a circus bear, as if it were unnatural to walk on hind legs. "Sir?"

"Find this man a bunk in First Division. Get him checked in with Doc Hodge. Then have him report to Morningstar."

"Aye aye." He gave Godfrey a mock salute, and the sarcasm surprised Carter. But Godfrey seemed okay with it.

"And get me some coffee, will ya?"

Kincaid led Carter through a maze of passageways and watertight doors. Carter tried to maintain his bearings—*parallel to the pier, now perpendicular, now three decks down*—but he lost track and resorted to simply being led.

"Godfrey's all right. Worked hard to get where he got." Kincaid stopped and smiled, eyes direct. "Now he don't have to work no more!"

Carter had never seen eyes so blue, though incredibly glassy and red. "Kincaid, what's your first name?"

"Waste." Carter looked puzzled. "Everybody calls me Waste."

Carter mulled it over while they walked. "Well, I ain't gonna call you that."

Kincaid was puzzled at Carter's insistence, at his desire to buck tradition. "Rick." And at that, Carter shook his hand. "Carter Monroe."

They found Doc Hodge, and he examined Carter while Rick watched. "You going ashore later, Waste?"

"Oh, hells yeah." He lit a smoke, and Carter registered the new cuss word—hell, plural.

"Except I don't drink any more, Doc!"

Doc played along, without looking at him. "Oh, really?"

"I don't drink any less, either!" Kincaid said it like it was the first time the joke was uttered, then pulled on his smoke.

Doc opened a drawer and produced a device shaped like an ear trumpet. "Hands on hips, please. Gonna have a listen to your ticker. Quiet, now." Carter felt mildly uncomfortable—the instrument on his chest and the man's head intimately close. He tried not to notice what was left of Doc's hair.

Finally, Doc stood upright, and he looked straight into Carter's eyes. "Ever have a doc listen to your heart before?"

"Uh, no."

Doc looked at Kincaid, then back at Carter. "Your heart," he began as he replaced the instrument in its drawer, "has an occasional *flutter* to it. Ever feel dizzy?"

"No. Never."

Doc crouched and tested the pulse in Carter's feet. From down there, he asked, "Ever pass out? Black out?"

"I've never done that." When Doc looked dubious, Carter snapped his fingers and donned his best Southern drawl. "Wait. This one time, a girl from a Tennessee kissed me. Just 'bout put me on me knees—does that count?"

Doc was standing now, chin resting in his hand. He weighed his next words, and Carter felt their criticality before they were released.

"I have to be honest—I hesitate bringing you aboard, Monroe."

WHAT! If Carter had never lost consciousness before, he wanted to drop right here, right now. To have trekked all these miles for this new life, and to have it snuffed? *Not an option.*

"Doc, listen. This is my dream job! And I've..."

Doc raised one hand, found a pencil with his other. But Carter pressed him. "Give me two weeks! I'll show what kind of worker I am."

Doc paused, unconvinced.

"Doc," he pleaded, palms up. *"Two weeks!"* He wished he'd brought something to bribe him with, but—today of all days—he had nothing to barter.

Doc removed his spectacles and folded them into his shirt pocket. "Kincaid. No one hears what went on here, today, got me?"

"Course," he said, exhaling the last of his smoke.

"Monroe, you've bought yourself two weeks." Carter said nothing aloud, but he exuded gratitude. "If you feel dizzy or see spots, you get yer ass down here, pronto."

"Yes, sir." He gripped Doc's hand, then left with his paperwork, Waste leading the way.

Kincaid took him down two more decks to the berthing compartment. When they walked in, the stale smell of perspiration hit them. Hard. It was dark, save the shafts of light that came through the few portholes near the ceiling.

Carter strained his eyes to make out the arrangement of aisles and lockers, hammocks perched three high. Kincaid lead him to the starboard side, the outermost aisle.

"Here ya go. Highest rack. That means you don't get stepped on!"

"Okay. Good." Carter threw his seabag up into it.

"I'm one aisle over. And I wouldn't leave that up there." Kincaid walked farther down the aisle, "You can stow yer gear in here. Careful what you bring aboard, though. Stuff tends to walk away if it's not nailed down."

Then he led Carter back out to the weather decks, where cargo was being strapped, hoisted by rope and pulley, lowered to the pier.

"Morningstar!" Waste called. *"MORNINGSTAR!"* he repeated, then under his breath, "You dumb-ass."

But Morningstar was occupied. *"Come on*, ladies! This ain't babies we're handlin' here!" He turned to Kincaid.

Kincaid pointed to Carter, who came forward and extended his hand. "Get a glove on, man!" were the first words his new boss spoke to him. And from there, things only cooled.

But Carter had reached his destination, and no man was going to stand in his way, now. He'd already met *everyman*. His theory was that we only meet ten people in this world. *They're the same ten, over and over — they just have new names and faces, that's all.*

And before he knew it, he was manning a line, hauling a rope, learning how to slip a knot, how to balance a load. And he let the others observe him, learn what kind of man he was. He was focused, now, on fulfilling his purpose.

And in the back of his mind, Doc's revelation replayed itself. And for the very first time, he listened to his heart as he rested between loads.

They spread a net. On it they stacked wood cases labeled "Fragile" four wide, four long, eight high. And when they hoisted, the edges of the net came up like giant gift wrap and lifted off the deck like it was magic, then gracefully presented to the crew on the pier.

They opened it, removed the contents, and greedily sent the thing back up, wanting more. Wanting all of it. Wanting everything they had, and don't stop until you're empty. And Carter heard a slave song in his head.

nightbird she knows
which star's my guide
when I learn her song
I'll be singin' on the north side

nightbird she whispers
and pulls at my sleeve
she'll sing which path to take
and when I'm to leave

nightbird she flies
through wood and hollow
and if she's goin' Pennsylvania way
on wings I'll follow

And with each ton of cargo, the ship would rise in its berth, displacing less water, stretching the mooring lines that kept it tied to this earth. And the ropes would register the new strain with an occasional "snap."

Then another pier crew would arrive. And this time, *they* would do the gifting. But the same shipboard crew would do the taking— always the same crew. And the ship would displace more water again, riding a little lower in the lake. And all hands on board would sense the load and the need to sail, carry it, deliver it.

Before the sun set, the gangplank was pulled aboard and stowed, the mooring lines untied and *faked out* neatly on deck. And deep inside the ship, the huge boilers—fired up hours in advance—would get the signal to finally release their steam, and by instinct the gas snaked its way to the turbine. And it had no choice but to turn. And the bronze propeller twenty feet below the lake's surface would churn air and water and power them out of the harbor.

Anyone watching from the pier would marvel at the effortless grace, the shapes of magic steam, the waters that parted for the blessed vessel. And only the sailors knew the conditions below decks, the bearing grease that would live in their pores, the desert heat, the insults in the chow line, the stench of the berthing compartment, the hell of the coal room.

And Carter would learn day two that the honor and dignity associated with being a sailor was a sham, a myth. After supper, a gang of three enginemen enticed him to their berthing compartment, one deck lower than his. "You need to be indoctrinated, friend!" Once there, they backed him into a corner.

Carter tasted adrenaline, but feigned passivity, surrender.

At the same time, he positioned himself so that the strongest of the three stood behind him and to the right. *Behind and to the right.* Then he wheeled in the same direction, his elbow like a sledge. And if it weren't for the man's cheeks, the jaw would have come clean off.

He'd never seen a greasing tool before, but he head-butted the man who held it—his nose broke like an egg. Carter stripped him of the tool and wrapped it scissor-style around the man's arm. He was prepared to break it at the shoulder, but he paused. The third man simply raised his hands as if to prove they were empty.

He yanked the scissor and spoke intimately into the trapped man's ear. "Where I'm from, you would say 'Uncle' right about now."

Blood came from both nostrils and sputtered when he talked. "Uncle! Jesus! *UNCLE!*"

But he twisted it tighter. "I know where you sleep. If you even look at me, again, I'll find you and I will deep six you."

Carter dropped the grease gun. And while the man soothed his shoulder, Carter drove a fist into his solar plexus. To convince bystanders, he did this with a single, staccato yell. Then he walked past the third man, who waited to be disemboweled, and climbed the ladder.

They can fire me. Hell, throw me overboard! Nobody greases my ass.

Carter hadn't been in a fight in a decade. But he'd walked so damn far to get here, three snipes weren't gonna get in his way. He'd once told Abram, *Sometimes, you get one chance to make a statement. You put your balls into it or you put on a dress.*

It was an hour before the adrenaline wore off, before his forehead scabbed.

He'd climbed to the main deck, then four decks higher, just outside the bridge. The interior was bathed in red light to prevent night blindness, and only half of the Captain's, Helmsman's, and Navigator's faces were visible. The rest were rutted, moon craters. In darkness.

It felt nice up here. The wind went around him. The waves let the ship pass, mostly unfettered. They enjoyed an unspoken agreement, safe passage.

He leaned on the life rail and felt dew penetrate his shirtsleeve, his pants, letting the night touch him intimately. Clouds hinted that they would soon part and reveal tonight's half moon, in good faith showing just a glimpse—wisps of hair, some cleavage.

He was patient. He took the bait, would wait. And when she finally stepped out front, she cared not that she had an audience of but one, for she held that one and held him good.

He stared, appreciating the lunar glow, but focusing on the dark half of her, there. The ruts and pockmarks made his mind go to the half faces on the bridge.

The moon, the bridge watchkeepers, and Carter—each bravely surviving. Each consumed. But alas… lacking, half.

And he thought of Rosetta. And he saw her on the sand, by the boat, on her little pond. And he stopped breathing that he might conjure her scent in his nostrils. And his lips gave it all away— pressed in a smile, then pursed for her. He held for moments his kiss-pose in the moonlight, a purr in his throat.

My second day as a sailor, and already I'm dreaming like one!

Rosetta, Dear

what's left to learn i cannot teach you
what's been bandaged i can't heal

It was in Toronto that he decided. Specifically, when he held the door for a couple entering Nectar & Rain. He and Rick Kincaid had just eaten an early supper, there. And when he saw them arm-in-arm, his heart-thoughts went to Rosetta.

The couple walked inside, brushing off snowflakes, laughing. And in that instant, he decided that he was now, in fact, established, equipped to support a woman, a wife. He was prepared. He no longer saw a reason why she should not come north to be with him.

It only makes sense!

And one night that week, while the ship rested at the pier, he wrote.

Rosetta, Dear.

I hope this finds you well, happy. Things here are quite wonderful. I am into the rhythm of shipboard life, and have saved every nickel I could so that I could ask a question vital to me...

Would you like to move to New York to be with me?

There are sacrifices... I am gone two nights a week. The town is quaint, far from metropolitan. The winter months are harsh, but the fireside is beautiful.

I can give you things beyond security. Since we met, I have held inside of me a light that is steadfast. And I would be honored to share it with you.

Consider this, Rosetta, for as long as you need. If this is the life you would like, I would love to bring it to you!

And I will send for you.

And I will love you.

Carter Monroe

When the letter was dry, he folded it and tucked it in the little leather satchel that his sister made for him.

And he wondered if his words were too brazen. And he considered starting the letter over, perhaps writing multiple versions and choosing the best.

But in the end, he decided that it was this letter that spoke his heart. *If she is offended, then it's at me—not some gentleman dressed up as me.* He needed his passion to show. He needed her to feel the things that he would give her.

The Full and the Emptiness

Dear Carter,

Thank you for your beautiful letter. I am touched. Beyond measure, I am.

It is so difficult to love at a distance, this geography, these slopes! It's harder, still, to have so little time to develop a love, to nurture it. And hard to share all of the parts of a person—the seen, the unseen.

If we had known each other longer, I would have learned so much more about you! And you would have learned this from me:

When I lost my baby and came to live with Doris and Dusty, a good doctor nursed me back to health. He was so caring that he made sure I was his last patient each night. (He even visited while you were here.) It's because of him that I am alive, sane.

Can you see how the above simply wasn't something I could share during the short week you were here? It's all rather intimate, especially for two who met just days earlier.

It so happens that the doctor is a widower and needed caring of his own. During the past several weeks, we have grown closer. And I believe he and I have a chance at making it as a couple.

These words are very difficult to write, dear Carter... I became so enamored with you, and so quickly! But think about it: I am basing my love for you on mere moments. A week of elapsed time, but our alone time was a couple of moments.

And I do trust those moments!

And I am quite sure that we could also do beautifully, wonderfully as a couple. But my mind whispers that it makes sense to remain here, close to my kin, in the known world.

Carter, I pray that you understand, that you forgive me for leading you down a garden path, for leading you anywhere you did not wish to go under your own power.

Please take some time, but please write back to me. I need to know that you are fine, at peace. Not for my sake, but for yours.

'Tis near the bottom of my inkwell. But please know that—after my feather fades and scratches dreamy-silent curves—

I shall document in daydreams the moment you sat so near, when this hand knew the chiseled structure of your face, when this heart knew fullness.

You will have love, Dear Carter.

And here is mine,

Rosetta

Light Fog, Heady Conversation

we gain perspective in this world or we do not—our choice
not all will acquire a taste for the blue notes,
for the barbs of sweet irony

He sat alone on the rock. On the beach. Knees tucked up under his chin. Sunday was the day the *Northern Star* rested. For six days, she would make the journey to and from Toronto. And Carter often wondered where all the cargo went.

Do people really consume this much? Is that even possible?

For six days, he was driven to deliver. Yet today he felt totally spent, having no reserves, empty.

How will I answer that letter? The one that so sweetly put a dagger in my heart.

He knew now why the bottle could be man's best friend in time of need, and he sighed for never having established that friendship. He had only his thoughts this day. Just puzzles—ones that logic and reason could not solve.

He thought of Kelly Wood, and how they discussed the challenges of life. And he played out a slow conversation with him.

So, hey, Carter! Got yourself a Dear John.

- I was a fool to think it was real, Kelly.

You thought it was real because it was, Pardner! Did you feel it?

- Yeah.

Did she?

- I suppose.

You know she felt it, Carter! But sometimes... sometimes, the world complicates the simple things. Love. Sometimes, love steps aside for the sake of convenience. I think that's what happened, here. She never fell out of love with you. You can't say that.

Carter exhaled, adjusted his sit-bones on the rock, got comfortable again.

- So, now what?

So, now... now, you're in the valley. You've already been to the mountain! You've tasted love! Now you wait. You prepare yourself.

- For what?

For the magic, Carter! You've had magic before because you're open to it! You're in a beautiful place, now... expectant. Get ready for the next beautiful thing. Get your ass ready for the magic, man!

Carter smiled, musing at Kelly, at Kelly cussing in the afterlife! And he brought his hand to his mouth and wept just a little. Still in mourning, but smiling that his friend could still help him focus, could steer him to a peaceful harbor.

Need and Deliverance

and when i bow down e'er so low
it will be before a God
who's ne'er insisted
i do so

Carter slid down off the rock, onto the sand.

Two moons have passed, and still I have not lifted my pen to respond to her. Couldn't!

He swiped at the back of his pants. The lake was smooth before him. He breathed deeply and felt a smile, a smile for no reason.

Kelly… gone. Abram… gone. Rosetta… God, gone.

He walked along Shore Road, then farther, past his own street, following the soft, pastel commotion up ahead.

And when he rounded the bend that mirrored the shoreline, three horses looked his way. Two were hitched to wagons, one was tied to a post, and their ears went straight up at the sign of the man, as if they'd been waiting.

And they made him smile. It was funny to him that—in this town, still lonely to him—it was horse and not human interaction that he experienced, that got him noticed.

He walked to the pair and let them nuzzle his empty hand. And in their eyes he saw only beauty, only truth, and when he approached the posted mare, he saw a sweetness that he recognized in all mares— ever a filly, but with the beauty of depth, one who can carry and bear another.

"Will you be coming inside, sir?"

Carter turned, suddenly enough to spook the mare. And there she stood—gloved and bonneted, just standing to be sure, but lit, somehow.

"Inside?"

"Service begins at the top of the hour." She stepped back twice, but left her eye on him. The confidence of her movement and gaze struck him. "There's a place for you."

He felt his chin and wished he'd shaven. He laid his hand on the mane of the mare and sought her equestrian guidance. Of course it was only to shake off a fly that she shook her head in the affirmative.

Of course. That's all she was doing.

But he believed in signs, and unplanned fate, and lightning striking. And if this magic happened on a Sunday morn, so be it. *What bravery doth a sailor have if adventure he hath not.*

He took the two steps up, removed his hat, and shook the hand of the greeter tending the door. Her face was sweet and powdery smooth and she smelled of lilac. "Well, good morning, sir. It's nice to see you."

An usher led him, but Carter quietly insisted on sitting near the back of the church. *Just in case I need to make a holy run for it.* The walls were sky blue and the windows open. No stained glass. Not a crucifix in sight. An altar, a chalice, a candle.

No lamb and sickle, he joked to himself. *That's a relief.*

And when music began up front, people arrived from an unseen place, and the air was charged with excitement. Carter leaned to his left for a better view of the organ, the organist.

No great pipes extended to the heavens. So he leaned left to see just how she was able to create such a sound—the air of woodwinds. He watched as her hands not only directed the ivories but pulled and pushed various knobs, her feet pumping a device underneath. And she continued quite seamlessly. And his eyes continued surveying.

The little chalkboard up front listed three hymns, and he reached for the book before him. Page 88 would be first. And he could not remember the last time he sang. *Had to be on the trail. Maybe... maybe Mississippi, Tennessee, Kentucky, West Virginia...*

"Do you mind if we sit here?"

Carter looked up at the women. "Sure. Please." Carter half-stood and moved to his right. The woman from out front followed the first into the pew, and she looked over her sibling's shoulder to grant him a smile.

And before he could think another thought, the congregation stood in song, ushering in the choir and the Reverend Brent Scott, who seemed to pick Carter out of the crowd as he ascended the steps and faced his flock. And Carter mouthed the words as best he could, unsure of the melody, uncomfortable at the required expression—especially when he looked left and both women seemed to be singing like birds and observing his own song.

The sermon began. And Carter was only too aware that the women now blocked an easy exit to the aisle. And to his right sat a couple too large for him to pass. So he settled in. And noticed how the Reverend's voice filled the space, the Yankee accent, the nods of the congregation.

Intermittently, he actually listened to the words.

"...a storm brewing where north and south meet."

A chickadee landed on the windowsill. Carter thought he was the only one who noticed, until a girl shrieked with delight three rows ahead of him. She clapped, hands open and fingers spread, making more of a spank than a clap.

"...testing the values of this young nation, our leaders, our citizens."

The wind blew hard, and the little bird tipped forward, tail feathers high above it; but the thing was sturdy, stayed put.

"...follow our true hearts! The heart knows what is right! So reach out! Reach out to those who have less! And pray that our government finds a peaceful solution."

At that, the bird flew across the pews, lighting on the opposite windowsill. "Oh!" someone laughed low and nervously.

"Let us pray."

The service was longer than Carter would have liked. *Why say in sixty minutes what you can do in five?*

It was redundant. *Why don't we just stand once, sing all the songs, and combine the prayers into one?*

But it had its moments. It was nice to meet fellow worshippers, people he would not have otherwise met. He had the pleasure of meeting the Moss sisters—Nina and Beverly. "But you can call me Bev."

And after the service, tea and cookies were offered to those who exited by the altar, where the Reverend shook every hand and met every eye.

"Well, Mr. Monroe, it was a pleasure to have you today!"

And it was heavenly to get back outside, on the waterfront, in the breeze. And Carter brought tea to the Moss sisters, and they exchanged all the relevant, vital information.

They'd grown up here, a mile from church, a schoolteacher and a nurse. They had a youth about them—quickness and easy laughter. But Carter noticed the kiss of wisdom around their eyes, the hint of experience on the backs of their hands.

He walked them along the side of the church, to the front steps, to the buggy and the black horse, Nathaniel. And it wasn't until the two ladies were seated that Beverly extended a dinner invitation for the following Sunday.

And he watched them ride off. And he replayed the simple moments that led the three of them together and marveled at the way the world works.

He started the walk back to his place, hands in pockets, considering the irony—*Why always sisters!*

Doris and Rosetta.

Claire and Kathryn.

Nina and Bev.

That afternoon, he rode Tara along the beach, as far north as he could venture before the shore turned to rock. And he felt intense gratitude for his new life, new location. Lake Ontario—from his perspective—was everything an ocean was, save the saltwater. He felt refreshed, a new character in his own book.

In a way, the South and who he was there felt like a distant memory, a previous life.

ghosts no longer reside beneath my skin
the distance I've covered served to wash them from me
they are but shadows, unable to penetrate me

He turned the horse around, this time riding in the lake surf, and Tara bobbed her head as she walked. And a pair of boys called to him, waved. He studied their faces as he passed, thinking he might see a telltale northern trait; but they looked like boys from anywhere, universal, held by no affiliation or flag.

"Great day, huh?"

"Can we pet your horse?"

He slowed Tara and turned her inland, and the lads patted her neck, her withers. She bent to sniff them and they laughed at that.

"What's his name?"

"This is Tara. She's from Mississippi. Are you boys sailors?"

"Ha! No."

"Actually, we still go to school," said the thoughtful one.

"Ah. You looked like sailing men to me."

The boys returned to their sand project and Carter rode on. He visited the bakery, where he bought bread and cheese for the week. He was fortunate to know of an apple tree not far from his place, and he went to it daily. During the week, he would pick an apple on his way to work. *My "walking to work" apple.*

But today, he spent as much time as possible with Tara. He missed her during the week. The thought of selling her crossed his mind. After all, everything he needed was within walking distance. But, honestly, he could not bear the thought of leaving her. *Even my practicality has limits!*

And when the day drew to a close, when the sun mixed pinks and purples in the western half of the lake's watercolor, his hand and body still rested against his horse.

And when he faced east, he rediscovered the first needlepoint pinholes pushing through the dark fabric of the sky. And so peaceful was the showing that he hated getting up and leaving.

But he led the horse by the reins, and she too knew that it was time to bid farewell—their one day in seven was ending. And in the lamplight of the barn she stared, expressionless, her lashes lit by the fire. And when he kissed that huge place between her eyes, she filled her lungs and exhaled. Then she went to her bucket and drank, not looking up when he left.

Sisters on a Sunday

you need not audition for a role of prominence
those positions are taken
and brute force will only tighten my knob and lockset
come and softly play your part and I will love you

Sunday came and he shaved and put on a tie. And after church he rode Tara next to the buggy and the black horse, along the winding little road that took them north along the lake.

When he saw their place for the first time, heard the hooves and buggy wheels on the gravel drive, he felt he was on a peaceful, northern plantation.

Austrian pines flanked the drive and the wind off the lake *shhh'd* in a near whistle, and Nina looked over at him and smiled, and her eyes were dark and deep, and he felt like he was in a good story.

A sleepy black spaniel met them halfway to the house, his entire rear half ruled by his happy tail. "Mozart!" Beverly called. He barked just once at Carter, but the wagging gave him away.

Carter unhitched Nathaniel for them, and both horses drank deeply from the same bucket. And Carter's head turned when Beverly took the rifle out from under the buckboard and locked it away. She noticed this and said, "In case of coyotes."

They came inside where everything felt feminine, delicate, precise. And he sipped tea while they warmed up the bird they had prepared last night, while they got the vegetables ready.

They offered their davenport, but he chose to stay near them, in the kitchen. And he found himself wishing that they were not sisters, for he could love them both and the thought of choosing was inconceivable.

He set the table, to be useful. And he held their chairs, and when Beverly said grace, he truly did feel blessed.

He told them of his journey and waxed melancholy when trying to articulate how huge but how intimate he found the world. And they watched his eyes as he conjured his interpretation of how he got here, what it all meant.

"It's somehow perfect, how every choice I made led me here, to this very table, to you two." He took a bite of turkey. "I'd never heard of Charlotte, but it's as if I'd been steering right for this place all along."

Beverly talked of her nursing, Nina of her teaching. Both had been married and both reclaimed their independence, their identity, their maiden names.

"That's so nice that you have each other."

And as the sisters sliced the pie in the kitchen, Mozart came and sat at his knee, and Carter scratched his neck. And each time he stopped petting, the animal raised a paw. The man leaned back and looked out the window. *It's possible that both women have sworn off men altogether!*

He smiled at the notion that he may not have a chance in hell with either of them. *Touche', Irony, my clever friend.*

When they brought the pie, the sisters concealed something humorous between them. And they kept their eyes downward, their smiles tight. Carter kept petting Mozart, but his eyes went from one woman to the other. If it weren't for the flattering, he might have felt uncomfortable.

After dessert and tea, Carter offered to wash the dishes, but the ladies wouldn't hear of it and they all went outside and strolled around the grounds. And when Tara saw Carter, she nickered, and the ladies laughed. And at a certain spot in the yard, they could look down onto the public beach, almost all the way to the pier where *Northern Star* was berthed. From here, his world looked like a still life.

Both women were Sunday-beautiful, and it was exceedingly clear that both were smart, alluring, intriguing.

And yet there was still so much to know. It was possible that they already had new men in their lives. And then—because there *had* to be an outrageous option—it's possible that the two would be content to split him, share him.

They were so very open, yet everything before them was a mystery, unwritten, undecided, and happy to be so.

The path, the long journey, brought him exactly where he wanted to be, but everything was different when he arrived. He was one man less, but along the way he found love. He'd not expected or even considered the love that he would find.

So, maybe the trade-off is worth it. Abram found love and decided that he would walk no farther. I walked on, never planning for love, but I seem to find beauty at every turn.

That night, he opened his back window and leaned half his body out, just to feel the cool, just to smell the night air. He looked down at his clasped hands, and prayed.

For all those who need love, make love apparent
And may the hungry be fed
Bring clarity to those who need guidance...

And he searched for the rhyme...
Let hands appear to those who need to be led

He dozed and slept and dreamed of a woman, of her face, her eyes.

She was gentle and sweet, and had just given birth to a son, already of age four or so, already reading, carrying a book. And when the three of them came together on the bed, arms and heads together, the book was open to page one, and the child had written his name inside. "Carter."

And out the back window, he could see his son and his wife, and out ahead of them, down to the pier, he saw generations—mere ghosts of children now, swirling, waiting to be born.

And he knew, as only dreams knew, why he had come here, why he'd been so driven, the reason for the pull. And never had tears felt so beautiful.

Hundred Hearts

if it happens once or thrice or twenty-nine times
love whispers (and rightly so)
"this is the once-in-a-lifetime kind"

He'd said to Abram "Sometimes, you'll make your best plans. You'll do everything you can to make them real. And then, when you're looking the other way, the world will make a move, will wave its hand and change everything in front of you."

And Abram surprised him, showed his grasp on the subject. "And, somehow, it will be for the better, won't it, Master Carter?"

Carter drained his cup of coffee, checked his tie in the little piece of mirror by the door, and walked out into Sunday.

He waited for them on the little steps. It got so close to the top of the hour that the music started inside. And then he saw them—the buggy and the black horse, the regal sisters. *One at the reins and one at the Remington.*

But there was a third, seated in the rear, half-turned to determine how close they were.

And when they rolled up, Carter took ahold of Nathaniel, tied the reins, then helped the women down.

"Carter, this is Marshall."

"Marshall. Of course. Marshall."

He had to do some quick calculations, had to clear some branches that obscured the family tree. And there he was... Marshall. Former husband of Beverly. Brother-in-law of Nina.

He's back? Carter thought.

"He's back," Nina whispered when she had the chance. "Came back Saturday morn." Carter held out his arm and she took it. And they came inside.

And for the first time, things seemed… complete. Two of them up ahead. And two of them here. And they found a pew that accommodated the four of them. And after they sat, Carter leaned forward and waited for Marshall to do the same, down at the far end of the group.

And Marshall did this—he sensed Carter, looked upon him, and leaned, smiled. And the two men sat back. Carter felt good. Felt complete. Felt happy that Marshall showed up.

And in a second, he wondered if he would be equally happy if… if… what's his name… Nina's man had shown up. But the fact that he couldn't recall his name told him not to chase the question any further. And he let it go.

And he turned his head to the right again, this time fixing his gaze on Nina. And she moved her eyes to him, and her little smile revealed only contentment.

Carter leaned in and whispered, "I really like your hat."

"You've seen this one."

Carter looked at it again. "I know. But… I really like it today."

"Not too quirky?" she whispered.

He laughed under his breath. "Sometime, we should talk about *my* quirks!"

They sang.

And Carter was sweetly, completely surprised when—during the last chorus—Nina bumped her hip against his. And it felt so funny to feel that in church. It felt perfect. And every exhale felt perfect as well, each one making room for the next breath, the next rush of magic, the next moment of life.

If he had to describe where he had been, he could. It felt like a long, rugged story. If he had to describe his path, his route to this new place, he had a map. He could trace it with his finger.

But if he had to explain—after all the miles and months and worn-out boots—how he happened upon love, how beauty and grace had found him, he could not articulate it.

Magic.

And they prayed. And his prayer of gratitude was real, from the purest part of his heart.

The ritual of this place had done its work. Something higher than the church beams, something more than the hundred hearts inside, something helped his own heart feel full, healed.

And, with eyes fixed straight ahead, he reached for and took Nina's hand. He didn't ask—he just moved to hers and wrapped her. And she felt tiny, delicate, perfect there.

And in his periphery, he saw the front of her hat tilt up slightly, he felt her inhale and hold it. And he was stunned at how peaceful the world could feel. And he was amazed at how pure and perfect—how calming and explosive and trusting, all at once—love could feel.

I am finally here, moving forward on a wave. And I sense that the one beside me rides the same wave.

Epilogue

no matter how many autumns we endure
or how profound our tragedies
men will ever rise to war's clarion call

Every story is more complex—leagues deeper—than the portion told. The untold are at least as fascinating, their volumes too huge to contain.

And there are no minor roles—each is pivotal, each is vital, and worthy. Every character has their moment, their glory, their intimacies —immensely pleasurable and deeply tragic.

Abram marched and fought with a Pennsylvania regiment, never dreaming that his literacy and navigation skills would serve him in battle. And his feet carried him down the map, to states not unfamiliar. And he brought home the horrors of war but in love fathered children with Tahira. The first was stillborn, never to pull a breath of this earth's air. But her spirit would live on with the sacred name Akua. Abram crafted her delicate coffin and enlisted his wife to help nail, to paint the bird and the cross. And he kissed her cold face, unafraid this time. And for their bravery, they were rewarded with a boy and girl.

On a windy autumn Tuesday in 1862, Danny Roots was pinned down with thirty-seven Confederate comrades in a valley too lush and wondrous to be dubbed "battlefield." They called his solo charge a pure, courageous sacrifice, enough of a distraction to allow his men to escape.

What they didn't know was that the lead Union horse—a Palomino—was a signal to him, a prophetic call to honor. His story would long outlive his breaths. And his eyes would lock on the sky across the road, above the men, above them all. And blue would be the last color registered.

In 1863, a generous young cook with tired eyes and a shrugged shoulder fired on Chauncey Kinsman as he led a night patrol. The lead ball occupied a place too vital to risk surgery, so he carried it home to Pennsylvania. Chauncey married Martha Cameron, the girl who once fell from his horse and now designed the houses and barns he constructed outside of Philadelphia. He died kneeling before her wheelchair, head in her lap, ever her caretaker and ever in her debt, in 1910.

The living and the dead—no matter how long or brief their stories—play out their time as scripted. Whether they bled in a meadow of mustard flowers with a lifetime of love letters unfinished or in a Sunday rocker, each life is a worthy, profound tragedy.

Carter Monroe's final curtain call shall not be revealed here, only because it matters not how or when he went. He was here; and with but the turn of a page, he went. The same for Sarah Jane, Rosetta, Kathryn, Nina—how they exited is not critical—it's their living, breathing stories that are important. Each carried on when certain they could not. And each enjoyed further chapters of joy and the richness of love.

Like each of us, these characters fade too fast but leave something beautiful behind. Be it seed or song or future story, *something* is carried forward, for the next.

About the Author

Dilmore grew up in a large, multi-cultural family in New York's Finger Lakes region, where he currently resides.

His first novel, *My Quirks and My Compass*, was published July 2009 by Pensive Pony Media (ISBN 0-9825224-0-1).

To purchase signed books or audiobooks read by the author, visit PensivePonyMedia.com.